Our Secret Winter

Ulwich Preparatory Academy: Two

S Bolanos

CHAOTIC NEUTRAL PRESS LLC

Contents

Content Warning

Ulwich Preparatory Academy is a mature new adult prep school series and contains situations that some readers might find offensive. This series is intended for audiences 18+ and features violence, sex, and blatant homophobia. This series also deals with themes of identity, self-doubt, consent, safe sex, and abuse* **.

*There will never be on-page depictions of sexual assault

**There is direct reference to an MC being a victim of sexual assault

Chapter 1

Calvin

The empty pudding cup sat beside me on the grass, forgotten as I leaned forward to give the impromptu lacrosse match below my full attention. With the arrival of the school's key Midfielder and two Defenders, the friendly game had evolved into a full-on practice match. No pads or helmets meant the body checks stayed fairly tame, but you wouldn't find me complaining. The sweaty bodies below glistened in the afternoon sun, a veritable feast for my eyes. It never ceased to amaze me how a school consumed with homophobia didn't see how shoving a bunch of developing boys in proximity to each other wouldn't foster at least a little exploration.

Andy, my companion and only real friend in this hellhole of repression, had long since abandoned me. Lacrosse held no interest for him, surprising considering the star player, Mitchum Hudson, had once been his best friend and seemed determined to be so again. I winced as a Middie and an Attackman came together hard enough to be heard even from this distance. Benjamin Price stared down at his latest victim, who remained on the ground in what was likely a state of shock. With his broad shoulders, thick torso, and muscular legs, Benny was a beast on and off the field. A veritable Laocoön or Farnese Heracles. My fingers tingled as I ran through the list of Grecian sculptures and imagined running them over the living model currently dominating the game.

What I wouldn't give to get my hands on that.

…Again.

A smile curved my mouth as I scooped the fallen art supplies back into my bag along with the cleaned pudding cup and spoon. I straightened up and cast a glance back down at the field below. The poor Attackman had found his feet, and the match had resumed, though it was clearly winding down. They'd be heading to the showers at the locker room next. If I meandered my way along, I'd arrive just in time for my appointment, and if I was lucky, a peek at all that exquisite flesh.

I yanked my loose tie off and stuffed it in my bag, where it hung out like a mustard-striped navy tongue. Next, I undid several buttons and yanked on the stifling collar. The uniform they forced us to endure was just another symbol of oppression and one I openly rebelled against. I rolled the cuffs of the navy jacket, exposing the white satin underlining, and pushed back the hair that had fallen in my face. The tight curls—a stunning Mars Brown with Burnt Sienna highlights—hung substantially longer than code dictated and were a constant nuisance. But it was either tie them back or cut them off, both of which were tantamount to admitting defeat. Unsurprisingly, the damn things tumbled back in my face and stuck to the sweat dampening my forehead. Not that I was out of shape, far from it, but the way was long and the afternoon exceedingly warm.

At last, my destination came into view. Rather than venture into the locker room proper and enjoy the view and the AC, I sought a bit of shade off to the side and waited for my quarry to emerge. The coolness of the painted cement offered a welcome reprieve from the heat and a convenient lean-to. I fished out a sketchbook and pencil, and made sure the rest of what I would need was within easy reach.

The pale cream of the fresh rag paper held all the promise of creation and none of the inspiration. I blew out a breath and stared at the soft white canvas. If I could not round out my portfolio, then I might as well kiss my chance at the Art Institute of Chicago goodbye. Of course, there was always Yale, but Chicago held my heart. I glared resentfully at the stubbornly blank page and graphite poised above it.

You'd think drawing people would be easy for me, considering how many I see all the time.

But not the way Jankowksi wants them, layered with nuances of vulnerability and authenticity.

Therein lie the rub, while I could see those things in others, translating it to canvas meant exposing a part of myself I'd locked away since I was nine.

And some doors should never be opened.

With a disparaging grunt, I fell back on tried and true. By the time my appointment arrived, my rendition of a Quaking Aspen was in full form on the once pristine page. I glanced up out of the corner of my eye without raising my head. My perch in the shade lay far enough from the main entrance to be inconspicuous and mostly hidden from view—unless, of course, you were looking for me.

Brian went rigid as he spied me lurking in the shadows. After a beat, he made his way over, movements jerky like an automaton in sore need of oil. His stunningly dark skin, an intriguing mix of

Vandyke Brown with Medium Hansa Yellow undertones, at once absorbed and reflected the afternoon sun. As the only other student of color in our grade, it was a true shame he hadn't been able to look past my orientation to foster any kind of friendship or camaraderie.

"Bridges," he grumbled under his breath as he stopped close enough to be heard, but far enough to deny association. I smirked as I took my time putting away my sketchpad with exaggerated care. The longer I took, the more growly he became. It was no secret Brian didn't like me, of course, he'd liked me even less since I'd caught him and another boy giving each other hand jobs.

At last, I procured the pack of smokes from my bag. His eyes lit up, then immediately darted around to make sure no prying ones were nearby. He reached out, and I pulled the open carton back out of reach. "Payment first."

His face twisted, and his hand fell back to his side. "I don't have it."

Cute how they always think I don't know.

"Don't be coy, darling." He winced at the endearment, and my lips tweaked up in a wicked half smile. "Post came yesterday and *someone* got a delivery." I held out a hand and waited patiently. He ground his teeth and grumbled incoherent insults as he liberated a small wrapped package from his bag. He plopped it rudely in my hand and glared daggers at me.

"Happy, you damn fairy?"

"Immensely." I curled my fingers around the vacuum sealed box and held out the carton of cigarettes with a few greener companions nestled inside. He snatched them from me and didn't bother to check the contents before shoving the poor, abused packaging into his bag. "Pleasure doing business with you."

"Fuck off," he sneered.

"Is that an invitation?" I bat my lashes as I pocketed the high-end cosmetics. It wasn't my fault he had connections to the esteemed company through his sister. Now, whether he stole, bought, or somehow coerced her into gifting the expensive items, I had no idea, nor did I care. It clearly was worth the price, since this was by no means our first such deal.

He rolled his eyes without deigning to answer, then turned to stomp sullenly off with his contraband.

"Oh, tell Tanner I said hello," I called out before he could get too far.

Brian stiffened once more, confirming my suspicion that the two hadn't ceased their extracurriculars despite being caught. Of course, I'd never out either of them on principle, but Brian didn't know that nor would he likely believe me if I told him as much. Plus, it was nice to remind him he was not as untouchable as he acted. He stole a few moments to pull himself together, then resumed storming off.

I chuckled to myself, pleased with a good day's work and content with the knowledge that my client base was well and truly in line. Secrets were a dime a dozen in this place if you paid attention, and it paid to do so. A deeper shadow fell across me, briefly dimming my merriment. Curious if it was another client in need of another trade or a new petitioner, I glanced up once more.

Ah, the latter.

"Benjamin." Nothing could be done to school the wicked grin that stretched my cheeks. Sadly, I didn't seem to have anything he couldn't acquire on his own, not to mention the only secret I had on him fell squarely in the sacred column. I straightened up from slouched repose to be of an even height with him, but didn't abandon my casual stance. "Fancy seeing you here. What can I do for you? Any particular *needs* I could help you with?"

The slight tightening around his eyes was the only indication he'd caught the targeted emphasis. "What are you doing here? You know your queer ass isn't allowed anywhere near the locker rooms."

I pushed off the wall to invade the fringe of his personal bubble, undeterred by the hostility and a touch emboldened by the fact that he'd sought me out. "There's no such rule against it."

"There is, if I say there is, you fucking fagot."

"Ooh…" I shook my head from side to side. "Tsk tsk. You sure you wanna do this, Benny? Here," I purred. "All alone, without your boys to back you up? Last time I checked, you liked to have… a hand." Shuttered fear danced behind his eyes as he no doubt remembered something he tried hard to forget. Meanwhile, the same memory was emblazoned in gold and given a position of prominence in a hall of fucking glory in my mind. "That's what I thought. Now, if you'll excuse me, I have other business to attend to."

Unable to resist riling him up more, I lazily dragged my gaze down his body. Once more, the fantasy of molding that incredible physique in smooth, wet, pliable clay filled my thoughts and made my fingers itch to reach out and test the firm muscle before me if only to make sure I got the consistency right. By the time my gaze found his face once more, his ears burned a fantastic Alizarin Red with steam practically billowing out of them while he fought not to swallow his tongue.

I winked and blew him a kiss, which he didn't catch. "See you around, Benny." I walked past him close enough to feel the tension and anger radiating off his statue-like form. No more slurs followed me as I made my way back to the school proper to inform my client that their shipment had arrived.

White silk hung in elaborate folds from King Kelani's sleeves as he met with the latest supplicant. The trade agreements settled without quarter or malice, but with a firm stoicism that bespoke of a wisdom beyond the young ruler's age. Many had made the mistake in the past of believing the ostentatious prince would become a weak and malleable king. However, Kelani had assumed his role with a dignity and form unbeknownst to his predecessors. After all, what need had he for an army when he held sole control of all the supplies essential to his hostile neighbors?

Chapter 2

Benny

My efforts at keeping my expression neutral went wholly unap-
preciated as the headmaster himself shot me a pointed look. I
diligently didn't roll my eyes and returned my focus to the cluster
of fresh faces currently filling the atrium. Ulwich Preparatory
Academy's latest batch of would-be gentleman looked about
with wide eyes filled intermittently with wonder and uncertainty.

New class, more like lambs fresh for the slaughter.

Anxious eyes darted toward me and I tried harder to remove
the scowl from my face, to no avail. I recalled my own amaze-
ment and expectation upon enrolling. A legacy whose place was
solidified by money and prestige, a fact my father never let me
forget for a moment. The Price name was precious, inscrutable,
and powerful, and I dare not do anything that might tarnish it.
All lies, of course, puffed up circumstance and money lining the
right pockets.

I rolled my shoulders, and one of the underlings shrank back
into the herd. He wouldn't last long. This school had a nasty habit
of taking anything it saw as weakness and crushing it beneath an
iron heel. You either grew thicker skin or learned how to put on

armor. Trouble was, no one bothered to warn you how much the armor would come to chafe.

"In conclusion, we look forward to having you all join our esteemed ranks next fall." Headmaster Torsney straightened and flattened his formal robes. The navy velvet hung heavily to the floor and swished lightly on the ancient wooden floors.

Fucker has got to be burning up in that shit.

"Mr. Price—that's Benjamin Wallace Price the Fourth—will now lead you on your tour of the grounds." Torsney gestured over to me and I plastered my fakest sincere smile on my face. The parents erupted into a muted tizzy over the news of who their personal guide would be, while most of the youths looked at me with the level of fear I expected from the lower grades.

With a resigned sigh I mostly kept to myself, I stepped away from the wall. "If you'll follow me, we will begin by visiting the dormitories. The youngest grades are situated closer to the teachers' wing in the event of an emergency, but as boys age out, they are transferred to one of three other halls." I turned down the wide expanse of walkway.

This particular route granted an impressive view of some of the school's trademark architecture, including the vaulted ceilings and elaborate stone archways. Never mind that the students themselves would have no occasion to venture this way, but then again, this wasn't for them, was it? This whole charade was so families could feel better about shipping their sons off to live without them. Some of these boys wouldn't see their parents and loved ones for months at a time, others for years.

Sometimes the years are preferable.

I shook off the melancholy thought and concentrated on the task at hand. Spinning on my heel, I began walking backwards.

"Traditionally, Ulwich aims to keep bunk mates with the same assignment for the duration of their education. A built-in friend, if you will." I smiled, and the parents tittered happily again. Meanwhile, several of the boys eyed each other skeptically. They had the right idea. Forced bunkmates rarely made for friends. Becoming a prefect certainly had its draws, namely that I had to do these ridiculous tours, but it did have the fantastic perk of coming with my own room. I barely even remembered my original bunkmate.

The tour dragged on for another two hours until I was satisfied that the parents and children were too tired to ask any more inane questions or complain. I left them back in the atrium for a pretentious lunch with the faculty and excused myself to my own diversions. Sadly, though, no reprieve was found in my room. Shortly after arriving, a knock came at the door.

"What?" I snapped, already knowing who would be on the other side. The door had scarcely opened when Neil and Todd came tumbling inside.

"Where have you been all morning?" Todd asked as he flung himself into my chair.

"Yeah, you missed class," Neil added, thumbing through my school books.

I scowled at the pair of them, completely oblivious to me not wanting to be bothered. "I had that stupid fucking tour this morning. You know how Torsney likes to parade me about."

The two shared a look, one of the few examples of successful bunkmates. I wasn't sure how they'd stayed friends or why they bothered to stick around me, likely for the same reason everyone else did. At least they didn't simper.

"Torsney is an ass hat with a prick so small not even a blue pill could save it," Neil declared with conviction.

I snorted a laugh, because it probably wasn't far from the truth. In a sudden spark of energy, I surged up from my seat on the bed. "Let's get the fuck out of here."

"Where did you have in mind?" Todd asked, promptly vacating his stolen seat.

"Somewhere fucking else. Town or something."

Neil rubbed his hands together. "And how long will we be somewhere else? Will we be back in time for, say… afternoon classes?"

I smirked and grabbed my discarded jacket. "We'll see. I've had enough responsibility for one day."

Calvin

Professor Jankowski looked back at the sketch, his brows coming together with an intensity that matched the puckering of his mouth. He didn't need to say it, I already knew, and it was written plain as day across his face.

"Calvin."

"I know," I cut him off, not wanting to hear the words I knew would follow.

"This is not what I meant."

"I know." With another huff, I launched out of my seat to stalk across the room. I stopped to survey the cluster of canvases left to dry. The skill employed wasn't remarkable, but what room did I have to talk? At least they'd *done* the assignment.

He let out a frustrated sigh, and I heard the unmistakable sound of paper whispering to the desk. "We've been through this." I braced myself for the lecture coming; cutting him off would only delay the inevitable for so long. "Art is pain."

"I'm aware."

"Then why won't you let yourself feel?"

"I feel just fine," I snapped back, spinning to face him. He grabbed the flat sketch of my priest from the table and waved it at me.

"*This* is feeling? Come on, Calvin, you're better than this, or at least I thought you were. I've seen your landscapes, the joy you suffuse in a sunrise, the sorrow of an empty hillside bathed in moonlight. Where is *that*? Because it's not here. I have first years that can't manage proportions putting more emotion into their sketches."

I glowered and turned away. The pointed insult needled my pride, but I couldn't do what he asked. Letting feeling out meant letting feeling in, and that wasn't something I could afford to do. I swept the dark curls out of my face and retrieved my bag from the floor. "Fine. I'll try again."

"I know it's hard, Calvin," Jankowski said as I reached for the pathetic attempt at a portrait. "People are complicated, and capturing those nuances is a momentous task. But I wouldn't ask it of you if I didn't know you could rise to the challenge." My fingers clenched into a fist, then I snagged the limp page from him and made my way out. "I'll give you a month's extension, but the deadline for applicants is dwindling. Make it count."

I nearly crumpled the evidence of my failure into an indistinguishable ball. Instead, I carefully slipped it between pages of my sketchbook where it could remain safe and whole. The only way to get better was to learn from mistakes, but fuck if I knew what this one could offer me. I left the art room and only paused twice on the way to my dorm to check key alcoves for customer requests. At finding none, my mood darkened further.

My roommate Greg glanced up at my storm cloud entrance, unsurprisingly without a word. Our entire first year bunked together I'd assumed he was mute given that he never said a word, then I'd overhead him talking with some of his classmates and realized it was me.

"What?" I snapped as I flung my bag on the bed, sending art supplies tumbling free.

In lieu of a verbal response, his dark gaze flicked to my desk equally strewn with pencils and charcoals and a sole envelope. I snatched the small missive up and sat back on my pillows. Greg rolled his eyes and returned to whatever mindless task he used to occupy his time. My fingers deftly fished out the folded square, and I flicked it open, a smile tugging the corners of my mouth.

1. I've done as you said. 2. Hauntings are always worst at midnight.

~L

Instantly, my spirits lifted. Granted, Leonel's code could use some work, but even if Greg had read the note, I doubt he would have been able to infer its true meaning. Considering today had been absolute shit, this wasn't so bad as far as consolation prizes went. After all, in a scant two nights, I'd be getting laid. To celebrate, I yanked out my sketchbook and turned to a clean page.

The portrait remained neglected while I drew the pencil in a broad arc over the page. Bold strokes tapered into delicate scratches that filled the room and went largely uncommented until a perfect rendition of the main atrium of the school dominated the page. I flipped my pencil around and used my pinky to smudge some shading, grounding the image solidly in the late afternoon.

The room depicted held no life, but the shadows of memories filled the emptiness. I'd been frightened to be surrounded by so many strangers, had fought my mother on coming to this place I was sure held nothing but horrors for a boy who couldn't pass even if he wanted to. I sighed and my pencil hung from limp fingers as I let the tide of the past wash over me. The horrors had come, but that day I'd gotten a different surprise. I'd caught another of the boys looking at me. The weight of the world seemed to rest on his shoulders, the burden heavy as if he was Atlas himself, but when he'd looked at me, his demeanor had softened.

At first, I'd believed the look to be one of curiosity. I looked like none of the other boys, with my dark mop of curls and skin like smoky quartz to his delicate fawn. But as the orientation went on, I realized he wasn't looking at my differences, he was looking at *me*. When I'd finally offered a tentative smile, his eyes had widened like I'd caught him doing something wrong. He stopped looking and melded into the crowd to be replaced by a different boy that seemed to wear darkness like a cloak. *He* had smiled at me, a feral thing that made me want to seek out the nervous boy and cling to him for both our sakes.

My pencil scratched violently across the page, digging deep enough to rip the resilient material and mar the once beautiful image. I took a steadying breath and decided to take advantage of my sudden rush of emotion. The portrait slipped free of the pages and I spent the next three hours trying to add any of the compassion or put-upon patience Father Miles had any time we spoke.

Chapter 3

Benny

I slumped in my desk, not even remotely paying attention to the proofs Stein was scribbling on the board. Of course, I wasn't the only one whose attention had found other venues of distraction. The angled calculus text before Gallagher undoubtedly gave Stein the impression that his pupil was fastidiously following the lesson. It also hid the paperback nestled in the bend of the sizable textbook. I wasn't surprised that he didn't feel the need to pay rapt attention, though I wondered if he had any idea that we were neck and neck for the coveted title of valedictorian.

Probably not. That assumes anyone realizes I'm more than just some jock.

Truth be told, the team kept me plenty busy and would keep me busier if I actually landed team captain. How Coach justified drawing out the announcement like this, I had no idea, but much longer and it would be more than students he'd have to answer to.

I was on the verge of excusing myself to literally anywhere else when the classroom door flew open to reveal a flushed student. He was younger than the class he'd burst in on by at least three years, though I recognized his pockmarked face from some of the lacrosse practices. His gaze swept the room until it landed on me.

"Excuse me, young man," Stein said, "you are interrupting my class."

The boy's gaze snapped to the irate professor. "Yes. Sorry, sir. Professor Nolan needs Benny, I mean Mr. Price, at once." His focus swiveled back to me. I hesitated only long enough to receive an approving nod from Stein before standing and making my way out of the room.

That's one way to get out of class.

The nameless youth scurried down the hall at a clip just shy of a run. We made our way down the hall to a room on the far side. He opened the door much like he had the one to my class and rushed in. "I've got him, sir."

Professor Nolan turned to face me, and I choked on a laugh. Black paint smeared across his forehead and jaw, which was currently clenched tight enough to crack rocks, a stark contrast to his exceptionally pale complexion.

"Benjamin Price, you will get to the bottom of this." He gestured to his desk, and I realized his entire hand was coated with black as well. I bit the inside of my cheek to keep from laughing aloud and addressed my attention to the three items that lay on his desk that I suspected to be the culprits of his appearance. Each one consisted of a dark material that had no doubt helped to hide the paint from detection.

I cleared my throat. "Of course, sir."

"Excellent. I want the miscreants apprehended and punished severely."

"Naturally."

He nodded his approval, then tsked loudly when he made the mistake of painting the arms of his chair when he leveraged them to stand. Bitterly muttering beneath his breath, he turned to the board and the entire class erupted in laughter.

Motherfucking Christ.

Nolan spun in place, simultaneously trying to bring the class under control and find the source of the outburst. While I could have helped, I wasn't suicidal enough to point out the cheeky smiley face now painted on his ass and staining his khakis. Thankfully, he didn't need the assistance after all, as he finally noted the pointing and looked down. Fury splotched his face purple, and he spun to hide his violated rump against the wall.

"Benjamin!"

"I'm on it, sir." I stepped forward to carefully retrieve a thoroughly painted book from the desk, leveraging an empty bag from the trash so I didn't end up looking like Nolan. Considering all the items, including Nolan's chair, were all originally either black or equally dark, I had a sneaking suspicion this wasn't everything. "May I advise not touching anything else dark in the room?"

Nolan was borderline apoplectic as he looked back at me. "They will pay for this."

"Yes, sir," I said again, taking my evidence and stepping back out into the hall. The door swung shut behind me and Nolan was already yelling at the students all sorts of vitriol for this outrageous stunt.

"Maybe, if you weren't such an unbearable prick, shit like this wouldn't happen to you," I said to the empty hall.

This certainly wasn't the first time Nolan had been the victim of a prank and I seriously doubted it would be the last. Though the last one to cause such a ruckus had been over four years ago.

The Dust Frog Caper, as the student body referred to it. The chalk drawing of a frog bearing Nolan's trademark mustache waiting for him on the other side of the pull down had been hilarious enough to solidify the prankster's place of infamy. But it paled compared to the sheer chaos that had erupted when a furious Nolan had then opened his desk only to have a dozen frogs spring free to spread chalk dust on everyone and everything. No prank had ever come close to that scale before or since… until now.

I reached out a finger to touch the exposed spine of the otherwise safely wrapped book. At first impression, nothing seemed amiss, then I pulled my finger back and revealed the tacky paint hiding in plain sight, paint that was now staining my finger. "Son of a bitch." I more securely wrapped the book, confident that the substance would stubbornly remain intact, and retrieved a napkin from my pocket. Unfortunately, it didn't do shit. In fact, it made it worse.

Now officially pissed, I stormed down the hall toward the art rooms. My temper and frustration grew in equal parts as I discovered the rooms were void of any occupants. I slammed the book down on a nearby desk. "Motherfucker."

"Sorry, no one here by that name."

I spun around at the cheeky comment and spied none other than Calvin Bridges perched upon a chaise, no doubt intended for posing models. He had the audacity to wiggle his fingers at me in a wave that set my teeth on edge.

"Where are the others?"

"Out." He didn't even blink as he delivered the flat response. Frustration bubbled beneath my skin. Asking Calvin anything was one hundred percent at the bottom of my list, but in lieu of someone more qualified to talk to, he'd have to do. I snatched the book back up and crossed the room.

"Explain this," I demanded, thrusting it at him. When he didn't take it, I dropped it with a loud thud on the table sitting beside the chair.

His outrageously long lashes fanned darkly over his cheeks as he looked down at the item in question. He inspected it a moment, then leaned back on the couch. I ground my teeth at his nonchalance, but refused to be goaded into asking a second time.

"That would be Lamp black acrylic paint," he declared. "Terrible stuff. Prefer oils myself."

I took a deep breath in through my nose to foster patience I absolutely did not have. "How do you know what it is?" He shifted his head slightly, causing the rampant curls to fall in his face as he quirked an eyebrow at the accusing undercurrent.

"You shouldn't have tried to wipe it away. You need paint thinner for that shit."

"Where is the paint kept?" I asked, determined to focus on the reason I was here and not on his attitude or the way his dark hair curled around his brown eyes. He gestured over his sketchbook with his pencil at a closed cabinet. "Care to be more specific?" I growled, already regretting this entire endeavor.

He rolled his eyes and made a grand show of setting his work aside. His long limbs stretched out like a snake uncoiling as he extricated himself from the plush chaise. I took a step back as he stood so we wouldn't be standing on top of each other. The only thing more remarkable about Calvin's lithe height matching my six-one was the confidence with which he carried himself, like he owned the damn school instead of it being the other way around. This wretched place owned all of us.

"Take your time, why don't you," I snapped irritably as he meandered at a snail's pace over to the indicated furniture.

He glanced over his shoulder, the navy broadcloth of his uniform jacket bunching. "I intend to," he purred, the words thick with insinuated promise while his dark brown eyes shamelessly took me in. My chest puffed up out of reflex while my ears burned. I hated when he looked at me like that, something he never failed to do when there was no one else around. Before I could say anything, he unlocked the cabinet and threw open both doors, then let out a gasp.

I surged up beside him, heedless of the proximity. "What? What is it?"

He held a hand to his mouth in mock coyness. "It seems someone has liberated that detestable paint."

"Are you fucking serious? I swear, you limp-wristed flamer, if you had anything to do with what happened in Nolan's class—"

"Ooh... What happened to Nolan?" he asked, his eyes sparkling with intrigue.

"Nothing."

"Doubtful if it has your knickers in such a twist."

I ignored the prod and looked deeper into the cabinet. To my relief, a few bottles lurked in the back labeled Lamp Black Acrylic. I snagged two bottles and noted the circles of dust highlighting another missing three. Given how difficult the shit was to get off, it was unlikely the culprit had gotten away unmarked. "Who else has access to this?"

"Besides me?"

I rounded on him and resolved not to show how much having him this close was affecting me. "Is that a confession?"

His eyes narrowed as a sinister smile pulled at his full mouth. "I'm very good at confessions, Benjamin. Have any you'd like to share?" Unable to stand his proximity anymore, I jerked back and used closing the cabinet to hide the reaction. "What's the matter, Benny? Are there some deep dark secrets you need to unburden? I'm all…" his gaze flicked down and back up again almost too fast to catch, "ears."

I curled my lip at him and squeezed the tubes of paint so hard I feared they'd burst. "Listen, flit-"

"Working our way down the alphabet today?" he interrupted, his Cheshire grin growing. "Wouldn't it be more fun to work your way down something else?"

Fucking Calvin Bridges and his fucking insinuations.

I pivoted on my heel, nearly forgetting the wrapped book in my eagerness to get the fuck away from him. His laughter chased me out of the room and continued to ring in my ears as I made my way to the headmaster's office to report.

Kel's laugh filled the atrium and abraded Einar's ears. The king's bejeweled robes swept in an elaborate arc as he turned away from the young prince. Prince Einar saw no humor in these proceedings, however, and resented the implication that he'd come, like so many others before him, to court the self-assured ruler. He tightened his hold on his sheathed sword and followed after to the throne room with its ornate adornments that lauded the king's power. King Kelani assumed his seat with all the regal bearing befitting his station and considered the prince, the supplicant, as one might consider a fish before gutting it for dinner.

Chapter 4

Calvin

Leonel glanced up at me, nervous anxiety written in every line of his body from the dark rose flush staining his cheeks to the tightness of his shoulders. "You're not going to tell anyone, right?" It was hard to miss the edge of defensiveness… or hint of threat.

I diligently refrained from giving face to my surprise. Not that the implied threat was new, but normally they asked that question *before* we had sex. I let out a slow breath and offered him a reassuring smile as I moved to squat down beside him. To his credit, he only flinched a little at the proximity. For some reason, having me near him without clothes was perfectly acceptable, with, however, apparently bore different implications. "No."

His gaze shuttled away to look opposite me. Anger and a fierce need to comfort him in this time of doubt warred within me. Against my better judgment, I reached out to comb his brown hair behind an ear. He stiffened at the touch and the anger inched a little closer to winning.

"No one you don't want to will ever know what happened here," I said softly and dropped my hand.

His gaze danced back toward me, fear to believe swimming in their mahogany rings.

"Do you remember what I told you to do next?" He nodded mutely. "Good." I caught his gaze to make sure my next words took. "However you feel about what happened here is your business, but aftercare is important."

"I got it," he snapped. His gaze fell once again, but at least didn't wander too far this time. "Thanks," he finally added, with the tiniest hint of humility.

I smiled and straightened up, then offered him a hand, that to my surprise, he actually took. "You say that like I got nothing out of this."

His cheek twitched, and I won my first genuine smile of the night. Teasing the men I slept with was always a bit of a gamble that paid off about as often as it blew up in my face. He glanced around, taking in the thin mattress and twisted sheets that still bore the evidence of what we'd done minus the condom. I'd disposed of that while Leonel had been pulling himself together. I'd learned the hard way that actually seeing it triggered the skittish ones more often than not. "Do you want any help cleaning up?"

Once again, I worked to school my face, but as generous as I found the offer, it was also abundantly clear that Leonel was ready to run as far and fast as his legs could carry him. "No, I'll take care of this. You go on and sneak in a shower before your roommate wonders where you've gone off to."

He offered another weak smile and gingerly gathered up the last of his things. Unexpectedly, he paused and glanced over at me, the shy nervousness back in full force, along with a heavy dose of fear that pinched his brows and clouded his eyes. "Does this mean… I mean, does this make me…" The floundering and inability to come right out and ask it would have been laugh-able if it wasn't so damn heartbreaking. Fuck this school and what it did to generations of confused adolescents. Leonel was technically older than me, though not by much, and *this* was how he had to explore his sexuality.

"No, Leo, you're not gay. Curious, maybe, but not gay."

Hope lit his eyes and soured my stomach. "Do you know?" he asked like I possessed some magic eight ball about what people's sexual preferences were.

"Not always, but sometimes," I admitted, an image of a young boy looking across a crowded room and truly seeing me flashing through my mind.

Fucking motherfucking damn. I never should have drawn that Christ forsaken atrium.

I pushed away the tide of resentment threatening to further dim the evening and nodded towards the door. Some days I wondered if I was taking this whole sexually liberating the repressed too far. "You should get going. Be careful of the prefect doing the rounds." Leonel offered one more nod and left without a backward glance, just like they all left. There had only ever been one that had stayed, had wanted to be held and comforted, who hadn't had shame in their eyes.

I swallowed against the sudden tightness in my throat and glanced around the empty room. Once a bustling classroom like all the others, rumors and superstition had led it to be abandoned, closely followed by several neighboring rooms as well, which made it the ideal place for illicit interludes. En-couraging those rumors had been a no-brainer the second I recognized the potential of such a space.

I scooped up the sheets and tried not to think about the boy with the penetrating gaze who felt so much as I balled them up. They joined a collection of odds and ends that would also find their way back into the school proper, be it the laundry or the trash.

An hour later, not a speck of evidence remained. The mattress rested between the multitude of shelves squished together and the lube rejoined the remaining condoms in a hidey-hole hidden behind loose backing. Satisfied the place once again looked every bit as derelict and haunted as it was supposed to be, I gathered my own things and made my way to the less used showers on this floor, confident they'd be empty.

Worry scratched at my nerves as I made my way back to the dining hall in the hopes my friend would be there. I rounded a corner and the solid form of someone moving much too fast slammed into me. My breath came out in a grunt and I looked down to see copper red hair no bottle could ever reproduce. Relief instantly flooded through me.

"There you are. Where the fuck have you been all day?"

Andy glanced up from his efforts to restore his bulging satchel, surprise clear on his face. "H-hey."

The worry I'd just lost came back in a rush. "Is everything alright? Where have you been?" I asked again.

"I... uh... fell asleep in the tower," he said, evading the real question as he hopped from foot to foot as if our conversation were an inconvenience. My frown deepened. Andy only went to the Tower when he was thinking about Mitch, though he'd never admit it. "Missed all my classes," he added, though we both knew that wasn't the root of the problem.

"No one gives a shit if you blew off a couple of classes. I've blown off plenty. What's really going on?"

He stubbornly shook his head. "You don't get it." True, I didn't get a lot of things. Like why people thought being gay was a big deal or why anyone believed acrylics were better than oil or how a single stroke could decide if a painting was a masterpiece or absolute rubbish. His green eyes flicked up, the tiny ring of amber encircling his iris holding all the pain of old wounds. "Mitch found me." *There* it was.

"I'm not surprised. He practically turned this place upside down looking for you." The strange part being that Mitch and Andy didn't really share any classes, so how had he known Andy wasn't in his?

Andy startled at the comment and the fidgeting returned with a vengeance. "You don't understand. I was dreaming about…" He glanced around and lowered his voice, "*that* night."

Well, fuck.

"What of it?" I asked. Andy had only told me the barest details of *that* night, but it didn't take a genius to figure out that something besides making out had happened, something that had destroyed one of the most beautiful friendships I'd ever seen.

Andy's gaze cut to sharp shards of uranium glass. "I think I was talking in my sleep. I… I don't know what he may have heard."

"You could always ask him," I suggested. *Maybe then we could finally get to the bottom of this ridiculous intrigue.*

"I can't," he countered, stubborn as ever.

Movement in the background caught my attention, and I glanced behind Andy to find the root of his troubles glancing frantically over the heads of the thickening dinner crowd. If I hadn't already suspected that more was going on, the panic shining in Mitch's autumn eyes confirmed it. I brought my attention back to Andy at odds with warning him and holding him hostage a little longer to give Mitch a fighting chance to fix whatever he'd broken. Suddenly, Mitch caught sight of us and immediately began pushing through bodies with determination. I mentally sighed in exasperation. Much as I wanted to help Andy by letting Mitch catch him, Andy wouldn't see it that way, and Andy was my friend, not Mitch.

"You better pull your shit together." Andy's face clouded in confusion, and I darted my gaze behind him. "He's coming this way." Andy glanced over his shoulder and hissed a curse. "What are you going to do?"

"Cover for me."

"Andy." His name came out flat and full of rebuke. I understood my role in Andy's life and how our friendship had come to be, but this was getting ridiculous.

"Please?" he asked, desperation emanating off of him.

The battle to do what I knew would help and what Andy thought would, raged once more. My teeth sank into my bottom lip as I searched his face and settled on something in the middle. "Tell him the truth."

The worry in his eyes vanished in a flash of anger. "No."

"All I'm saying is-"

"I don't give a shit what you're saying," he cut me off. "Just be my fucking friend." I took a physical step back at the force of his words and he pushed past me to leave me to deal with his mess. I barely got my shock under control by the time Mitch approached, his eyes feverish.

"Hello, Mitch," I said, absently leaning against the wall and blocking his path to buy Andy his precious seconds.

"Where is he?"

"Who?" I raised my eyebrows and projected an innocence that no one in their right mind would ever buy.

"You know damn well who." Anger tightened his shoulders and clenched his jaw. Then, as suddenly as it had taken him over, it was gone. Those same shoulders sagged in defeat and he ran a hand through his hair. "Please, Calvin, where did he go? I need to... I need to talk to him."

"I'm not sure where he went," I admitted. "He seemed to be in a hurry. You two have been spending a lot of time together lately. Maybe he needs space."

Mitch's eyes darkened, not with anger this time, but with doubt. "What did he say?"

Not seeing the harm in it, I related as much of our conversation as I dared. "All in all, I gather he's embarrassed." I angled away from the wall and wrapped a hand around the strap of my bag. "Give him time," I suggested gently.

His shoulders drooped even more as the defeat took root. He nodded quietly, causing his light brown hair to fall in his face. Rather than push it clear, he seemed to shrink behind the wall it offered. Then, without another word, he turned and made his way into the dining hall. Almost immediately, his teammates swarmed him. His responding smile was as broad as any of theirs as they launched into animated chatter about the Senior Captain finally being named, but I couldn't help but wonder if any of them could see the sadness that lingered in his eyes.

Unwilling to subject myself to anymore drama for one evening, I adjusted my course for the library. There was a windowsill there with my name on it. And with everyone else preoccupied with dinner, there would be no one to stop me from climbing up to the coveted perch.

The ambassador spun away in a whirl of green robes and stalked off. Kel remained resolute, standing beside the parapet, and watched in silence as his greatest councilor left to fulfill other obligations. The kingdom itself would keep so long as the king betrayed no signs of weakness. Much as it pained King Kelani to send his reluctant ambassador on such a perilous mission, there were treaties to be made and alliances to seal. Would that his own marriage could bring such fortuitous tidings, but the king as yet remained unaffected by his many suitors.

Chapter 5

Benny

I stomped down the hall toward the cafeteria, my stomach bubbling more with acid than hunger. Today was about as shit as a day could get. First, Coach had finally made an announcement about who would be Senior Captain—Brian, not me. Then, I'd fallen half a letter grade in chemistry thanks to a couple of ambiguous questions on an over-weighted exam. Then, I'd been called to report to the headmaster's office about the motherfucking prank on Nolan, of which I had nothing. We'd spent literal fucking hours turning that classroom upside down for any clue as to the culprit and only gotten painted hands for our trouble as we found the two-dozen other booby-trapped items. And as if all that wasn't bad enough, Anderson fucking Gallagher had just threatened me. Maybe not in so many words, but the intention was clear—he knew what I'd done… and with who.

And what did I do about it?

Did I feign ignorance about "eventful" showers?

No. I stood there like a goddamned idiot.

My fist collided with the stone wall of the atrium, and pain radiated from the point of impact. I snatched it back with a grunt and inspected the torn skin around the knuckles. Bright pink shone through raw skin and pricks of red grew in tiny puddles that burned. I flexed my fingers and shook out the shock waves of hurt. The move only made it feel like my pulse was throbbing in my hand.

"Fuck!" The curse rebounded off the distant walls and was flung back at me. Having lost my appetite, I turned around and headed back into the heart of the school where hopefully I wouldn't run into anyone that I'd be more willing to hit.

Thunder boomed through the encroaching night, shaking the walls and matching my mood perfectly. I'd almost made it to the library when the phone I wasn't supposed to have vibrated in my pocket. A quick glance around didn't reveal any peers or professors; with luck, they'd all still be in the dining hall for at least another hour. I slipped into the library and found a shadowed alcove. Only then did I remove the contraband.

I squinted against the bright light of the screen and the missed call notification. As if possessed, the device began vibrating once more. My stomach rolled as I stared in unsurprised, muted horror at the caller id. I swallowed down the bile creeping its way up my throat and accepted the call.

"Hello, sir."

"Benjamin, what is the meaning of this?" I winced at the fury-laced question and wished the alcove were deeper.

"Father-"

"I have to hear from O'Connell that the Daniels boy has been named Senior Captain."

"We only found out this morning," I argued, but the words went unheard.

"And what's this nonsense I hear about you being unable to apprehend petty vandals? Children, Benjamin, fucking children," he said in his usual gritty manner right over me.

I ground my teeth and forced myself to keep quiet. Pointing out that the prank had been far too sophisticated and well-planned to be committed by first years would be pointless. I'd yet to meet an entitled brat capable of picking locks, which they would have had to have done in order to access Nolan's room, not to mention the paint they stole.

"Are there any other failures you'd like to regale me with?"

The question dripped with scorn and disappointment that slithered into my belly. "No, sir."

"With conviction, boy. You're a fucking Price, for God's sake."

My shoulders tightened as steel ran up my spine. "Yes, sir," I replied.

"Get your act together. I didn't send you to that school so you could make a mockery of our name."

"Yes, sir. I wo—" The line cut out before I could finish. I looked at the phone in my hand and seriously debated breaking the piece of shit in two and flinging the pieces as far as I could into the stacks. I'd never wanted to come to this school, had begged to attend a regular school, one that would...

The soft shuffling of shoes whispering on carpet as someone entered the library intruded on my thoughts. I quickly pocketed the device and ventured deeper into the quiet. Still seeking sanctuary, I wandered to one of the few places in the library that actually managed to be isolated. By the time I emerged in the sheltered hollow of shelves, my anger had faded, leaving me empty. Truth was, it didn't matter what I did—I could be Captain, Prefect,

Valedictorian, Prodigy—it still wouldn't be enough for Benjamin Wallace Price III. Nothing ever would be.

Calvin

At the sound of a muffled voice in the library, my pencil paused over the page. Not that I was worried. Short of someone thinking to look up, no one would ever find me stretched out on the wide ledge of the stained-glass window that dominated and looked out over the library. Balanced an impressive ten feet above the ground, it would take a flash of lightning backlighting me and broadcasting my shadow to betray my presence.

I studied the image that filled the over-sized sketchpad with its eleven by fourteen page. Stacks of shelves wove and twisted in intricate patterns, revealing the unseen labyrinth of books we called a library. From this vantage, I could see a lot that no one else thought to consider. The toy covered in dust, spirited away to the tallest shelf, where it had remained hidden for who knew how long awaiting its owner's return. The arched alcoves that provided a refuge for friends and lovers to whisper in corners. And of course, my own retreat, nestled just below me, a veritable island of isolation surrounded by literature. There, I didn't have to put on a show, be the loud and proud gay man they all needed me to be. There, I could be myself. Andy and I had spent many an afternoon sequestered in the oasis, quietly appreciating the luxury of peace.

I flipped to a fresh page and debated what to draw next. The altercation with Andy came to mind, but I really didn't want to think about how he'd basically shoved our friendship in my face. I'd kept his secrets and made sure they didn't spread, no matter how much the rumors wanted to sprout like weeds. For four years, I'd ensured that only three people in the entire school knew that Andy was gay, despite our friendship and the speculation it inevitably created. My pencil scratched an oval on the fibrous material, Andy's anger clear in my mind.

At the whisper of fabric, though, I paused and looked out at the refuge below. I recognized the student slinking into the space immediately. He walked to the center of the bedroom-sized space and paused. I watched in silence as he raked his hands along his short hair that I imagined felt like crushed velvet. Then he intertwined his fingers behind his head. The move stretched the muscles across his chest and strained the cotton button down to its limits. A heavy sigh drifted up, perfectly matching the obvious distress that had hold of him.

He squeezed his eyes shut, clearly fighting some unvoiced emotion. When he finally dropped his hands, it was to brace against the bookshelf before him. Tension defined every taut muscle starting at his neck and working its way through his shoulders and back on down through his legs. The shirt clung to his form, an insubstantial armor against the demons that plagued him. Where his jacket had wandered off, I had no clue, but without it, the purity of pain lay exposed. Each line of definition stood in high relief thanks to the ivory fabric clinging to his torso, a testament to the immense well of feeling before me.

My pencil whisked softly of its own volition along the page, having found its muse. His fingers dug into the shelves, sliding books free of their path, as if seeking a purchase from the insurmountable weight determined to crush him. He remained miraculously still, while the graphite continued to glide with a life of its own, filling in every speck of white space with the agony of a boy who felt too much and had no way to express it, standing not seven feet away.

The longer he stood there, the more life the likeness gained. It captured the tightness of a jaw working hard to keep from giving voice to the sorrow permanently etching itself into broad, sculpted shoulders. Each pass plucked out details of pain. Eyes scrunched against the agony. White-knuckled fingers, torn and marred with a raw pink. A mouth pressed to a thin line. My fingers grew weary and smudges stained each finger as I worked tirelessly to have the 2D image echo reality. Layers upon layers of shading added light and dark to a tortured soul. A boy with all the weight of the world sitting on his shoulders and no idea how to put it down.

Chapter 6

Benny

"You wanna hit up the game store?" Todd asked as we left Malcom's Sporting Goods empty handed. Neil glanced over. No doubt curious what my response would be. I'd been an outright cantankerous son of a bitch since news had dropped about the captain's assignment. Of course, they didn't know the full extent of my anger and frustration, and I preferred it that way.

"Nah. Don't really feel like it." Truth be told, I didn't much feel like anything. Their faces fell and I only just didn't roll my eyes in open exasperation. "You two go on. I'm gonna…" I searched for an acceptable single pursuit that didn't require them fucking dogging my every step. "Walk around."

They shared a look, surprise clearly written on their faces. In all fairness, it was rare that I ventured off on my own. "You sure, boss?" Neil asked.

"Would I have fucking said it if I wasn't?"

Neil held up his hands. "No offense, just checking." He shared another look with Todd. If either had an actual pair between them, they would have called me out for acting like a bitch. Unsurprisingly, they didn't. "We'll see you around," Neil said at last.

"Whatever." This time I did roll my eyes before stomping off without another word, not giving a shit what they did as long as they left me alone. I thrust my hands in my pockets and wandered down the semi-populated sidewalk, the greatest mercy being that it wasn't stifling hot.

Thank fuck this fall is almost over.

The unremarkable town of Hylestead passed by me in an indistinguishable blur of colors and shapes. Nothing held my amusement and if I was being honest, I didn't have a damn clue where I thought I was going. On a whim, I turned toward the cafe that occasionally had decent pastries, not that I was supposed to be eating those. I could practically hear my father's voice gruff with scorn in my ear as he reminded me for the millionth time that an athlete's body was sacred, that a powerful mind required proper nourishment, that sweets were for the weak. Never mind the man himself had no such qualms indulging in most decadences.

That's all I need, my father bitching because I've put on weight. What the fuck does it matter as long as it doesn't affect my performance on the field?

With that, I stepped into the quaint cafe. Pristine little white tables filled the intimate space while thin blue curtains gave it a welcoming glow. The tension that had been riding my shoulders for days relaxed slightly as I spied the glass display and its impressive assortment of forbidden treats. Mental calculations of how much exercise I'd have to do to burn off the excess calories ran through my mind as I inventoried the options and stepped up to the counter.

"Pastries, Benjamin? You know better." The reproach crashed through my determined indulgence. Guilt surged up inside of me, quickly followed by overwhelming anger.

I spun around to give the insolent voice a piece of my mind. However, when my gaze fell on the Amazonian blonde, long hair cascading over her shoulder, hip popped out and hands placed upon them with a button down on the verge of losing its battle with the barely contained cleavage, I couldn't help but smile. Her lips quirked into a wry smirk and her blue eyes flashed as she stepped up to the counter and feigned looking at the display. She bent at the waist, purposefully putting on her own display of all her best assets. She glanced over her shoulder at me and I half expected her to wiggle her ass, which the short plaid skirt did next to nothing to keep hidden.

"If you must indulge, though, I'd say get creamed." Her eyes glinted wickedly, and my smile broadened. "I mean, the Boston Cremes," she amended as she straightened up, her ample breasts bouncing almost out of her shirt.

"Savannah." Her smirk widened to a grin, and she held open her arms. I gladly stepped into the embrace, the press of breasts against my chest further distracting me from my otherwise dreary day. "What brings you here?" I asked as she stepped back, taking the modicum of comfort with her.

She rolled her baby blues and gave a dismissive wave of a hand decorated with sparkling rings and bracelets that clinked together. "Needed a break from those bitches."

I snorted and the attendant that had been standing in the background trying not to swallow his tongue at Savannah's provocative display leveled her with a scorn-filled glare. Sensing censure, Savannah twisted and arched an eyebrow of challenge at him, then turned back to me.

"We should do lunch," she suggested in a perfect imitation of her high society mother. "It's been too long since we caught up."

My eager smile twitched a hair wider. "Okay. When were you thinking?"

She deflated with an exasperated sigh, her hand falling to hang listlessly by her side. "Uh, how 'bout now, dipshit?"

I laughed outright, a full sound that burst out of me and prompted the judgmental assistant to shift his glare. "You really don't want me to have any sweets."

"Fuck that. We're getting the sweets and a sandwich. Your treat." She winked.

I laughed quieter and stepped up the rest of the way to the counter and the thoroughly scandalized attendant. "You heard the lady. That'll be two Boston Cremes and two turkey clubs."

"Two, Benny? You flirt. You'll have to fuck me extra hard to work that off," Savannah said, smooth as silk when she accepted the food. The attendant fell into a coughing fit and dropped my card twice before ringing us up.

"You just couldn't help yourself, could you?" I commented as we took a seat at one of the painted white ironwork tables on the private patio.

She shrugged. "Not my fault he's a prude. People fuck and not all girls are dainty flowers."

"No, some of them are captain of the State Championship Girls' Volleyball team, could give sailors a run for their money, and just happen to have perky tits and a nice ass."

"Damn straight." She took a massive bite, shoving renegade bacon back in her mouth and I shook my head. Savannah Strickland was a picturesque debutante at all social events and gatherings, smiling sweetly and saying all the right things to all the right people. She could work a room with the best of them and had. But beneath the fine veneer polished to a mirror shine, she was every bit as crass as Calvin, maybe more.

"The highlights look good," I said, indicating the honey streaks combed through her impressively straight curtain of hair, hair that also happened to be hugging her full breasts.

She gave me a wry smile and slid the hair back over her shoulder, offering me an unobstructed view. "You always have been good at noticing things like that."

I smiled back at her not fooled in the least. She continued to study me and I shrugged since there was no sense in denying either the spoken or the unspoken accusation. I knew what I liked, always had. Finally, she blinked and cocked her head to the side.

"Really is a shame we don't work." Her gaze slid over me appreciatively much like her hands once had and I felt myself hardening beneath the unabashed scrutiny. Tempting as it was to forget my distractions in her inviting body, we really were better friends.

"Please. You broke up with me the same day—at the same time, I might add."

She laughed and shook out her hair, causing the honeyed locks to glow golden as they hit the light. "Okay. Fine. I did. Doesn't mean I can't be sad about it. You've got a nice dick. The rest of you isn't so bad either," she added belatedly.

"Oh, I see," I said as I polished off the last of my sandwich. "It was purely physical."

She let out an exaggerated gasp that put her already strained buttons to the test and reached out to place a hand over mine. "Benny. Did you catch…feelings?"

We both let out a hearty laugh that raised my spirits even more. Savannah really was a good friend, even if we were a terrible match romantically. Though for a time, it hadn't really been up to us. The Stricklands and the Prices aligned would have been a power couple to shake the status quo. Or it would have been if our grandfathers hadn't gotten into a snit about someone cheating at cards—or maybe it was a bet? Either way, no one remembered who did the cheating or what had started it all, only that whatever machinations that had existed in regards to creating permanent family ties were to cease and be forgotten immediately.

We sobered up and tackled the remaining sweets. She glanced up at me as she licked her fingers clean of the white filling and my mind instantly sank into the gutter again, no doubt her goal. "So, have you talked to the big man lately?"

The gutter dried up and cracked, rents ripping through the foundation to expose bedrock. "I take it, you've heard."

"News travels fast."

"No shit."

She reached out a hand again, this time all elements of playfulness gone. "I'm sorry, Benny."

I gave her hand a light squeeze and pulled back. She left her hand on the table another moment, then pulled it into her lap without pursuing the conversation, a gesture I was more grateful for than the original outreach. Savannah was one of the few people from my family's social circle that I could speak with honestly. She understood the unbelievable pressure I was under, because she experienced it too. The fact that she'd found a way to both conform and rebel was one of the many reasons I genuinely liked her. But for as much as we had in common, we saw the world in very different ways.

While I adored her and she was strikingly beautiful, she believed in pedigree and materialism. Those stunning highlights probably cost at least a couple hundred dollars and would undoubtedly get replaced in a month or so when she grew bored of them. Each ring on her finger bore a genuine stone in a solid gold setting. Even the bangles were a far cry from costume jewelry and likely worth a fortune on their own. The cheapest thing on her was the mandated school uniform and even that cost a shiny penny if my own was a mark to go by.

Where she basked in the world wealth and status brought her, I resented it. Then again, that resentment hadn't stopped me from taking advantage of the doors that opened for me at the mere mention of a name, which I suppose made me a pampered hypocrite. I glowered at the remnants of our shared meal, now even deeper in the darkness than I'd started.

"I know you say you don't gossip, but you're a blue-balled liar. Tell me all the latest dirt that's been happening at that warped cock fest of a school," Savannah artfully navigated the waning conversation. I gave her a look and she leaned forward to prop her amble bosom on the table. "I'll tell you mine if you tell me yours."

We spent another hour trading nonsense about our respective schools. When we finally parted ways, I simultaneously felt lighter and heavier. I enjoyed spending time with Savannah, but she was also a painful reminder of the world that awaited me when I left the refuge I'd carved out here.

Calvin

Holy Trinity rose up before me, no less grand for its small size. Like the rest of the town, it boasted a mix of aged brick and granite as well as stained glass that rivaled the school's. A sense of peace settled over me as I stepped through the banded, double doors into its hallowed halls.

Ornate pillars rose up to support the vaulted roof decorated with exposed beams and more stained glass, inviting pockets of multi-colored heaven into the space of worship. To the far left, a smattering of prayer candles offered their own flickering glow, while soft organ music kept the handful of parishioners company.

I double-checked the time and made my way over to the confessional booth. This time of day many were still at work and I slipped inside the sound-padded room without delay. The interior thick velvet curtain settled into place to add another layer of crimson silence. The firm seat beneath me held no comfort despite the thin cushion, no doubt to discourage confessors from devolving into scruples.

I clasped my hands together in my lap and not for the first time longed for the rosary my grandmother had gifted me with before she'd passed. The traditional olive wood beads weren't the least bit ornate, but nonetheless beautiful in their simplicity. A shadow passed behind the lattice to my right as a figure settled on the other side.

"Good day, my son." The warmth of Father Miles' voice brought a smile to my lips as did the subtle admission that he'd seen me arrive. It had been an unexpected gift to find a sympathetic priest when everyone else seemed determined to condemn me.

I drew the cross over myself. "Forgive me, Father, for I have sinned. I'm still gay."

The partition snapped back to reveal Father Miles in full-on grumpy bear mode. "Calvin, if you cannot take this seriously…"

I smothered the rest of my laughter. "Sorry, Father. It's just too easy."

He narrowed his Azo Brown eyes at me and his mouth drew into a thin line in his pale face. "You know where his Holiness stands.

You can either confess real sins or make way for those in need of genuine contrition." He waited for me to nod before settling back with a harrumph and snapping the divider closed.

I took a deep breath, let it out slowly, and crossed myself again. "In the name of the Father, and of the Son, and of the Holy Spirit. Amen. Bless me, Father, for I have sinned. It has been…" I faltered a moment then pushed forward. "Three weeks since my last confession. I am an artist in my final year of primary school and pursuing a scholarship for secondary." My words filled the hushed space, then were swallowed by silence.

"What sins would you like to confess, my child?" Father Miles gently encouraged once more back to his easy, affable self.

"Last week I… I helped a boy at my school."

The shadowy figure shifted, and I did the same in my own uncomfortable seat. "This does not sound like a sin."

"I fear the Lord would disapprove of my methods. We engaged in sex outside the bounds of matrimony." My fingers tightened around my imaginary rosary. "I'm not sorry for the act itself, but… I know I should be."

"We've been through this. Forgiveness requires contrition."

"I am sorry, just not for me. I know who I am. I'll never apologize for being myself, but others are not as blessed."

"You cannot confess the sins of others." The gentle reprimand wasn't anything I hadn't heard before, but it still smarted.

"I know, Father, but they have no one." I let out a heavy sigh and leaned back against the unforgiving wall. "They have questions, doubts, and only me to answer them."

"The Lord works in mysterious ways."

I snorted at the implication that fucking my way through the senior class could in any way be part of God's greater plan. "There are some that fear too much to come forward. My heart breaks for them." I squeezed my eyes shut and fought the image determined to surface, the same one that had led me to confession early.

"Anything else?"

I pushed the image away and focused on smaller sins. "I was disrespectful to my mentor. He provided guidance, and I lashed out. He is a good man and does not deserve to be punished for my failures. You see, I've been avoiding an assignment for weeks—one that seems particularly difficult for me." The image I'd been fighting for days pushed forward and refused to be denied a minute longer. "And… one more thing. I saw a boy suffering. But I did not offer aid. I… I drew him."

"Was this suffering physical?" Father Miles asked, an edge of rebuke to the question.

"No, Father," I hastily clarified. "As far as I could tell, it was only suffering of the heart." Not just the heart, though, a deep soul hurt that had come to life on my page, captured for eternity in graphite and pulp. Guilt tore at my insides. "But I feel terrible. I should have extended comfort or at least warned him he wasn't alone as he believed." I stared down at my hands and pictured what Benny's reaction would have been if I'd been insane enough to do either. Fury without question.

"Why did you refrain?"

I curled my fingers until the knuckles turned white. My mind's eye filled with the tightness lining his shoulders, the subtle twitches of hard-won muscles fighting an unseen force. The wealth of sorrow and heartache that had filled the intimate space while Benny quietly fell apart and tried to keep it all together. Finally, I gave the only excuse that made sense. "Because he deserved to hurt in peace."

Father Miles' silhouette nodded beyond the lattice. "Your heart is good, though your... methods could stand improvement. As penance, you may not use the ill-gotten image for your assignment. You must obtain an honest rendition."

"But, Father," I argued, turning toward the division.

"Contrition, Calvin."

I crossed my arms and grumbled beneath my breath, though not quietly enough.

"This is your penance. You would not have confessed this sin if it did not weigh so on your heart. Thus, your atonement must start there."

I sighed in defeat and slumped against the wood at my back. "I really hate it when you're right. Okay. Fine. I won't use the portrait for the assignment." Even though it's the best fucking thing I've produced in months.

"Or..."

I stiffened and clenched my jaw. "Or the Admissions Portfolio."

"Better." I let out an aggrieved sigh at the unfairness of it all. How the fuck was I supposed to get an "honest" rendering of Benny without him beating the shit out of me? "Calvin. Is there something you'd like to say?"

"No, Father." The silhouette nodded once more, and I straightened.

"God, the Father of Mercies, through the death and resurrection of his Son, has reconciled the world to himself and sent the Holy Spirit among us for the forgiveness of sins in the name of the Father, and of the Son, and of the Holy Spirit, Amen."

As he finished, I crossed myself once more and echoed, "Amen."

"God has freed you from your sins. Go in peace."

"Thanks be to God." I took a moment to gather myself, then exited the confessional, the weight of my guilt lifted to be replaced by the pressure of figuring out how to fulfill my penance and the assignment.

Back out in the nave, I pulled my rebellious curls back and held them at the back of my head for a minute. My gaze flitted around the church, taking in the statues and crosses while I debated lingering a while longer rather than returning to the school right away. Eventually, I dropped my hair to fall loosely around my face and headed for the door. At some point, someone had pulled the massive doors shut, likely to keep the unusually warm fall out.

I pushed open the smaller door and stepped into the fading afternoon. Shadows stretched in long swatches across the sidewalk like a bright paintbrush dragging charcoal. I tucked a renegade curl behind my ear, still struggling with how to fulfill my penance, then looked up. And froze. At the end of the breezeway stood none other than Benjamin Price.

He stared at me in silence, then his gaze slid past me to take in the elegant facade of Holy Trinity and the placard boldly proclaiming it as a Catholic church. I swallowed and braced myself for the inevitable ridicule to follow as his gaze once more settled on me. Ten years I'd kept my faith quiet, avoiding the derision bound to accompany the observance of an openly gay man having religion. All of it gone, in one chance meeting.

Benny remained quiet and my anxiety rose, all the peace I'd found in absolution diminishing with each passing second. Then he blinked and continued on his way without uttering so much as a syllable. I remained frozen for another few seconds before rushing to the end of the sidewalk and looking after him in wonder. Maybe there really was such a thing as holy ground.

Kel straightened to his full height and braced for the battle to come. Not a king in this moment, but a man burdened by the expectations of an ungrateful king-dom. Though even without his majestic robes he was no less a king in control of every moment and still the strongest ruler Prince Einar had ever had dealings. The young prince debated seizing advantage of the king's precarious position and leveraging this per-ceived weakness to aid in his own trade negotiations. Expectation filled the silence as decisions waited to be made until, at last, Prince Einar bowed his head and let the proud Kelani pass unhindered. Even a king deserved to set his mantle down once in a while.

Chapter 7

Calvin

I placed the book on its precarious perch and inspected my work. Designing an alarm system out of books, while inspired, wasn't easy. I frowned and switched out one paperback for a heftier hardback. The collection of color improved, but the structure wobbled. With a frustrated huff, I removed the entire top layer and set about reconfiguring the base.

A glance to the side showed Andy every bit as lost in thought as he had been all the other times we'd hung out. I'd wanted to talk to him about what had happened in town with Benny, but he clearly had other things on his mind. He lifted his head to look in my direction without truly seeing.

Maybe what Andy needs is a distraction from his thoughts.

"So… I ran into Benny in town the other day." I paused, a fresh book in my hand. "Well, not actually ran into, but you get the idea. He saw me after my visit with Father Miles." I gently leaned the heavier book against a red-backed monstrosity. Encyclopedias always made the best noise when they fell. "Can you believe it? He didn't say so much as a word. Not one. Hell, he barely even blinked at me." I sat back on my haunches, pleased with how this latest book-trap was developing.

Andy turned a page of his own book, though I doubted he'd read so much as a word. I rolled my eyes and returned my attention to the masterpiece before me. It didn't take a genius to know Andy's preoccupation centered on his increased time with Mitch, but I'd learned the hard way not to bring up the Attackman out of the blue.

"It was weird," I continued with my recounting. "I don't think I've ever had an interaction with the guy that didn't also include a slur and profanity." Except one, I could think of one. The memory flitted through with its fuzzy feels and I sighed.

Why couldn't we have stayed like that?

We didn't have to be lovers, but would friendship really have been so far-fetched?

Of course, the very thing that would make us tolerable friends was also the number one thing stopping us. Benny saw my truth…and I saw his. "I'm telling you, one of these days he'll realize the error of his ways."

Andy glanced up again and this time his gaze actually focused. "I still don't get it. I mean, Benny… Of all the people to have a crush on."

My hand twitched at the accusation and nearly sent the whole sculpture crashing down. What I had with Benny wasn't a crush, more like morbid curiosity, bordering on obsession. Explaining that to Andy, though, would only solidify his belief, so I said nothing.

"Seriously though, he's such an ass."

The fuzzy memory came back, and a wicked grin spread across my face as I turned to Andy. "But you see, that *is* why." I held out my hands, miming Benny's spectacular ass, which had most definitely made it into my spank bank, though I only pulled it out on the rare occasion when nothing else would do. "Mm, you don't even know. Boy's got an ass you could bounce a quarter off of." I squeezed the imaginary butt and could almost feel the firm flesh giving way. Blood rushed through my veins and my cock twitched.

Fuck me. Looks like I'll be jacking off to that later.

Andy's laugh—which had become rare these days—filled the intimate nest of shelving and books and brought a different smile to my face. At the muffled sound of books falling though, our momentary happiness fled, and we each returned to our previous occupations, me to my structure and Andy to his book. As expected, the crash was followed by the emergence of Benny and his friends, if they could be called that.

"Look what we have here. It's Club Fagot." Neil and Todd mimed fucking each other in the background while Benny leaned a shoulder on the nearest shelving. I rolled my eyes at the lewdness and paid them no mind.

Amazing how it is perfectly okay for them to pretend to bend each other over, but when I do it for real, it's suddenly a crime.

"Bugger off," Andy said without raising his head. "We're not bothering anyone." I mentally frowned at the sharp dismissal and realized how tight his shoulders were.

So, that's what it is. Should have known he'd be sensitive about sex after breaking up with Connor and spending so much time with Mitch.

"You're bothering me," Benny spat, his face twisting into a sneer that marred his features. Andy's wince was barely perceptible beyond the tightening of his fingers on his book.

Oh, fuck that.

I dusted my hands and prepared to take the focus away. Benny I could handle, the others would follow him. Before I could intervene, Andy spoke up again.

"Then leave."

Benny stepped deeper into our sanctuary of literature. "What if I don't want to? What are you going to do about it?" In a flash of movement, he flipped a precariously balanced book and sent all my efforts crashing to the ground. I choked on my outrage and lurched up from the ground to deal with the brute head on.

"I'm gonna start by getting Professor Jackson. I don't think he'd appreciate learning how you're treating the materials." Once more, Andy's calm intervention stopped me.

What's gotten into him? Since when does he go at it with Benny?

Unsurprisingly, Benny bowed up at the blatant threat. "Oh yeah? And how do you think he'd appreciate finding out about you two fucking up here?"

Shock hit me in the chest, and I let out a gasp. "We are in a sacred space of learning. And… ew." I glanced over at Andy and hoped he'd understand that it was nothing personal. Andy was cute, but not remotely my type, nor was I his. And while I'd absolutely fooled around up here with others, I also wasn't dumb enough to get caught.

Andy rolled his eyes and turned back to his book, like that was the end of it. Benny's glare, on the other hand, couldn't seem to decide which of the two of us was most deserving. Determined to get to play at least a little, I gave him my best come-hither smile.

"If *you're* volunteering, though, I could be persuaded to violate the sanctity of knowledge." I could be persuaded to do a lot of things if it meant getting to taste Benny again.

His lip curled as if the suggestion was hands-down the most revolting thing he'd ever heard. Of course, we both knew better. "Whatever, homos." He flipped me off, and I clutched my chest as if restraining my beating heart. His face soured further, then he and the others stalked off.

"One of these days," I sighed as I watched Benny's tight ass walk away.

"I'm not one to judge—really, I'm not—but seriously? How can you still say that? He's a jerk and he'll always *be* a jerk."

I shook my head, because there was no way I could ever make Andy understand. Instead, I held up my hands once more in the shape of Benny's perfect ass and wiggled my eyebrows.

Andy threw up his hands in response. "To each his own."

"Speaking of which, you still carrying that flame for Mitch?" I asked, seizing the opportunity to dig into what the hell was going on with him, more concerned than ever after that little showdown with Benny. I glanced over my shoulder to find him staring down at his pages, his face twisted like he was going to puke all over it.

Shit.

"You're friends again, right? You've been spending a lot of time together at the very least," I commented, trying a different tactic.

"You could say that. And for the record, I'm trying to keep that particular light extinguished."

I diligently didn't snort. Andy not liking Mitch was like watercolors not running.

He shook his head and added, "But he makes it really hard. I don't think he has any idea how hard he makes it."

"I *bet* he doesn't," I snickered, less successful at keeping my opinion to myself a second time. Out of nowhere, a book smacked into my arm and nearly destroyed the tower of books I was working to rebuild. "Ow-wa." I glared at him as I rubbed the shallow injury. If that was what he was playing at, then kid gloves were coming off. "Have you told him?"

He instantly looked like he'd swallowed something tart. "I'm trying to make things better, not worse." We'd been through this—many times. He'd balked at all of my "methods" and refused to budge beyond the current nothing he'd held onto for four years.

"Just saying. Maybe if you slept with him…" I ventured again. His green eyes lit with anger and I thought for sure a hardback would be flying my way shortly. I held up my hands to prepare for the onslaught. "It was just a suggestion."

"The whole thing is a mess." The defeat in his voice as he hung his head hurt my heart. What good was I as a friend if I couldn't help him with this? Never mind I'd been trying to do just that for the last four years with no success.

I gave up my tower and sank down beside him. "If you would tell me more about what happened that night, maybe I could help better." He untucked his head enough to peek at me over his arms.

"I've been dreaming about that night again."

Fuck.

"Judging by the way you say that, it's not the good bits," I said, hoping that I was wrong. Andy had only shared the smallest amount of what had happened, but it had left an impression.

He shook his head and buried his face so that only his vibrant, burnished copper hair remained in sight. "It's always the same. I wake up cold and alone. I search the room, but there's no clue to where he went. He's just… gone." My heart ached for Andy. Whether or not he chose to admit it, he'd been in love with Mitch, and if his current miserable state was anything to go by, still was.

Thank God I've been spared this agony.

"I remember thinking at the time how smart he was to already have gone, that he was protecting us, so that we wouldn't be caught together," he said after a while, the edge of his voice raw with emotion. I placed a hand on his back and offered what comfort I could. His breath hitched, and he shuddered at the touch. "He's going to do it again. He's going to ghost me. I can feel it," he croaked.

"Maybe you should do it first," I whispered, still rubbing his back.

"We both know I can't do that anymore than you can let go of what happened with Benny." Like I needed the fucking reminder. Unlike some, I didn't lend more weight than the interaction deserved. It had been a dalliance, nothing more. Granted an unexpected, fucking amazing dalliance, but that was all, and it was time to remind Andy that.

I gave up my attempt at comfort, which was obviously doing nothing, and wrapped an arm around Andy's slumped shoulders. He let out a wheeze as I squeezed tightly and sighed. "Benny. Did I ever tell you about that shower?"

Andy laughed despite himself and glanced over at me. "Only like a hundred times."

Seeing his smile again gave me hope. I may not be able to fix whatever was going between him and Mitch, but I could offer a distraction from his troubles. So, I recounted the one and only sexual encounter I'd ever shared with Andy like I had every other one of the hundred times. I hadn't told him everything, but enough to arm him in the sevent he ever needed it, not that he should considering the "no-touch" order Mitch had issued to the lacrosse team shortly after they'd had their falling out, but I was positive Andy wasn't aware such an order existed. Normally, I didn't condone leveraging someone's sexual history for blackmail, but if Andy ever had occasion to need a secret that could save him from harm, I wanted him to have one. Besides, this wasn't just Benny's secret, it was mine.

Chapter 8

Benny

Going up to the library oasis had been a mistake, not the least of which because I'd gotten my foot crushed by a fucking encyclopedia of all things on my way up there. I'd taken one look at Calvin and immediately been transported back to the sidewalk in front of the church. He'd been so shocked to see me, which was fair, considering the only reason I'd been anywhere near the place had been because of my lunch with Savannah. The insults practically wrote themselves. *Calvin.* Lewd, crass, unashamedly gay, running a black-market trading scheme, not to mention all the other shit he got up to that no one would ever admit to knowing about, Calvin…was Catholic? Not possible.

But then his shoulders had tightened defensively, and the briefest flicker of fear had flashed in his eyes. I was many things, but I wasn't so much of an asshole to mock a man for having the audacity to believe in something. That fear hadn't been in his eyes at the library, but challenge had. Calvin had everything he needed to bring me to my knees and turn me into a laughingstock for the entire school. It wouldn't even take an hour before my father would be calling and demanding retribution.

I pushed away the idle thoughts and focused on the task at hand. The hallways opened before me, shrouded in darkness and devoid of life, with only the occasional lamp to light the way. I'd gotten a much later start than usual for the evening rounds due to being called to the headmaster's office—again—to explain that the culprit of what was now being heralded as the greatest prank in school history could not be found. That had gone over like a ton of bricks and I'd dragged my feet going about the rest of my school appointed duties.

The telltale squeak of a shoe scuffing on the floor rang through the hallway. I immediately altered my course and turned down the West Dormitory. A shadow darted across the hall and I quickened my pace. It hovered by the wall, oblivious to my silent approach, and peered down the dimly lit corridor.

"Looking for someone?" I asked loud enough to be heard.

The kid jumped practically out of his skin and whirled to face me. This time, the shrill squeak didn't come from his shoes. "B-Benny."

"What are you doing out of bed, third year?"

He swallowed and the little blood remaining in his face drained away. "I-I was j-just g-going to the b-b-bathroom."

"Are you finished?" I asked, knowing full well that if he hadn't already been, he'd likely pissed himself when I showed up. He nodded vigorously. "Back to your room. Lights out is lights out. No exceptions. Keep a fucking bottle in there if you have to or, better yet, don't drink before bed. Grow some fucking senses."

"Y-yes sir."

I crossed my arms and glowered at him. "Well? What are you standing around for? Get." The preteen fell over his feet in his eagerness to comply. I waited for him to vanish into what better have been his fucking room, then resumed the nightly ritual.

The North dormitory and the dining hall were both quiet. I glanced down the main hall for the East Dormitory that was still consisted entirely of older boys. Seeing nothing amiss, I made to keep going. That's when another squeak reached my ears. Unlike the scuff of a shoe, this noise had a higher pitch to it, like hinges in need of oil, or… the sound came again.

Or a bed rocking.

Anger surged through me as I stomped down the hallway, tracking the intermittent sound. With the addition of a faint moan, indignant outrage replaced my anger. Over my dead, fucking body was someone going to have the balls to sneak someone in their room on a night I was doing rounds. The sound mocked me all the way to the door itself. As I reached for the door, a thump reverberated through the floor and another moan came. I immediately twisted the knob, my gaze already sweeping the room in search of anyone that had no right to be there.

"What the fuck is going on in here?"

Moonlight poured through the drawn curtains, illuminating an immaculate room and one perfectly made bed at the far side. I scoured the space until my gaze landed at last on the room's supposed sole occupant. Too late, I realized the error of barging in. Anderson Gallagher sat buck ass naked on his bed, unabashedly stroking his cock despite the fact that someone had just walked in.

"Fucking hell, Gallagher," I snapped and lurched my gaze to his face.

"Ever heard of knocking?" he asked without stilling his hand. I thanked the darkness that he couldn't tell my face was burning.

"Jesus, you fucking fag. Stop."

"Since when is it a crime to get off?" he fired back.

"I'm right here," I snapped in a desperate attempt to get him to at least acknowledge he had an audience.

He raised an eyebrow, then without so much as a goddamn blink, he deliberately stroked himself, adding a loud moan for good measure. As his fist tightened around himself, his eyelids fluttered, but didn't close. "Are you just going to stand there, or are you going to help?" He might as well have gotten up and slapped me for all the effect his words had. I fought to control my temper and the horrifying realization that Andy didn't just know that "something" had happened in those showers, he *knew*.

"Fucking queer, keep that shit to yourself." As far as rebukes went, it was limp-wristed. Not that Andy seemed to be having a problem with that at the moment.

Fuck. Stop thinking about cock. Andy's or anyone else's, for that matter.

"That a no?" the persistent fucker asked, still working himself and adding the odd moan.

"Go fuck yourself."

"Trying. So help or get out. What'll it be?" he threw down.

Help or get out. Almost verbatim what I'd said to Calvin two years ago. Seemed Andy's threat in the hall that day wasn't idle. He *knew*.

Heat surged up my neck, and I had to clench my jaw tight enough to keep from screaming. Finally, I managed, "Keep it down," then slammed the door shut and got the fuck out of there.

Calvin

I glanced over at Greg's bed, where his silent, judgy-self had been asleep for at least a couple of hours now. With the stealth of practiced ease, I slipped from the sheets and quietly gathered my things. The shower caddy already held shampoo and body wash. I added the conditioner worth its weight in gold and slipped on the house shoes I'd purchased for the sole reason that they never squeaked. The towel I'd procured earlier got tucked under my arm and I was set. I chewed on my lip for a moment, then caved and returned to my desk. The sketchpad lying there still held the image I wasn't allowed to use, but that was neither here nor there. I'd figure something out. I pulled open the drawer and added the lube I found there to the caddy. I'd earned some me-time.

And who knows? Maybe I'll get lucky.

Doubtful, but a guy could dream. All else failed, my hand was more than sufficient to get the job done. Still smirking to myself, I ghosted out of the room and began the journey to the rarely used second floor showers. During the day, the bathrooms themselves were frequented enough, but at this hour they were blessedly empty—which was the whole reason I was here now.

I made it there without event, avoiding the elevators, as the damn things would alert anyone within a hundred feet that they were in use. I'd learned that lesson the hard way. But for all the years I'd been sneaking around the school—be it for my client exchanges or hookups—I'd only had a few close calls. I was nothing if not a master of stealth. Not even the awful squeal of the rusted hinges of the restroom door gave me pause as I reached my destination, though, perhaps it was time to add a bit more oil.

Inside, the mint green tile shone almost clear beneath the fluorescent lighting, and a wave of serenity washed over me. Though outdated by a couple of decades, the tiles never failed to remind me of a spa I'd once gone to with my mother. Sadly, the school did not boast seaweed wraps, but the water was hot and the pressure steady. I made my way past the sinks and walked around the wall separating the showers from the rest of the bathroom. Six shower heads lined the tiled walls, including a handicap accessible setup at the far end.

I took my time removing my night clothes, folding them, and placing them on a bamboo bench that rested against the dividing wall. Then I walked over to the shower in the middle of the nearest wall and turned on the spray. While the water heated, I removed everything from my caddy and placed it within easy reach. By the time I returned from securing the caddy with my clothes, the water was sufficiently hot. I stepped beneath the spray and released a sigh that bordered on a moan as the scalding water pounded my muscles. After a few indulgent minutes, I reached for the shampoo. The bottle of lube caught my eye, and I winked at it.

"It's you and me tonight." I laughed, then moaned again as my fingers massaged the lather into my scalp. Best part of showering at this unholy hour? I could make all the noise I wanted and no one would say a damn thing.

Chapter 9

Benny

There is no way Andy was telling the truth. It's been two years since that happened.

I swallowed. Sometimes it didn't feel quite that long ago, others longer. I shook my head as I turned down the latest abandoned hallway.

This really is a useless practice. No one is ever out of bed after curfew. Well, except for that one dumbass.

I continued down the vacant corridor, my mind wandering back to its original track, the same one it had been on since I had made the mistake of confronting Andy about Mitch virtually abandoning the team. I'd done a fair job of pushing the interaction to the far reaches of my mind and pretending it had never happened, but tonight had brought it roaring back to the forefront to torture me during this waste-of-time round.

Everyone knew Andy and Mitch had been friends before, but that had all changed when Mitch had become the school's star lacrosse player. Now, apparently, it was changing back. When I'd bumped into Andy that day, it'd seemed like an ideal time to confront at least one of them about it. Mitch may not have exactly been a friend, but he was vital to the team, and the team was suffering due to his lack of focus. Andy had never stood up to me before. I hadn't expected our chat to be any different.

Wrong.

I blew out a sharp puff of air. When he'd first voiced the low-key threat, I hadn't wanted to believe it. How could he have gone so long without saying anything? I'd certainly given him and Calvin plenty of reason to use the information against me. I ground my teeth together. Truthfully, it was a goddamn miracle the entire school didn't know.

Calvin's a damn gossip queen.

Even as I thought it, I knew it wasn't true. Calvin didn't share secrets. He collected them. For what horrid purpose was anyone's guess.

Probably blackmail. Definitely for his illicit trading scheme. Which I'm sure he doesn't think I know anything about.

I hooked a right and suddenly found myself in front of the second-floor showers. The same showers that he'd found me in two years ago. I glanced around the barren hallway.

It couldn't hurt to look, if only to confirm that Andy was just having a go at me. All threats aside, there's no way he was actually serious.

Confident in my assumption, I boldly strode to the door. I cringed as the rusty hinges squealed and glanced back down the barren hall, positive that the ruckus would have alerted the entire fucking school to what I was doing. When the obscene sound faded, there was still a steady noise filling the room: running water.

Someone's taking a shower.

The ridiculous thought floated by unattached. My legs moved with a life all their own, powered by I didn't even know what.

No fucking way. It has to be someone else. There's no way that he's continued to take showers here at three-fucking-am for two years. Just. In. Case.

I rounded the privacy wall and stopped dead. Sure enough, Calvin Fucking Bridges was standing by a stream of water covered in soap—naked. *Very naked.* My gaze followed the path of suds as they slid their way down his slick back. They swirled in the dip above his ass, then streamed down his long legs with their light layer of dark hair. The bubbles I'd been tracking finally left his body, and I dragged my gaze back up. Muscles in his back rippled as he went through the motions of cleaning. He didn't look the same as before; he looked better. Though how that was even fucking possible was beyond me. My heart pounded. I'd have given almost anything if I could just look away, or at least fucking blink, but my eyes stayed glued to his light brown skin with its warm peach undertones.

He still hasn't seen me.

No sooner did I think it, then he turned around.

Fuck me. When did he start working out?

Calvin did not look like the kind of guy to possess a six-pack—perpetually skinny, maybe—but not toned. Even with suds still obscuring half of him, I could clearly see the definition, the outline of firm pectorals, the perfect ridges of his abdominals, the pronounced V that invited a wandering gaze to keep exploring. Heat rushed through me as I continued to take in every sculpted inch of him. The same heat that had sprung to life as I'd stood outside and stared at the door just thinking of the possibility that he might be within.

"Benny."

At the sound of my name, I dragged my gaze up to his face, where his brown eyes were wide in surprise.

He's still not afraid of me.

The thought came unbidden. Then the reality of the situation hit home, and that this was an almost perfect role reversal of what had happened two years ago.

I need to leave. Turn around and go. I have my answer. Turn and GO.

The urgent logic asserted itself and yet, my rebellious gaze fell to the tiled floor and landed on a bottle by the soap.

That's not shampoo.

Calvin watched in silence as I stripped off first my shirt, then my pants, quickly followed by my boxers. I threw them to some dry corner and stalked up to him. I snatched the bottle of lube from the floor and tossed it at him. "Expecting someone?" I wasn't sure why I asked or why it even mattered. I just knew that it did.

"Never hurts to be prepared," he responded, a cheeky smile teasing his lips. His eyes blatantly traveled down and back up my body, inspiring another wave of heat. I stared back at him and tried not to think about what I was doing. "Same as before?" he inquired with a raised eyebrow.

God, yes. I still had fucking dreams about his mouth on my cock and what it had felt like to have him inside of me. I was getting hard just thinking about it now. Correction, harder. Blood had rushed to my cock the moment I'd laid eyes on him.

"Not quite," I responded, then before he could say anything else, I placed a hand on his surprisingly defined chest and pushed him back under the water.

He stared at me unblinking, still not an ounce of fear in those dark eyes. The last of the soap washed off of him and I wrapped my hand around his cock. He stiffened beneath my fingers and my pulse spiked. I tightened my grip and stroked up his length, rubbed my thumb across the tip, then slid back down again. His eyes lidded and he gave a low moan.

"Tell me when you're getting close," I ordered. I waited for the commentary, the judgment, anything. All he did was nod.

I looked down at where I had hold of him. His cock, like the rest of him, was several shades darker than me. I gave the spongy cap an experimental squeeze. It was different touching someone else like this, yet there was still an echoing stir in my cock. Not to mention, there was something intoxicating about hearing him groan as I worked him, but that wasn't what I really wanted.

I knelt down and studied him for a moment. Still no quippy remark. I wanted to know what he tasted like, had thought about it far more than I cared to admit. Slowly I took the head into my mouth and was instantly surprised at the difference in feel from my fingers. I swirled my tongue around the tip, and he rewarded me with a throaty groan. My cock twitched in response. My lips slid further down his shaft as I took more of him in. I ran my hands up the front of his muscled thighs and stroked his Adonis belt with my thumbs while I admired the neatly trimmed nest of dark curls surrounding my captive prize.

His hips threatened to buck as I added the flat of my tongue and established a rhythm. The sound of the water spraying around us mostly hid the noises I was making, but did little to cover his increasingly husky breathing. It was fucking hot. To know that I was doing that, I was making the self-confident Calvin Bridges lose his cool. He let out a heavy moan as I methodically worked my tongue up and darted it across his slit. Finally, I had my answer to what he tasted like.

He's salty, almost sweet.

I took all of him back in again and his breath hitched. "I'm gonna come," he groaned. I quickly released him, a little sad to have to stop. His groan this time was decidedly more disappointed.

I stood up, and he watched me in perfect silence like he'd done everything else, like he'd done two years ago when I'd been unwilling to turn him away. I snaked an arm around his waist and tugged him away from the wall. Our cocks brushed together, and a thrill surged through mine. For a moment, we stood chest to chest, face to face, his golden-brown eyes seeing everything inside of me I worked so hard to keep from the world. My gaze flicked down to where his lips hovered on level with mine.

I wonder what the rest of him tastes like.

I ignored the thought and took his place by the wall, facing it instead of leaning on it as he had been. Whatever insanity had brought me here tonight, I was done waiting. It was time to see how good my memory really was. The lid of the lube made a snap as it opened and trepidation shot through me.

*What am I doing? This is wrong. This is insane. This is—*a seriously lubed finger circled my hole, then slipped inside—*fucking incredible.* I groaned and pushed back. My memory didn't do it justice.

"Easy." The soft word was like a caress, matching the way his other hand was massaging my ass cheek. He added another finger, and I got harder.

Fuck. Why does that feel so good?

Then he moved, slow and shallow at first, then deeper until he stroked that spot inside me I'd been too afraid to touch myself. I redefined my definition of good. He took his time working me open, gradually increasing his pace, then slowed again when I started pressing back in time with his thrusting fingers.

God damn it, Cal.

I wanted to shout at him to stop fucking with me and just take me already, but I was struggling with coherency too much to try to form a proper sentence. Another finger. My whole body simultaneously reveled and rebelled at the invasion. Another delicate brush of my prostate.

God, I'm not gonna make it.

No sooner did I adjust to the feel, than all three fingers were gone. I sagged against the wall, resting most of my weight on my forearms.

I don't know if I should be relieved or upset.

His fingers kneaded my cheeks, and my moan turned desperate. Then he pulled them back apart. My breath caught when I felt his swollen head at my entrance.

About fucking time.

Impatient, I made to push back, only to have his hands turn to iron and prevent me from moving. No comment or anything, just a silent command to hold still. A shudder ran through me, but I didn't force the issue.

If he goes any slower, I'm going to pass out from anticipation.

He slid past the first ring and I let out a whine.

Fuck fuck fuck. Oh god, was he this big last time? I don't remember this at all.

My hand fisted against the slick tile, and I forced it back flat.

"Breathe, Benny," he whispered.

I wasn't aware I had stopped. I dragged in a shaky lung full of air. As I let it out, he drove the rest of the way home and stopped moving. His lithe fingers started massaging the small of my back while he stayed deeply rooted, his impressive cock stretching me. I focused on the touch instead of the burn. I knew Calvin was an artist, but this was different. He confidently traced patterns in my skin, as if he could see something no one else could.

Maybe he can.

I drew in another deep breath in time with the swirls he was creating. When I exhaled, the last of my tension went with it. I relaxed, and he slid a fraction deeper, his cock expertly angled to rub across my prostate. A groan from somewhere deep inside of me emerged as I hung my head.

That, that is what I remember.

Pleasure spiraled as the memory I'd clung to and this new reality merged. Then he moved. He pulled out halfway, and I whined again. *What the fuck is wrong with me?* He pushed back in all the way to the hilt. *Fuck me, that's good.* Gradually, he established a rhythm of long, deep strokes. His painter's hands digging into my sides started to feel like the only things holding me up. I let out another moan and reached for my cock. *How is it possible for anyone to be this hard?*

"Fuck you're tight." The low hiss nearly sent me careening over the edge. Already, I could feel it building to a breaking point.

I don't want to come so soon, but if he keeps talking like that, I won't have a choice.

His grip loosened, and he pulled nearly all the way out. I could have cried with frustration. Before he could stop me, I rammed back and took all of him at once.

"Fuck!"

I echoed his exclamation as I came hard enough that the light green tile turned white.

Our ragged breathing surrounded me as we came down from our respective climaxes. His hair brushed the middle of my back as he folded to rest his forehead on me. He finally slipped out and an overwhelming emptiness took its place. The ache of absence warred with the satisfaction of fulfillment. Suddenly, I realized the water was still falling all around us.

Neither of us said a word as we stepped far enough apart to clean up. He passed me the soap in perfect silence and we took turns in the spray that miraculously still held warmth. We rinsed off and got dressed, the haze of release still firmly wrapped around my mind and keeping my body a relaxed collection of muscles. It was a motherfucking miracle I didn't collapse as I put my pants on. I still felt like I should be lying in a heap on the floor, though it wouldn't have helped the ache in my ass, an ache that wasn't entirely bad.

That hadn't been at all like I remembered it. It had been a hundred times better.

I looked over at Calvin gathering his things where we'd just…
What the fuck did I just do?

I walked over to him and he raised an eyebrow in that infuriating way he had. "Not a fucking word of this to anyone." A smile played at the edge of his lips. He mimed zipping his mouth shut, locking it, then throwing away the key.

Real fucking cute.

"This doesn't make me gay," I said emphatically.

He snorted a laugh, and I glared at him. He held his hands up defensively, but kept to the silence.

I glared at him again for good measure and had to resist the urge to give him another once over.

You'd never know…

I dragged my thoughts away from what he really looked like beneath the plain cotton tee and loose lounge pants. Without another word, I exited the showers and made a beeline for my room. I was already deep under the covers by the time it occurred to me I hadn't ever actually finished the round.

Well, fuck.

I sat up, and something pulled at my side. My hand quested beneath the covers for the source, but came up empty. I flicked on the lamp and investigated more thoroughly, my hand patting along the under sheet.

Nothing in the bed. Maybe it's on me.

At last, I found the cause of my inexplicable discomfort. Three perfect scratches, easily an inch long, graced my hip with a matching set on the other side. I snickered to myself.

Perfect composure, my ass.

I wasn't even thinking as I pulled out the notebook I kept under the bed. Pages filled with scribbled words flipped past until at last I found a blank one and continued the story I'd been working on for the last two years.

The indomitable Kel had met his match…

Chapter 10

Calvin

The filing cabinet squeaked and groaned in protest at the sudden force of me plopping atop it. Almost instantly, the sound of my great aunt's voice scolding me for sitting on the furniture filled my mind. I smiled as my over-sized sketchpad landed with a hard smack on the desk before me. Great Aunt Winnie hadn't been able to break me of the habit and I didn't expect Ulwich Prep to have much success either. I leaned back on my arms, my legs kicking aimlessly, while I awaited Professor Jankowski to return and give me my passing grade. Unsurprisingly, my mind wandered back to the same merry-go-round it had been circling for the better part of three days.

Benny gave me head. Benjamin Fucking Price actually got down on his knees and put my dick in his mouth. Willingly.

Giddiness bubbled through me like Dom Perignon. I still wasn't sure what surprised me more, that it had been *the* Benjamin Price or that he'd been so goddamn enthusiastic. Probably had as much to do with all my thoughts being centered on my dick, but I could have sworn he'd sighed—in disappointment, no less—when I'd warned him I was on the edge. To be fair, I'd been pretty fucking disappointed myself, so it was possible I'd actually heard my own sigh. Hard to tell with the water crashing around us, but I was inclined to believe it was Benny. Of course, getting to slide into that tight hole, his intense heat wrapping around me...yeah, that might have made up for it.

Benjamin Fucking Price.

A smile tripped over my lips. Bringing the lube had been a stroke of genius. Shame I hadn't thought to keep a spare condom in the shower caddy. Even as I considered starting to do so now, I dismissed the reckless idea. Getting caught with it wasn't worth the risk. So what if we'd gone bare? Benny was officially one of two guys in my entire life I'd ever done that with and I took my health seriously. I trusted he did as well.

With a body like that, he'd have to.

"I see you've done it."

The comment merged so perfectly with my latest mental victory lap, it took me a second to process the intended meaning behind the words. I blinked the fantasy away and realized that at some point Jankowski had arrived. Though how I'd missed it when he was standing right fucking in front of me... I shook my head at my distraction and focused on what had captured his attention—the sketch of Benny in the library.

"This is incredible," Jankowski said, like I'd expected he would when I'd completed the damn thing in the first place.

Shit.

"Wait. Not that one." He glanced over, his mouth pressing briefly into a thin line as I hopped off the cabinet and stepped forward. I took the pad from him, careful not to crumple the exposed page and opened the book to the more recent, honestly obtained portrait. "This one," I said as I passed it back.

Surely Benny knowing I was there this time counts as honest. Right?

Jankowski gently took the pad back and glanced down at the fresh image. The moment his gaze landed on the page, though, he jerked away. "Calvin, how many times do I have to tell you? You cannot give me pictures like this."

"Oh please, art is art. And he's not even a minor. Even I have some moral standards." I gestured at the image, because *obviously* that wasn't some kid. His scowl deepened as he stared at me. "What?"

"But it is still a student. Correct?"

"Irrelevant," I countered.

"Calvin, I do not want to see my pupils this way. It's unethical."

"It's *art*. At least look at the damn thing before you decide I'm too morally depraved."

"I didn't say…" He let out a heavy sigh and pinched the bridge of his nose as he often did when we debated subject matter. With obvious reluctance, he finally looked down. He gave another put-upon sigh like I was torturing him instead of offering some of my best work, maybe ever. "It's exceptional. Your attention to detail is as astute as ever. But the eyes… those are incredible. You've captured a world of emotion and you can only see half his face."

I knew exactly what he was talking about. Lines arched gracefully up the page to form the sculpted landscape of Benny's back. Shading had brought the two-dimensional sketch into a world all its own where I could reach in and touch the quivering skin, flush from heat and arousal. You could just make out his hands in the background, bracing him against the wall while he turned to look over his shoulder at me, his lips parted slightly, still spit-slick.

Everything about his face was incredible, the openness, the raw vulnerability, the way his eyes shone with lust and sheer desperate *need*. I'd jacked off to it no less than three times. First time I'd ever jacked off to one of my works, so I guess, point Benny. Fine, two points Benny. The first for taking me by surprise and making me finish before I'd intended.

"Why not the other?" Jankowski asked, bringing my thoughts back to the present.

I crossed my arms and leaned against the cabinet. "This one's better."

"I'd say they both admirably display your talent. But the first… might be better received."

My spine stiffened. Why couldn't the male form be beautiful? It was okay to depict women like this, but heaven forbid a man be portrayed as vulnerable, as wanting. Being those things didn't make him weak, they made him strong. Not to mention, I'd intentionally left out anything that might be conceived as explicit, stopping well above the spectacular curve of his ass. No Dimples of Venus, no exquisitely muscled thighs, not so much as a goddamn nipple. I'd even left out the water, for fuck's sake.

"I'm not using the other. You can judge me for this one or not at all."

"But why?" he asked, his gaze flicking up at my serious tone.

"Personal reasons." I shrugged and left it at that.

He simply shook his head and returned his focus to the piece. Suddenly, he jerked and ripped back to the previous portrait with as much care as anyone can frantically flip between two pages. "Is this…Please tell me this isn't…" His voice dropped to a whisper as he turned eyes wide with horror on me. "For the love of God, Calvin, please tell me this isn't Benjamin Price."

An evil grin spread across my face. Though admittedly, I was impressed he'd gathered that from half a profile. "Well, they are the same person, if that's what you're asking."

He snapped the book shut and dropped it to the table like a living, breathing Benny might actually emerge from the layers of graphite. "I understand you pride yourself on the outrageous, but have you no sense of self-preservation? At all?"

"I survive just fine." I plucked the discarded sketchpad up and tucked it securely back in my bag.

"And what do you think Mr. Price will do if he finds out about those?"

"Beat the living shit out of me, I imagine."

"Jesus," he hissed. "I can't display this. If Benjamin isn't even in my class and *I* can figure it out, others will as well." He glanced at me out of the corner of his eye. "Are you two… No. Don't answer that, I don't want to know." He straightened up. "I will accept this as your assignment—you clearly have the skills—but it will not be included in the fall exhibit." I made to argue, and he held up a hand. "It's not up for debate, but it is time we cultivate this skill set. For your next assignment, no more of this side view nonsense. I want a full frontal."

"You sure about that?" I asked with a smirk.

He nearly swallowed his tongue as his words caught up with him. "Clothes *on*." My smirk broadened to a grin. Clothes on could be just as salacious with the right details. Jankowski finally found his voice and his glower. "In addition, I want a self-portrait."

"Now wait a minute. I'm not creating some pretentious piece of—"

"I'm fully aware of your opinion on the style, however, this too is also not up for debate. I've been far too lax in accepting your excuses and *that*," he gestured at my satchel and the sketchpad within, "proves it. Your portfolio is nowhere near complete. You have your grade, but if you want to keep it, you'll create the pieces."

My jaw tightened along with my death grip on the strap of my bag. This was blackmail, pure and simple. I should know. I leveraged this tactic all the time with my clients.

Jankowski softened the tiniest bit. "Remember, artists—even great ones—rarely get to choose their own subjects."

I huffed and pushed my way past him to make my way down the hall. He might as well have added that great artists were also usually dead by the time they were recognized as great. Begrudging acceptance gradually tempered my anger. There was no way Jankowski would ever understand my abhorrence of self-portraits. Most really were of pretentious ass wipes puffed up with their own self-importance, but there were the odd few that stood out as genuinely remarkable. Those told a story and I didn't want my story to be told.

Too late, I heard the telltale catcall. I lurched to a stop, my hand going instinctively to protect my satchel and its precious contents. I'd die if something happened to those sketches. Before they could gain more on me than surprise, I squared my shoulders and locked eyes with Benny. My fingers curled over the flap, my thoughts instantly going to the condemning pictures within, and I smiled.

Benny

I'd run into Calvin over the years a hundred times, no, make that a thousand, and it had never affected me before. But today, it did. I swallowed hard at the lascivious grin pulling at his lips and, for probably the first time in my life, was grateful that he always looked at me like that. Nate and Todd would never be able to know something was different, even if I did. There was no distinguishable difference. He always leered like a lech because he knew it got under my skin. The more I squirmed, the more he did it. It was an awful game and one we couldn't seem to stop playing. And now, now all I could think as he looked at me like that and caressed his bag was how fucking envious I was of the damn bag.

Fuck. Double fuck.

It had taken over a day for my ass to stop smarting and half that for me to start aching to have him fill me again. All my years of avoiding this part of myself were gone in an instant. Blood roared in my ears and he arched one dark eyebrow, that knowing smile still painted on his face. With growing desperation, I slammed down all my walls, barbs and everything, then fell back on the familiar.

"What the fuck are you looking at, queer?"

His eyes glinted with a malevolence that immediately froze my heart and stilled the air in my lungs. What if he told? I had nothing to stop him, no argument, no leverage, only this unbearable want crawling up my spine bolder than ever. He removed his hand from the satchel and inspected his nails like he had all the time in the world. Only Calvin Bridges could calmly face off with three grown athletes without an ounce of backup and remain cool as crystal.

"That really the best you can do, Benny?" He tsked his teeth and shook his head slowly from side to side. "If you're going to insult me, Price, the least you can do is get creative." He glanced up at the ceiling as if pondering the ultimate insult. Then he dropped it again, eyes wide with inspiration, long fingers of both hands spread out in the air. "I know! You could tell me I have a small dick."

Todd and Neil snickered behind me at Calvin's self-imposed insult. I couldn't bring myself to even do that, no matter how smart it would have been. We both knew that Calvin didn't have a small dick by any stretch of the imagination. Fuck, even thinking about it made my ass clench greedily. If he kept making cracks about his dick like that, I'd end up sprouting wood. I needed to get control of this now. I took a step toward him and his open grin settled back into a smirk.

"What'll it be Benny?"

"Telling you that you have a small dick assumes you even have one."

"Ooh." Calvin placed the fingers of one hand against his chest in mock injury. "Benjamin, do we need to play doctor?"

I rolled my eyes. "When's the last time you even saw a doctor?"

His eyes sharpened, betraying that I'd struck a nerve. He didn't have many, and they were damn near impossible to find, but he did have them. "Three months ago, you fuck twat. Clean bill of health. What about you, Benny? Up to date on your rabies shots?"

"Like I would put my teeth anywhere near you." A traitorous image of his cock gagging me while my nose pressed into his pubes and he moaned above me flashed through my mind. I fisted my hands and pushed the image away, determined not to let him get the best of me. "Speaking of people willing to be near you, where's your little sidekick?" I leveled my hand at my waist.

"Yeah," Neil snickered, "Where's fire crotch?"

Calvin's gaze flickered to him at the pedantic insult. "How the fuck should I know? We're not attached at the hip."

"Really?" I crossed my arms. "You two seemed pretty... *tight* once upon a time. Let me guess, he gave up when he figured out you didn't have a dick to find."

The muscles in Calvin's jaw worked furiously while his eyes burned with anger. As soon as the emotion surfaced though, it was gone, no more than a pan flash. "Andy has absolutely zero interest in my dick. I can be gay and have friends without wanting to fuck them, asshole."

"You sure about that? Last I checked, you only had the one friend, and he's nowhere to be seen." I held out my arms to encompass the hallway that currently only held the four of us.

"Hasn't been for a while," Todd chimed in. I glanced back at him and he tipped his chin at me. I barely didn't roll my eyes at the unnecessary assist and returned my attention to where Calvin was working harder than usual to remain neutral.

"How much has to be wrong with you that not even other queers want to be around you?" I asked.

"Go fuck yourself."

"Seems to me like he's moved on... or is it moved back? Now that Mitch is back in the picture, he doesn't need or want you. Face it, you were never anything more than a placeholder to him." With each word, Calvin's shoulders tightened more and more until the tension practically rolled off of him and he had a death grip on his satchel.

"You don't know what you're talking about." His glance slid behind me. "At least my friends aren't a bunch of boot-licking sycophants. Did you get a say or did daddy buy them outright for you?"

"Watch your fucking mouth," Neil growled while Todd bowed up.

I held up a hand to forestall them before it escalated to actual violence and continued to worry the open wound I'd uncovered.

"Bought or not, at least I know they have my back. Tell me, does Andy have yours when it matters, or only when it suits him?"

Dumb and Dumber fist bumped behind me. "That's right, ride or die you pansy bitch," Neil added like the idiot he was. I barely checked my eye roll and took another bold step toward Calvin, who glared absolute death at me.

A part of me instantly missed the lascivious look that seemed a permanent part of him, capable of stripping you bare and fucking you where you stood. The other part recognized that I wasn't supposed to want that, wasn't supposed to want *him*. He remained rooted to the spot as I leaned forward and dropped my voice so it wouldn't carry. His sharp gaze cut to me and I almost checked to see if the look had drawn blood.

"Does anyone at this school actually know who you are? Do they care? You talk a lot of smack, but admit it, at the end of the day, you're an island, always have been."

"Haus," Todd called. "We throwing down or what?"

I stepped back and looked down my nose at Calvin, not easy considering we were the same height. "What's that? Nothing to say, Bridges?"

The rage simmering in his eyes crystallized into ice. "Oh, I have plenty to say."

A spike of fear shot through my chest. Despite my gnawing uncertainty, I didn't back down. Calvin could've destroyed me years ago. He hadn't then, and I didn't expect he would now. "Let's hear it." The challenge fell from my lips and every muscle braced for the worst.

His icy gaze studied me, then his lips twisted into an almost smile. Releasing his white-knuckled grip on his bag, he flipped his hair back. "No, I don't think I will." The air of nonchalance was pure grade-A bullshit as he made a grand show of stepping around me to continue on his original journey.

Todd and Neil moved with the same coordination they did on the field to stop him. I waved them both off and they looked at me askance.

"Let him go. He's not worth our time. He's not worth anyone's time."

Calvin's shoulders tensed as he passed between them, the only sign I'd struck a nerve. No one moved as he walked unhurriedly down the hall. When he finally disappeared around a corner, the tightness in my chest eased and Neil and Todd rushed me.

"Damn, boss, that was cold," Neil said, clapping me on the back.

"I don't remember that last I saw him actually shook. How'd you know the dig about Andy would get to him?"

I blinked away the last sight of him. "Good guess. Figured if Mitch flaking to hang with his old buddy fucked with the team, then Andy was probably doing the same." It was more than that, of course. Being unique brought with it a level of isolation whether you wanted it or not, and Calvin was nothing if not unique.

King Kelani's rage could have burnt down the entire palace if it hadn't been so cold. The aloof king had fielded countless attempts to undermine his rule over the years. In fact, such attempts had only reinforced his reign, made him bolder. Prince Einar had longed to be the one who brought the emboldened king to heel, who reminded Kel that he was not the only significant player in this game of crowns. But now that Einar had at long last accomplished his impossible task, he could not maintain the King's level glare. He had not anticipated his victory to taste so bitter.

$$Chapter\ 11$$

Benny

I stood in front of the door to the second-floor showers and hesitated. More than anything, I wanted to go inside, to be claimed by him again, to just *be*, but I faltered, unsure of the reception I'd receive after what had happened in the hall. Calvin and I'd had several run-ins throughout the week, but that one haunted me. The ghost of hurt in his eyes had been real and I'd put it there. And why? Because I was afraid he'd reveal what we'd done to Todd and Neil? That was part of it, but not the part that mattered. Calvin could have exposed me for the liar I was years ago. Hell, I kind of hoped he would. Then I could finally stop pretending. No, after nights of tossing and turning, I could finally admit the truth. To myself, if not to Calvin. I'd violated our unspoken rules of engagement. Made him hurt because I could, because it was expected of me. I'd gone for the one thing I knew would bring him to his knees in some misguided attempt to prove he didn't have power over me. Except he did. He always had.

My fingers wrapped around the handle. Would he send me away? Demand retribution?

Is he even here?

I pushed the door open. The damnable hinges squealed with a horrible cacophony of metal against metal, alerting the whole fucking world of my weakness. It swung shut with a decided thump and the sound of running water filled the room. The tension wrapped around my chest relaxed slightly, but didn't dissipate altogether. The need to know quickened my steps until at last I rounded the wall dividing the showers from the rest of the bathroom.

My breath caught and my stomach lurched into my throat as my gaze fell on Calvin's light brown body leaning against the pale green tile. Water cascaded over him, caressing every exposed inch of his gloriously naked body before running off to vanish down the embedded drain. He raked back damp curls from his face while his other hand stroked up his length with a firm grip. His fingers slid all the way up his cock with practiced ease until they encapsulated his swollen head, then purposefully slid back down.

By the time I dragged my riveted gaze away from the mouthwatering sight, my pants were uncomfortably tight and Calvin's eyes were boring into me. Apologies for the awful things I'd said bubbled up, closely followed by the overwhelming desire to beg for his forgiveness, offer him whatever he wanted so long as he'd touch me again. I swallowed down all of it and it swirled unpleasantly in my stomach.

We stared at each other with nothing but the sound of spray hitting tile filling the air. The whole time he continued lazily stroking himself like he didn't have an audience. He squeezed the base of his shaft and arched against the wall, his heading falling back at the pleasure of it. I didn't even bother to check my groan as sheer fucking want turned to liquid fire pulsing in my veins. Calvin raised his head and looked at me once more, his eyebrow characteristically raised.

"You just going to stand there and cream your pants or are you gonna come over here so I can fuck it out of you?"

One minute I was across the room, the next Calvin was shoving me under the spray, his hand like a vice around my aching cock, making me gasp. I didn't remember taking my clothes off or what I had done with them. I didn't remember when I'd decided to come here. I didn't remember anything for the next hour.

Calvin

My thoughts were a muddled mess, like paint splatter on a white wall, the color running together and no discernable image in sight. I absently checked the enclave that held a statue of some forgotten scholar who'd undoubtedly paid a shit ton of money for the ugly piece. But not even the three folded slips of paper could pull me out of the quagmire. Benny had come back, the unmistakable glint of fear and desperate want shining in his eyes. Part of me hadn't expected him to show. Hadn't wanted him to. His taunts about Andy had cut deep and still stung. I hated him for taking our typical banter that far. Despite forgiveness being a tenant of my faith, I'd never been very good at it. It galled a bit that I'd not only been pleased that he *had* shown, but that all my plans to punish him by turning him away had gone down the drain the second I'd laid eyes on him.

I slipped into the art room and let out a relieved breath to find that no one else had arrived yet. My usual desk toward the back of the room squeaked as I sat, reminding me of the door to the showers. Hate fucking wasn't something I really ascribed to. I made a point to always be tender with the men I slept with, recognizing it was likely their first time and no one should have to endure a first like I had. But ascribed to or not, that's exactly what I'd done with Benny. He hadn't protested the rough handling or punishing pace. He'd taken it like a champ, almost like he thought he deserved it.

… And that's where my brain dissolved, like a water-based blue paint reaching across soaked paper until it was translucent. I wasn't that person. As mad as I was at Benny, I didn't use partners that way. Not even Benjamin Price *deserved* to be treated like that.

"Penny for your thoughts?"

I blinked and glanced at the desk beside me where Keagan sat waiting for my response. At some point, the rest of the class had come in and somehow I'd missed it. I returned my focus to him, noting that he'd copied the way I'd done my tie, or more accurately, hadn't, as well as untucked half his button-down. Though I doubted he realized it was actually a French Tuck and intentional style choice on my part rather than a means of rebellion. They said imitation was the highest form of flattery. I found it fucking annoying.

"Have you decided what you'll be submitting to the art show in the spring?" Keagan asked when I neglected to answer his first question.

The sketch of Benny looking over his shoulder while water cascaded around him flashed through my mind. I ground my teeth, more than a little perturbed with myself that I couldn't seem to keep my thoughts away from Price. "No," I responded flatly, then turned to remove a less damning sketchbook and the art text.

"Huh, normally you have like ten things already lined up and the rest of us are trying to squeeze in anything." He gave a humorless laugh, reminding me that despite being in a room full of shared interests, I had no friends here. Whether it was because I was gay, better than them, or both was anyone's guess. "Maybe this will be my year to take the showpiece."

I barely contained a snort. Snow stood a better chance in hell than of Keagan being awarded the coveted showpiece slot. "What are you planning to submit?" I asked, feigning interest. Anything was better than thinking about my last encounter with Benny.

"Like I'd tell you. Last thing I need is you pulling another stunt like you did our sophomore year."

"The assignment was landscapes. It's not my fault Hunter, and I chose the same one to paint." It didn't matter how many times I said it was an accident, pure coincidence. No one believed I hadn't done it on purpose to show him up. The debacle had solidified my reputation among the school's art community as an egotistical upstart. It certainly didn't help that the piece had captured the aforementioned showpiece.

"Yeah, yeah. You start your self-portrait yet?"

I stiffened. "Not yet."

Keagan gave me a quizzical look. "For real? It's due in like two weeks. No way you'll finish in time."

"Yeah, well, I guess I'll be asking for an extension then, now won't I?"

His blue eyes turned cruel. It was a subtle shift, but one I'd learned to pick up on early in life. "Thought for sure you of all people would've had that done in no time."

My grip on my sketching pencil tightened until it snapped, compounding my irritation. That was my last 6H graphite. I'd have to order more and they definitely wouldn't arrive anytime soon, thanks to the brand I preferred. I chunked the broken pieces into my bag and pulled out a 2B. If I was lucky, I could salvage the other and eek out a few more sketches before it was unusable. I didn't bother responding to Keagan's less than subtle dig at my "over-inflated pride", instead sliding down in my seat to review the pieces of paper I'd retrieved on the way to class.

I unfolded the first, mindful of prying eyes. It was from Connor, thanking me for the boa and letting me know he had more pot whenever I needed it. The next was more crumpled paper than folded note. The shaky handwriting betrayed their nerves as they asked for flavored lube for their girlfriend. Despite the nom de plum they'd used, there wasn't a doubt in my mind it was a request from Tanner, and it definitely wasn't for a "girlfriend". The note joined the first, and I reached for the last. My eyebrows rose in surprise at the request. It wasn't every day a student at Ulwich had the balls to ask for anal beads. Hell, I didn't even have any. Then again, I'd never had a partner interested in exploring anything beyond my dick in their ass.

Shaking my head, I stood and walked over to the art supply cabinet. There were still a few minutes before class officially started. More than enough time to take care of this. I fished out a paper mixing cup and poured undiluted acetone into it, then dropped the scraps in one at a time. The paper may not have completely dissolved, but they were a far cry from legible. Best way to keep secrets was to make sure there was no evidence. I was nearly done cleaning up when I spied my pouch of backup art supplies shoved into a corner of the cabinet from when I used to sneak into the classroom to draw in solitude. That was before I'd been tall enough to get onto the ledge in the library.

Back in my seat, with scant seconds to spare, I unzipped the uncharacteristically demure pencil bag and let out a whoop.

"Mr. Bridges, was there something you wanted to share with the class?" Jankowski asked from the front of the room with an exasperated expression that could rival Father Miles'.

"Found another 6H, but I don't plan on sharing," I replied with a cocky grin.

Jankowski stopped just shy of rolling his eyes and turned to the board to start class. "For today's lecture we'll be covering..." His voiced drifted out of focus as I twirled my unexpected prize and flipped to a fresh page.

Chapter 12

Calvin

The door squealing open barely even registered as I entered the showers. *Will he be here?* Part of me was genuinely curious; then again, he'd either already been here or shown up shortly after me the last four times.

I don't hear anything. Maybe he won't show.

I tempered my disappointment. I always knew what this had been. Having fun with Benny was bound to have a short shelf life, even if it was nice to learn someone's body, all the tiny things that drove them wild with pleasure. That wasn't something I'd had before. Twice was my previous all-time high, and that had been as much desperation as good timing.

Oh well, it was fun while it lasted.

I folded my clothes and rounded the division, where a grin immediately split my face. I quickly reined it in. It would never do for Benny to know how much I was enjoying our random hookups. So maybe the enjoyment wasn't strictly getting to know *any* person's body, but Benny's specifically. Stripping away his reservations to reveal the unbridled lust lurking beneath the surface was a special kind of high. I'd debated what I would do if he showed up again after that day in the hall. All sorts of scenarios had come to mind, but in the end, seeing the aching want in his eyes had decided me. Whatever else I could do, it wouldn't ever have near the satisfaction of bringing Benjamin Price to his knees.

He's so fucking proud.

And already naked, I was pleased to note. My grin threatened to make a reappearance as I shamelessly appreciated the view. Muscles wrapped around him like they'd been sculpted and rippled as he moved, every motion intentional and confident.

An athlete's body without question. And those squats are definitely helping. He has a fantastic ass. Like a perfect bubble. Tight and round.

My cock twitched at the thought of what I was going to do to that ass and I slowly worked my gaze back up his spectacular body. Either Benny hadn't heard the damnable door or he was ignoring me. He walked over to the same shower we'd used the last couple of times.

"Not that one," I called out. He spun around, clearly startled, and I smirked.

Little distracted, Mr. Price?

He glanced back at the shower. "What?"

I walked across the light green tile to a larger station on the far side of the room. "This one tonight." There was no missing the reproachful look he gave the handicap set up. Truthfully, the bench was too small to be of any actual use, but that wasn't why I chose it.

As if reading my thoughts, he asked, "Why?"

The knob twisted in my hand, sending out a wave of steam as the cascade of scalding water hit the floor. I looked at him through the curtain. "Because you're gonna wanna hold on to something." He swallowed as anxiety and what could only be excitement flashed across his face. I quickly yanked him under the waterfall before he could find some witty retort. "I'm going to fuck you until you can't stand, Benjamin Price. Now hold on tight." I spun him around so he'd be able to hang onto the support bars and sat on the absurdly small seat in front of him.

He made a dramatic show of placing his hands on the metal, but otherwise didn't comment. I ignored his condescending look and eyed his erect cock before me, already beaded with a perfect opaque drop.

I haven't even touched him yet.

I could barely hear his light moan over the water as I took him in hand. I squeezed the base and pulled up.

"Tall order," he finally quipped in response to my bold promise. I was impressed he managed to say the goading statement as flatly as he did, especially since it was immediately followed by a deeper moan.

So so proud Benny Price. I licked up the length of him and he shuddered.

"Do you have a book of tricks or something?" The breathy question lacked the sting it was undoubtedly supposed to have.

Or something.

"It's called imagination." I placed my lips around his swollen head and gave a light suck, earning me another moan.

I slowly took in more of him, hollowing my cheeks out and adding pressure with my tongue to the underside of his shaft. His moan became more pronounced. I settled into a pattern of lick, stroke, suck. Above me, his breathing became more ragged with each second. A quick look showed that he was finally taking the support bars seriously. I smiled inwardly and, without losing my pace, reached out for the lube I'd sat beside me.

"It's about being comfortable with your body and knowing what it wants," I said between mouthfuls.

"And you think you know what *my* body wa—" His snarky comeback died as I slid a finger past his entrance. His head fell back and his mouth opened in a silent moan as he gave himself over wholly to the sensation. I brushed across his prostate with a featherlight touch. His entire body shook and his cock twitched against my lips. I curled my tongue around his pulsing shaft and he dropped his head back between his arms where another moan fell out of him.

My mouth stayed on his cock as I began to work his ass. The water drowned out most of his fantastic responses, but I could still feel his heavy breathing on my wet hair, each moan a caress urging me on. When I was confident he was ready for it, I added a second digit. He let out a guttural groan from deep in his throat and squeezed around the pair.

He makes the best fucking sounds. What I wouldn't give for three hands.

My cock was twitching eagerly and aching. Finally, I slid in a third finger. He let out a tiny whine, and I tasted more pre-cum. I immediately abandoned my rhythm, but kept moving my fingers, wanting him nice and prepped for the pounding I had in store. His body tensed at the intrusion and relaxed in record time, without any coaxing or guidance.

He's getting better at this.

No sooner did I have the thought, then he gasped. I glanced up to see him white-knuckling the bars. "I'm gonna…" he groaned, fighting back his own need for release. "I don't… I don't want…"

Not so proud now.

His cock made a wonderful pop as I released the head, only to recapture it.

"What do you want?" I asked, alternating between stroking and sucking, careful not to overstimulate that glorious bundle of nerves inside of him.

He can't possibly hold on much longer.

The moan he let out was nothing short of primal. The sound wrapped around my neglected cock and squeezed without mercy. I choked on my own groan of need, but refused to relent.

Hell, I'm not gonna make it much longer.

"Tell me."

He groaned and shook his head, eyes squeezed shut. I threatened to remove my fingers, and he gasped out, "Your cock! I want your cock." The words rang with desperation and defeat.

Not good enough.

I slowly licked him from base to tip. "And where do you want my cock? In your mouth? In your ass?" It definitely had not eluded my attention how much Benny enjoyed having my dick in his mouth. Hell, with his enthusiasm, he'd be graduating from novice to fucking pro in no time.

"God damn it, Cal. You know where I want it," he said through gritted teeth.

"I do. But I want you to say it." I gently brushed that small globe of pure pleasure, determined to make him beg. He sucked in air and his whole body stiffened, squeezing my fingers so tightly that I simultaneously feared for circulation and despaired for my cock.

Shit. I've pushed him too far.

Benny took a deep, shaky breath that expanded his flushed chest and stretched his pecs. He held it for a few seconds, then released it in stuttering bursts only to do it all over again. I watched, fascinated as he fought back his climax.

He really doesn't want to come any other way.

"My ass. I wanna feel your cock in my ass," he said when he exhaled for the third time.

Better.

"Ask nicely."

He whimpered as I withdrew my fingers. "Please. Oh god, please, Cal." He tried to look at me, but could barely keep his eyes open enough to focus.

That'll do.

I slid my fingers across his slick skin, tracing the contours of his body, and repositioned myself behind him. He moaned as I drew light patterns on his quivering flesh, buying time for him to come down from the edge. I stroked myself and considered how to proceed. I'd never brought him so close before taking him, nor had I ever neglected myself for so long while doing it.

This should be interesting.

I pressed my body against his, tight enough for him to feel my insanely hard cock digging into his back. True to form, he groaned in anticipation, and his grip slackened. "You're going to want to hang on," I whispered in his ear. I cupped his ass and gave it a slight squeeze, stealing a minute to appreciate just how wonderfully round the damn thing was. When his fingers encircled the bars once more, I took him in one long drive, the heat of him swallowing me deep. His gasp echoed back on the tile. I held him tight against me once more and waited. He took a couple shaky breaths before I asked quietly, "You okay?" His only response was to moan and hang his head. "Good." I stepped a fraction back, pulling out until the head of my cock was barely inside him. His sound of frustration was maddening, but I refused to move.

You want it? Come get it.

I placed my hands on his ass and gave it the barest tug towards me. He got the message. I stared transfixed as he settled into his own driving rhythm, pushing back against me in order to claim the dick he so desperately wanted.

"You have no idea how fucking hot it is watching you fuck yourself on my cock." He pushed harder, and I struggled to maintain my footing without holding onto him.

"Stop… talking," he gasped, even as he rolled his hips.

"Why would I, when you so clearly like it?"

He made a small noise that might have been another whimper.

"You like hearing how fucking tight your ass is. About how good it feels to have my cock so deep inside you."

He groaned, and his pace quickened.

"Harder," I ordered.

He obliged and moaned again.

Oh fuck.

I wanted to slap his ass, but wasn't sure if he wouldn't turn and slap me back or just outright come. Neither was ideal, so I ignored the impulse. He slowed, and I realized he was starting to shake.

"Cal… I… I can't…" he panted.

Oh good, my turn.

I closed the distance again so that my body was touching as much of his as possible, sliding my cock back in deep. His panting was edged by a moan he couldn't hold back. I barely didn't shudder at the delicious feel of him squeezing me.

Why do I insist on playing these games with him? Even with all of his impatience, sex with him is like fucking endurance training.

I licked the salt from his back before pressing my lips against his shoulder blade. "Don't let go," I whispered. He had all of half a second to comply, then I took him hard and fast. I held onto his body for support as I drove in and out of him like it was a race to the finish line. And it felt like it. God, it felt like it. Each driving stroke sent crackles of energy radiating through my nerves, pushing me closer and closer to the pinnacle. I kept to the brutal pace until my rhythm abandoned me, then gave one last pound and finally gave out.

"Mother of fucking Christ," I hissed as Benny let out his own cry. The sharp sound somewhere between ultimate pleasure and pain ricocheted around the room and pulled every ounce of cum I had out of me. It took longer than usual to blink the world back into focus, and I noticed that his hands were practically ghost white from how hard he was gripping the bars.

Good call on those. Though I think I might have over-delivered. Not sure how well my legs will hold up after that.

My breathing gradually returned to something akin to normal, and I stepped away, albeit shakily. Benny's hands slipped from the bars and fell to his side like they were made of lead. He finished rinsing and started about getting dressed. I followed suit and finished in time to watch him try not to fall over putting his pants back on.

He doesn't look steady at all.

"Aren't you a smug fagot." The snide remark caught me off guard.

Oh, hell no. He could talk to me like that in the daylight, but not here, and certainly not after begging me to put my cock in his ass not twenty minutes ago.

"This still doesn't make me gay."

I raised a disbelieving eyebrow at the adamant declaration. Funny part was, I didn't believe Benny *was* gay, something in between for sure, but that was a moot distinction at this point.

Someone is definitely overdue for their reality check.

I stepped towards him and grabbed his buckle. His eyes went wide as I used it to pull him towards me and completely invade his personal space. "You're right, Benny, having my cock in your mouth and in your ass doesn't make you gay. Nor does having it there several times a week. But do you know what does?" He swallowed as I stared into his eyes. "Thinking about it every single day in between."

I released him and he staggered back, having to catch the nearby metal bar for support or risk falling over. His eyes flashed to it and back towards me, but I was already walking towards the door. Despite my outburst, there wasn't a doubt in mind that he'd be back.

I've got your number, Benjamin Price.

Whispers of war filled the hall. King Kelani studied the room with a practiced air of indifference, though the set of his mouth betrayed his concern. Things had not unfolded the way he'd expected, nor the way he'd been promised. Before long, an alliance would be necessary, but no suitor could tempt the young king's frozen heart. To love was to show weakness. To care, to invite snakes into his bed. But much as the young king would have it differently, the kingdom could not survive on the shoulders of one man. An alliance would have to be made.

Chapter 13

Calvin

I sat back against the stonewall and officially gave up my attempts to math. Far as I was concerned, the only tolerable math was geometry, since it was the closest to art, and Algebra II could go stuff itself. As a solidly average student, I neither possessed the drive nor the skill to dominate every exam the way others did. Now dominating a class of would-be artists with a stellar interpretation of the Starry Night—*that* I could do.

My fingers hovered over my bag while I debated filling the rest of the time with a fresh sketch. It was a beautiful day and the clouds scuttling overhead begged to be drawn in all their fluffy wonder. But I didn't reach inside and grab a pencil or mentally review which colors would best capture the opaque wonders. Instead, I sank my teeth into my bottom lip and glanced over at Andy, still completely immersed in his Lit II textbook.

Benny's words from the hall came back to me and soured my stomach, all the more cruel for their truthfulness. I curled my fingers inward and withdrew my hand to nestle it awkwardly in my lap. It wasn't like I could begrudge Andy our somewhat stilted friendship. I knew what I'd signed up for just like he recognized the inherent risks to his reputation in associating with me.

But still…

"Hey Andy."

He lifted his head, his bright red hair catching the light like burnished copper. It took him a few blinks before his focus centered on me. "What's up? Give up already?" he asked cheekily, a small grin tugging at his mouth.

"Ha ha." I made a production of setting aside the textbook and turned back to him. "*Actually*, I wanted to check in on you. You seem… better," I hazarded.

His shoulders stiffened slightly, and the vague smile fell from his face. A breath later, his entire body seemed to sag against the wall at his back. "I suppose I am. Mostly anyway." I glanced around, then scooted closer.

"Still worried Mitch is going to ghost you?"

"No?"

"Well, that sounded super convincing."

He let out a heavy sigh and let his Lit book tilt over his lap. "It's… complicated."

"I believe we've established my affinity for complicated," I teased. His cheek twitched, but no smile emerged. I debated letting him in on the unexpected intrigue I found myself in with Benny. Maybe if Andy knew how much I *understood* complicated, he'd be more willing to open up about whatever was going on with Mitch. Much as I wanted to be there for him, I also didn't want to betray Benny's trust… again. I'd had my reasons before, but Andy didn't need my protection anymore, hadn't for a long time.

Before I could decide what to do, Andy glanced over at me, his Phthalo Emerald eyes holding a hint of anxiety. "Calvin?"

"Yes, Anderson," I replied with all seriousness. Like I hoped, a tentative grin tweaked the corner of his lips.

"I... I wanted to apologize."

My brows immediately scrunched together. "What for?"

He scratched a nail along the seam of his trousers, where all of his focus was now centered. "I've been a pretty shit friend lately."

"Andy-"

He held up a hand. "Don't. Don't do that thing you do where you say it's no big deal. It's a big deal to me. You've been the most supportive, quirkiest, understanding friend I've ever had—I honestly don't know what I would have done if you hadn't come along—and I've been so wrapped up in my own issues that I haven't really held up my end. So, yeah, I'm sorry."

Warmth pulsed out from the center of my chest, spreading like ripples on a pond to fill every part of me. Even my toes tingled. A sudden lump formed in my throat and I blinked back an uncomfortable stinging in my eyes. "Is it weird that I kind of want to hug you?"

He rolled his eyes, abandoning his miserable demeanor, and gave me a wry smirk. "Go on already."

I eagerly reached out to claim the generous hug he was offering. While I side-hugged Andy all the time, our physical interactions were very limited, both out of necessity to maintain some kind of decorum and because he generally didn't like to be touched, though I suspected that would be different if Mitch were the one doing the touching.

I sank into the embrace, resting my chin on his shoulder. To my surprise, he actually squeezed back. The feeling of warmth intensified, and I blinked away the stubborn mist clouding my eyes. When it cleared, I saw Benny standing several yards away, staring at me, his expression unreadable. I cleared my throat and pulled away from my friend and the unexpected gift he'd given me.

"Thanks. So… things are going well with you two, then?" I asked in an awkward attempt to get things back on track while at the same time glancing over Andy's shoulder. Benny looked to be putting down roots, his gaze unblinking on a face of neutrality. I tucked a rebellious curl behind my ear, inexplicably self-conscious.

Surely one hug won't call into question whether or not Andy and I are an item…

Still, I couldn't shake the fear that Benny might be thinking I'd lied about it. But I hadn't. Andy and I just weren't interested in each other that way. Sure, it would've been convenient as fuck if we were, but that wasn't the case. He had his type, and I had mine… which was currently staring me down like I had a sign over my head blinking *Liar Liar* in bright neon.

Benny finally blinked and glanced back the way he'd come. I sagged with relief, then immediately tensed back up when I realized Todd and Neil were joining him. If ever there was a time for them to go after us, this was it. We'd let our guards down, we were exposed; we were sitting too close, we'd just hugged for fuck's sake, and Benny had witnessed it all.

His buddies caught up and, without so much as a backward glance, he led them away before the two could spot us. Mild disappointment wiggled in my chest, pushing aside my relief at not being harried.

Is he really not going to come over here?

"Hell-O." A hand waved in front of my face and I dropped my gaze from Benny's receding form back to Andy.

"What?"

"I said, things are going about as well as they can be," he responded to the question I'd entirely forgotten asking.

"Oh. That's good," I replied absently, my gaze sliding over his shoulder once more.

Is he avoiding me? Did I push him too far? What the fuck? That fucker better not be avoiding me. How does he expect to keep doing this if he's gonna be weird about it?

Maybe he doesn't want to keep doing this…

I dumped a mental gallon of paint thinner on the murky thought. It didn't matter what I said; I had Benny's number, no question. In fact, I had half a mind to go after them and provoke an altercation myself just to prove I couldn't be ignored. Forget the fact that I'd been relieved not ten seconds before that he wasn't going to say anything about the hug. Calvin Bridges was *not* someone so easily pushed aside.

"So…"

I let out an exasperated huff and returned my attention to Andy. Couldn't he tell I was having a minute? "So, what?"

His flame-colored brows rose at the sharpness of the response at the same time a smile flitted across his lips. "So, you going to tell me what's been going on with you?"

Oh. Maybe he could tell.

Fuck.

That's worse.

"You know you can tell me anything, right?" He placed a reassuring hand on my knee. "Judgment free zone. Always." My gaze flicked to the last place I'd seen the trio and back to Andy's face, open and waiting for an answer. "Well?" he prompted.

I've been fucking around with Benny for weeks and it's been freaking amazing, but I think I might have fucked it all up by calling him out on his homophobic bullshit and normally I wouldn't care, except I'm not ready to give it up.

… Yeah, I can't say that.

"Um… I don't think I'm ready to talk about it." Andy nodded in quiet acceptance, and I immediately felt like an ass. Here he was actively trying to be a better friend. And how did I react? By spinning the tables and pulling the same crap he'd been doing. I mentally smacked myself in the face and tried for compromise. "But… I promise to tell you about it when I am."

His face relaxed into an amiable smile. "That's fair. Same here. Deal?" He held out a hand, and I took it.

"Deal."

Benny

I couldn't take it anymore. Day by day, it chipped away at my sanity. Every time I closed my eyes, held my breath for too long, or dared to stop moving, Calvin's lips pressed into my shoulder, hot, velvet soft, firm. I'd almost come on the spot at the intimate touch and I hadn't stopped burning since. I wanted—no, needed—more with a desperation that terrified me. One absent kiss was all it had taken to turn me into a walking torch. Except there was only one thing I could think of to tame the inferno and that was to level the field.

It wasn't the first time I'd thought about kissing Calvin, or even the fourth or fifth. Fuck, it wasn't even the fiftieth, but it was the first time it had dominated all of my thoughts, nearly to the exclusion of all else. I couldn't function like this. Something had to be done… and soon.

"Heads up!"

I got my stick up just in time to catch the rogue toss and send it back out.

Fuck. I need to get it together.

I jogged after the others as we wrapped up the last of the drills. The season was still several weeks away, but Ulwich was determined to bring home that trophy and we were the team that was supposed to make it happen. Plus, now that Mitch was back to attending the informal practices with more regularity, everyone was getting their heads in the game.

Everyone but me.

We made it through a few more plays, followed by yet more dexterity drills. Donovan got tagged for suicides, Neil ended up running laps with his stick over his head for failing to keep his arms up, and Connor almost beamed the coach with the ball when he called him a pansy and was now doing pushups until the snow fell. How I escaped unscathed when my playing reflected my split attention was beyond me, but I wasn't about to look a gift horse in the mouth. I trudged off with the others toward the lockers, feeling frayed at the edges and eager to wash off the sweat and grime already drying on my skin.

A spun towel darted in front of me to land with a sharp crack on McNeil's ass. He let out a yelp and reached for his own towel to return the favor. I quickly vacated their area before I could become collateral. All around me the team stood in various stages of undress, nearly all of them bitching about the brutal practice. Occasionally, the conversations drifted to what people were doing over the weekend or whether we really stood a chance at taking the title this year. We'd come painfully close in the past, but we were all done with second place and for most of the starters, this would be our last chance. For many, the scouts coming would be their only ticket into a decent university. Heaven knew they didn't have the grades.

I glanced over at Mitch horsing around with Brian and Nate while Kyle hovered imposingly on the periphery. John stepped up and said something that had all four of them laughing. The whole scene should have been shocking, considering the lot had been in a full-on brawl in the hall only a few weeks ago, but that was how this place worked. On the surface, it looked like they'd all made amends, but I knew better. There was a tightness around Mitch's eyes that betrayed the strain of the front he was putting on, not to mention that fight had started over Andy. Mitch wouldn't forgive that so easily, but the only way his standing protection of his friend would hold was if he kept playing his part—which was exactly what the team wanted.

I shook my head and moseyed over to my locker, where I peeled off my clinging tee. It fell in a sweaty heap and I massaged the back of my neck. Sadly, my fingers did absolutely nothing to alleviate the built-up stress. Mitch wasn't the only one struggling to keep up appearances. My own game performance needed some serious work or coach was going to notice and a higher authority would have something to say. Last thing I needed was my father breathing down my neck about me being a failure at this too. Forget the fact that I wouldn't be allowed to take a sports scholarship even if I was offered one, I'd either be going to the University of Chicago as a legacy or Yale for the prestige. While one actually had a lacrosse team, the closest I'd get to it was watching from the sidelines. Even if I made the team, my father would never allow it. I tossed the rest of my clothes into the bottom of the locker hard enough to make it shake.

Maybe if someone else's fingers do the massaging, it would work. I wonder if Savannah is available.

Except I didn't want Savannah to work out the kinks tightening my shoulders and making my neck stiff. I wanted the long fingers of an artist to knead out the stress, to whisper filthy promises as he traced patterns I couldn't understand on my needy flesh. I wanted his moist breath to send a cascade of goosebumps down my back before he pressed those mouth-watering lips into my fevered skin.

"He lives!" Todd shouted.

I jerked at the sudden burst of sound right beside me and pushed away the fantasy. The last thing I needed was to chub up in the locker room. I'd gone this long without incident and I planned to keep it that way. If my father had found out about me losing the position of captain as fast as he did, I didn't want to think about how quickly rumors of his son getting a boner in the shower surrounded by his naked teammates would reach his ears. Not that some of them weren't worth getting a boner for, but that was a headache I didn't need.

I glanced in the direction Todd was looking and found Neil rolling up like he'd been run over by a fucking truck. "You look like shit," I said as he dropped onto the bench. His lip twitched in a half-hearted snarl as he worked on unlacing his shoes.

"Coach is really out for blood these days," Todd commented as he reached into his locker for a fresh towel.

"Probably has something to do with you-know-who," Neil grumbled.

As one, we all glanced over to the school's lead Attackman, acting like he didn't have a care in the world. On cue, Hendricks walked into the locker as well and glared absolute death at Mitch. While his absence had undoubtedly brought Coach down harder on the rest of us, it struck me as unfair that one man was expected to lead the school to victory. This was a team sport, after all, and that kind of pressure had a tendency to break people rather than help them rise to the challenge. My shoulders gave a sympathetic twinge to the weight he was carrying. I got it, I did, but I had my own burdens to bear. I couldn't carry his too. Mitch Hudson would have to figure it out on his own.

I was mid wrapping a towel around my waist when my gaze snagged on something shining coppery bright on Mitch's jacket hanging in his locker. While Mitch had dated almost with perfect singularity strictly redheads, there was only one person I knew of at either school with hair that color… and that short. Suddenly, I knew without a doubt that Andy had not been alone that night I'd busted in. And I knew who he'd been with.

"Motherfucker," I growled.

Todd straightened up from his lean on the lockers. "What's up?"

"Yeah, something wrong?" Neil echoed.

"What? No, I smacked a blood blister is all." Their faces twisted in sympathetic winces. "Forget it. Let's get this stink off and get out of here." I snatched my soap out and stomped over to the already half-occupied showers the sound of Mitch's forced laughter raking down my spine.

Chapter 14

Calvin

Excitement simmered beneath my skin, giving my step an extra spring as I all but sprinted through the dimly lit hallways. Moonlight poured through large windows to create large pools of Radiant White that rippled at my passing. Funnily enough, the very reason I could walk about so boldly after hours was the exact reason I was practically vibrating with anticipation.

Perhaps a little more caution wouldn't be a bad idea. If it gets out what we're doing, the fallout will be epic. Also, pretty sure Benny will beat the shit out of me.

Thinking of Benny sent another thrill through me, and my pace quickened. Finally, my destination solidified before me and my heart skipped and started only to race some more. I bit my bottom lip and willed the damn thing to slow down before it exploded and approached the door with none of my usual caution. It swung open in perfect silence and glanced up to find the hinges shiny with grease.

Benny.

A smile stretched across my face at the image of Benny doctoring the hinges to literally keep this quiet. Without the typical squeal echoing on the tile, the room held an uncanny absence of sound. My grip tightened on my towel as I stepped deeper into the vacant space.

Maybe I beat him here.

I shrugged to myself. Getting here first wasn't unusual, though it begged the question of when Benny had found the opportunity to oil the hinges.

Guess I'll just get started without him.

I walked past the stalls and rounded the corner that separated the sinks from the showers proper. My smile instantly slipped and my heart stilled with a sickening thud. I struggled to get my disappointment under control and took another step like my entire evening hadn't been completely derailed.

"You're still dressed," I said, taking in Benny from head to toe. Dressed was an understatement. He still wore his complete uniform though the tie had been loosened, his shirt was partially untucked, and his blazer was noticeably rumpled.

He pushed off the wall where he'd been leaning with his hands stuffed in his pockets. "I wanted to do something different."

"Different," I echoed as I continued to approach.

Different could be promising. Even as I thought it though, trepidation shot through me. Different could also be trouble.

"Yeah," he said softly as pulled his hands free and used his body to herd me until my back was pressed against the wall he'd just vacated. My heart sprinted at an alarming pace and my breath caught in a telling gasp as the cold tile leeched its chill past my thin shirt to suffuse me with dread. This was why I never let my guard down. Now it was too late. I was cornered and alone. No one would hear me scream.

I crushed the increasing anxiety before it could take anymore root than it had.

Benny has never physically hurt me.

The reassurance did nothing to temper the inexplicable panic now racing through my veins.

Get a grip Calvin. You're still in control.

"I'll make you a deal," I said, catching his eye. "Tell me a secret—something I don't know—and you can do whatever you want." He stopped a foot away, not technically crowding me, but close enough to be uncomfortable without knowing what he was about.

Benny's eyes narrowed with obvious skepticism. "Whatever I want?" Unwilling to let on how much the situation was unnerving me, I played along.

"Depends on the quality of the secret. But sure, why not?" I shrugged and gave him a smug grin. It was a tall order. There wasn't much that happened in this school that I didn't know about.

Benny shifted and looked me dead in the eye, as if weighing his options.

What secrets do you have, Benjamin Price?

"Alright. Connor and Andy were sleeping together."

I snorted a laugh. "I already knew that. You're going to have to do better." Admittedly, I was a little impressed that he not only knew that they had been, but that they weren't now.

"You know about that fight a few weeks back? The one in the hall by the East Dormitories?"

"I mean, I didn't see it, but yeah. A bunch of guys from the team got into it. What about it?"

"Did you know Mitch threw the first punch?"

"What? Why would he do that?" I asked, frowning. Mitch wasn't known to be violent or even to be in fights at all. Sure, he'd had a couple, but nothing to suggest he would ever *start* one.

"Probably because they were digging into Gallagher."

Okay, that part is news. But something still isn't adding up. Mitch knows Andy is gay. He's known for years. Even if they were laying into Andy, that's nothing new. Why would it bother him now?

"That's not the interesting part."

I threw my hands up. "Jesus Christ, get on with it already."

"Andy was in the fight too," Benny said, leaning forward. "He dragged Mitch out of there at the first chance. No one knows where they vanished to, but when Mitch made it to practice later that day with a black eye, he came from the woods on the east side of the field."

What the literal hell? Andy was in a fight and didn't tell me?

I put a hand on Benny's chest to prevent him from getting any closer. He stopped at the touch, but didn't back off.

The East Woods. What's in the East Woods? The only thing there is that godforsaken derelict shack. Why would they be there? Unless, of course...

My jaw fell in shock at what felt like the likeliest answer, the only thing that would explain both of their unusual behavior of late.

Holy shit. Mitch is sleeping with Andy.

Motherfucker.

"I'm going to assume by your reaction that was something you didn't know." Benny's words startled me back to the present where he was standing very, *very* close to me.

"What? No. I mean, not in the way you're thinking." Truthfully, I had no idea what Benny was thinking, only that I suspected he might be a hidden treasure trove of secrets. He knew about Andy and Connor. He clearly had suspicions about Andy and Mitch. What else could he know?

"Does it qualify?" Benny asked, one sandy eyebrow raised.

"I suppose it does." I eyed Benny nervously. I hadn't actually anticipated having to deliver on my end.

This is what I get for being an over-cocky ass.

"What do you want?" I asked, a little afraid of the answer.

"Your mouth."

I barked a short laugh. "Sure, I mean, that's kind of normally how this goes, but if that's what you want to waste your secret on."

What a relief.

"I don't want you to give me head, Calvin."

If his expression hadn't been so deadly serious, I might not have believed him.

Who turns down head?

My eyebrows shot up in surprise as an alternative came to mind. "Rimming?" I hadn't ever actually done that before, but there was a first time for everything.

I'm sure I can manage.

"No," he scoffed, leaning even closer. He was practically laid out against my entire body by this point, despite my hand still on his chest. Before I could guess again, his lips brushed mine.

My surprise turned to full-blown shock. I pulled back as far as the wall would allow. "Benny."

"You said whatever I want," he whispered, closing the distance to hover a hair's breadth away. Short of physically removing myself from the situation, I was out of options.

"I did. But..." I faltered.

What the hell is happening right now? How does this fit into our arrangement? Does it fit? Kissing is… kissing is… Well, kissing is kissing.

His hand slid along my jaw to hold my face. He seemed to be waiting for the rest of my argument… except I didn't have one. I searched his face and reined in my sudden panic. I swallowed.

"Okay."

Benny's mouth closed over mine without any of the hesitation I felt and it was like someone dumped high gloss varnish over a lusterless painting. My world exploded into vibrant hues as his lips moved with defined purpose against mine. I fisted my hand in the fabric of his shirt while I struggled to think of the last time someone had actually kissed me. His tongue slid in and I gave a muffled sound of surprise.

He's on a goddamn mission.

I tangled mine with his and let go of my reservations, sinking into the exploration and letting the colors sweep me away. I got so lost in it that for a moment I completely forgot that we both were still dressed.

"Whoa," I whispered when he finally pulled away. "You're really good at that," I added.

Perhaps he's more experienced—in some areas at least—than I gave him credit.

"I can't be bad at everything," he said as his hand slipped from my face. My cheek tingled where his fingers had trailed. I was tempted to tell him I thought he was actually quite good at a lot of things, but was more interested in getting back to the kissing.

I nearly forgot how much I like this.

I relinquished my death grip on his shirt and dropped the towel I was somehow still holding in order to capture his face with both hands. He didn't stop me when I mashed our mouths back together, hungry for more.

Fuck me, that feels good.

I let out a moan as he deepened the kiss once again and arched off the now warm tile into his even warmer body. The heat of his hand burned through my tee and into my lower back as he pressed me harder against him. My breath caught at the overwhelming intensity of it, and I nipped at his lip before getting sucked back in. By the time he pulled away again, we were both struggling for air and every cell in my body felt saturated with the purest color. I couldn't have said what day of the week it was, let alone how long we'd been at it, nor did I care.

"You should get back to your room," Benny said quietly and far steadier than I could have.

"I still haven't showered," I snickered, sliding my hands from his lightly stubbled cheeks to cup his neck.

This is going to be a great fucking night.

He didn't so much as blink when he countered with, "I have to finish the rounds." My enthusiasm, along with the riot of color inside of me, dimmed.

Is he serious? No, he can't go, not after that.

"Or you could stay." I gave him a wicked smile, determined not to give up so easily, and rubbed against him suggestively. Even that small move sent tendrils of aching pleasure through me. He leaned forward and gave me a smaller kiss, barely more than a mild pressure, but didn't respond. "Stay," I whispered, my eyes already half-lidded with the hope of another mind-altering kiss.

"Your room, Calvin," he responded sternly.

Fuck. He's serious.

"Fine," I huffed and dropped my hold on him.

Back to being the prefect already. So much for my great night.

He put distance between us, and I waited. "What?" he asked, sounding a bit irritated.

"Aren't you going to say it?" I asked.

"Say what?"

He's playing stupid, he has to be.

"Say what?" I mimicked in my poor imitation of his gruff voice. "You say it every time."

"I don't know what you're talking about." He turned to leave.

I caught his arm, and he looked back at me. "Yes, you do. You always say 'This doesn't make me gay.' Well, let's hear it." Benny gave me a level look and didn't respond. "You're really not going to say it." I searched his face, but found nothing even remotely enlightening.

I don't believe this.

"Go to your room. It's past curfew." He straightened his shirt, though it did nothing to smooth the fist of wrinkles I'd put in it and walked out of the bathroom, leaving me standing there like an idiot.

What the fuck just happened?

I twisted my hands with impatience as I waited for my turn to speak with Father Miles. It would be my luck that every Catholic in town and their brother would come to confessional today. I stifled an aggravated groan as yet another person made their way over. With a forced smile that I hoped at least looked genuine, I gestured for them to go before me and kept my position at the end of the line. They nodded in thanks and I reminded myself yet again that this was a house of God and throttling petitioners for taking too long would be frowned upon.

Finally, the last person left the booth. I danced from foot to foot and offered a weak smile as they took their sweet ass time getting the fuck out of the way. When they moved far enough off that I wouldn't have to push past them, I surged into the booth, snapping the door shut and whipping the curtain closed. I did the fastest cross of my life and rushed out, "Forgive me Father, for I have sinned," before Father Miles could utter so much as a syllable.

He cleared his throat. "What sins would you like to confess, my child?"

"I kissed a boy, and I liked it." The words burst out of me in a giant whoosh, taking all of my air.

Father Miles sighed on the other side of the latticed partition. "Calvin, how many times-"

I yanked back the divide and Father Miles' gray-laced, bushy eyebrows shot up in surprise. "Sorry, Father. I don't mean to be flippant and it's not really a confession. But I did. I kissed a boy, and it was amazing." I flopped back into the hard seat and ran both hands over my face. "Like really, really amazing and I hadn't been expecting it at all and I'm not entirely sure what it means, but I *really* want to do it again." *And again, and again and again.* I glanced over at the open divide as my exuberance trailed off. "Sorry, I just really needed to tell someone."

Father Miles held up a finger and leaned forward to open the door of his side of the confessional. He poked his head out a moment, then ducked back in. "What do you say we move this conversation to somewhere with more comfortable seating?"

I smiled and eagerly launched out of the booth to follow him through the nave, past the prayer candles, and into his personal office. He removed his ceremonial robe, hung it up, then turned back to me. His Raw Umber eyes crinkled at the corners as he opened his arms. I stepped into the hug not so different from the others he'd given me over the years, though I was substantially taller than I'd been at nine. He gave my back a firm pat and released me to take one of the seats in front of his heavy desk.

"I'm so happy for you, Calvin."

Light filled my chest as I took the chair opposite him, which was in fact way more cushioned than the one in the confessional. "Yeah?"

He pushed back up from his seat and walked over to the cabinet that traditionally held the communion wine. "Yes," he said as he pulled out a bottle and two plastic cups. "This calls for a celebration."

I laughed as I took the proffered cup filled with crimson liquid, bubbles floating across that taught surface. "You sure, Father?"

"I won't tell if you won't." He winked and took a sip. I mirrored the motion and had to laugh again.

"Grape juice."

"What else would it be?" he replied with a smirk. I shook my head and took another sip, leaning forward to rest my forearms on my knees. "Tell me about this boy."

I let out a sigh and stared into the sugary depths of my drink. "Where to even start?"

"The beginning perhaps?" Father Miles suggested as he settled back in his seat.

"That might take more time than we have and I… I kind of want to protect his identity. If that's okay? Not that I think you would tell anyone, but I feel like I owe it to him, if that makes any sense."

Father Miles held up his glass in a salute. "I will respect your wishes. You need only say whatever you feel comfortable sharing."

I nodded, appreciating the understanding and the inherent support. I'd come to Father Miles many times over the years for both spiritual and secular guidance. That he had remained such a resolute advocate for me over the years meant more to me than words would ever express, especially since my bio-father hadn't really ever been part of my life. I took a steadying breath to calm my nerves and took another drink.

"For starters, it's the same boy from the drawing I'm not allowed to use."

"That so?"

"Yeah." I rolled the plastic cup in my hands. "It's also the same boy from my first day at Ulwich, the one that I connected with. I don't think I mentioned that before."

"You did not. Go on."

I chewed on my bottom lip and tried hard to fight the smile threatening to dominate my face yet again. "I still can't believe it actually happened. I mean… it was kind of a bummer that it was *all* that happened, but…"

"Calvin," Father Miles admonished, a frown pulling his mouth down at the corners.

"I know, I know. He's not like the others, though, Father. He doesn't need my help." *Not anymore.*

I couldn't help but think back to the first time I'd been intimate with Benny. But it wasn't the sex I thought about or the way I'd coaxed him gently through it, reminding him to breathe and helping him to relax. It was the moments after that. The way he'd slid down the wall, his legs too weak to hold him, and I rushed to break his fall. The way he'd curled against me and rested his head on my shoulder. He'd let me hold him until the water ran cold, my fingers gliding through his short hair and trailing down his arm. When we did finally part ways he hadn't been embarrassed or ashamed of what we'd done, he hadn't raced off without a backward glance, he'd looked at me with sadness in his eyes like he really didn't want to leave. The same sadness that had been in his eyes the other night when he'd told me to go back to my room.

The plastic crunched in my hand as I tightened my hold on the flimsy cup. I quickly downed the contents before they could spill all over Father Miles' elegant rug and placed the cup on his desk with a shaking hand.

"Is everything alright, my son?"

"I…" The words lodged in my throat.

Father Miles' features gentled, and he reached out to place a hand on my knee. "What is it?"

"I'm scared," I admitted, unable to hold his gaze.

He squeezed gently. "What do you fear?"

"This… changes things. I don't know what the rules are anymore… or if there ever were any."

He patted my knee and sat back, his warm smile shining in his eyes once more. "Perhaps a little faith would be warranted?"

"Should have known you'd say that," I said, rolling my eyes, though I knew he hadn't meant it as an empty platitude.

"Trust that the Lord will lead you where you need to go." He spread out his hands. "Now, what you do when you get there is up to you."

And that was the rub, wasn't it? What was I going to do?

Chapter 15

Benny

I tugged on the striped, cotton pants, opting to change straight into my pajamas rather than stay up and study or immediately tackle my nightly obligations. Still, my gaze drifted to the closed door and the undoubtedly barren hall beyond.

It won't hurt anything to miss one night. No one will know.

The bed let out a puff of air as I landed unceremoniously on it and stared up at the ceiling.

The responsible thing would be to do the round.

But I couldn't. I knew what would happen. I would do the round—or only half—then end up in the showers… again, just like I always did lately.

Where I'll find Calvin.

Or I won't.

I wasn't really sure which was worse. The bedsprings squealed into the deepening night as I rolled over. I shut my eyes tight and wished for the escape of mindless slumber, but sleep was proving more than elusive. With a huff that hit the wall and bounced back at me, I rolled to my other side in the vain hope that it would prove more conducive to passing the fuck out.

I can't do this anymore. I'm not even sure what this *is. Why did I have to mess everything up? Why couldn't I just leave well enough alone? Things were fine the way they were, still confusing as fuck, but at least I understood the rules.*

I squeezed my eyes tighter, like it could block out the persistent thoughts. If anything, it made them louder.

Why did I have to kiss him? Why?

Even wondering was dangerous, as it immediately provoked memories of Calvin's warm body pressing against me while his hot mouth devoured mine and his delicate fingers held my face. After denying the urge to kiss him for borderline a decade, I'd feared that finally kissing him wouldn't live up to the impossible standard I'd concocted over the years. But it had, it had been absolutely everything it needed to be, raw, surprising… perfect.

I let out a sigh and turned over again.

This is fucking miserable. What time is it?

I sought the clock, barely visible in the gloom. Three a.m.

Of course it fucking is.

I raked my hands over my face and flopped them back to the bed, a chant of "Don't do it," playing on a loop in my head.

I have to tell him.

The determined thought came in direct contradiction with every ounce of self-preservation I had. But I couldn't lie here for another second and wish it all away. I stood up and shook myself, doing what I could to steel my resolve.

That's it. I'm gonna tell him. I can't see him anymore.

I didn't even notice if the hallways were empty, but it was unlikely there was anyone about to see me stomp through them. It was well past lights out and no one was brazen enough to be out of bed on the nights I was scheduled for rounds.

No one except Calvin, of course.

My pace quickened until at last I was standing in front of the door to the showers. My nerves returned with a vengeance along with the chant that had implored me to stay safely sequestered in my room.

I should have stayed in bed. What if he's not there?

What if he is?

I swallowed my anxiety and pushed the door open. The bathroom's sole occupant didn't hear it close behind me.

Why does he have to be attractive?

Every line of Calvin seemed so intentional, from his perfectly straight nose and angular jaw, to the way his leg was propped on his other knee where he lay on the bench by the sinks. Even his button down had a precision to it.

Wait a minute.

"You're still dressed," I said, officially announcing my presence.

Calvin's head swiveled towards me. He then immediately scrambled up off the bench. His long fingers fidgeted with the shirt, straightening the barely creased fabric, then moved on to tuck his hair behind his ear. The dark, silky strand immediately slipped free. Its length was just past code, but no one ever said anything to him about it. I suspected no one ever had. Calvin had beautiful hair.

"Hey, I..." He stopped and cleared his throat, then tucked the rebellious strand again. It didn't cooperate any better the second time. He rubbed his arm, scrunching the fabric of his navy jacket, and his gaze flicked towards me, then down again.

What the hell is going on? I've known Calvin for years and never seen him act like this. Even when I'm saying horrible things to him, he's still the picture of self-confidence and always has a witty retort ready to go.

What's wrong with him?

My eyes narrowed. I reconsidered the fact that he was still completely dressed.

Is he trying to tell me he doesn't want to see me anymore?

The thought brought with it a small rush of anger. He took a deep breath and tried again. I braced myself, fighting back my contradictory emotions. After all, wasn't that the exact reason I'd come here?

"I wasn't sure what you would want to do." Finally, his gaze met mine. In contrast to his behavior, their honey brown was steady, sure.

Calvin is still in his school uniform—the uniform he hates—because I was in mine last time.

All of my nerves and anxiety fell away. I knew exactly what I wanted to do. My single-minded determination of why I'd come here evaporated, leaving the real reason I'd gotten out of bed at three a.m., the same reason I was always here. I searched Calvin's face with its unusual mix of uncertainty and confidence.

How can he be so open? Never any judgment, just acceptance...
And he's still in his fucking uniform.

As I walked towards him, I knew what I had known at the beginning of the night when I'd refused to leave my room—I couldn't stop seeing him. I would keep coming here in the small hours of the morning until he stopped being here. Hell, I might even go off and find him if he wasn't. No matter how much I might wish otherwise, I couldn't quit Calvin Bridges.

He didn't say a word when I grabbed his arm and dragged him around the privacy wall. Nor did he argue when my mouth closed over his and forced him flush against the tile. My fingers slid along his face and into his stupid, soft hair as I kissed him deeper. He kissed me back, and I felt the featherlight touch of his hand on my wrist. I trailed my fingers across his neck to his collar. One button was quickly followed by another.

He let out a sigh edged with a moan as I tasted first his throat, then his clavicle, pushing the blue and cream fabric out of the way as I quested for more. His head turned as I worked my way back up his neck, tasting him the way I'd wanted to for years.

"Tell me a secret," I whispered.

"What do I get if I do?" The husky question made me light-headed.

"One in return," I said, then promptly recaptured his mouth. I'd known kissing him would be a mistake, not because he would use it against me or anything else so gauche, but because I wouldn't be able to stop. My want of Calvin had started when I was scarcely more than a boy and had only grown over the years. When I released him, I wasn't sure whose breathing was more ragged. I returned to his neck. This time, his sigh was definitely more of a groan.

"I wasn't sure you'd come," he immediately offered, albeit a little breathless.

And yet here he was.

"Now you," he prompted.

"I almost didn't."

"Why did you?"

"Uh-uh. One secret, that was the deal," I countered, unwilling to admit the truth.

Uncertainty flashed in his eyes. It disappeared to be replaced by acceptance. He grabbed my face and pulled it towards him like he had the other night. I let out a groan as his teeth pulled on my lip and pressed him harder into the wall. I wanted to make him feel good, but not just good, really good, needed him to know how far gone I was.

I mindlessly conquered buttons until I reached his buckle. He arched back as my mouth followed the same path as my questing hands. He sucked in air in a small gasp when my teeth closed on a nipple at the same time my hand wrapped around his cock.

God, everything about him…

I couldn't decide what of him I wanted next. I wanted all of him, had wanted it for so long. My fingers tightened around his shaft and I dragged up until it popped free. His resulting groan decided me. I kissed down his torso, stalling at his navel, tasting every part of him on my journey even as my hands ventured to explore his newly freed chest.

He didn't stop me as my lips closed around him. I didn't expect him to. He never had before. I sucked on his wonderfully swollen head, taking my time and enjoying the soft sounds of pleasure he was making that were gradually increasing in volume. His hips bucked when I took the rest of him inside and added my tongue. His fingers scratched along my scalp. They tightened and released as he rode the rising wave.

"I'm gonna come," he groaned.

I knew it was true, could taste it in the beads leaking out of him. I hollowed my cheeks and pulled harder. His whole body seized, and he gasped as he gave out. His release shot down the back of my throat. I swallowed and didn't let go until it was clear he was done. I slowly pulled away, sucking him clean as his cock fell free. Then my fingers deftly righted his trousers while my mouth resumed its languid trail up his quivering torso.

Damn, his skin is smooth.

My hands glided beneath the open shirt to his sides, then I used his body to pull me up. By the time I made it fully upright, his mouth was waiting for me. I pressed him tighter against my aching body and devoured his lips with the same need I'd swallowed his cock.

"You made me finish," he said, his voice deep and frayed at the edges.

"I did," I responded as his lips molded perfectly against mine, adding to the high that had hold of me, a high I'd gladly chase for as long as possible.

"What about you?" he asked, teasing another kiss.

"Next time," I said, stealing it from him.

"Next time?" I could feel the hint of his smile against my mouth, and it made my heart skip. My hands drifted along his abdomen and chest, mapping the contours of his body with my fingers.

Calvin is a fucking hairless wonder.

"I like that you don't wear an undershirt," I said, leaning down to place a kiss on his chest.

He gave a low chuckle while his fingers danced featherlight over the back of my neck. "Pure laziness, I assure you."

"You know," I began as my hands continued to rove. "No one would ever guess you look like this underneath." His eyes glittered with mischief.

"*That* is purely selfish," he said, arching into the touch so I could more easily explore his back. "Call it my secret."

"Your secret, huh?" My lips ghosted along his angled neck while my eager fingers traced the definition of his back. "I suspect there's few people who know it."

"A few," he said with an arched brow and a wicked gleam in his eyes. "Perhaps a couple more than who know what a gifted kisser you are."

"That many?" I teased. He gave me a crooked smile.

"I suspect your numbers have been grossly exaggerated."

"You seem awfully confident about that." I hovered a breath away from his lips.

"I know you, Benny," he said, punctuating the remark with a kiss that only made me ache more.

He was right. Calvin knew me better than my own friends and family. What's more, he understood and accepted me exactly the way I was. He'd never asked for more and didn't expect perfection. With him, I had the luxury of being enough. I slid deeper into the kiss.

"Tell me a secret," he whispered.

"I masturbate to you," I said without hesitation.

He groaned and fisted his hands in my shirt as he conquered my mouth. "I really wish you hadn't finished me," he said as he drifted a hand down and squeezed my ass, pressing me tightly against him. "I could still…" he offered when I moaned.

"Next time." The shaky assertion seriously lacked conviction, but he took it anyway.

He nodded. "I'll make it worth the wait."

"You always do," I responded before tasting his lips again. While I explored his mouth, my hands reluctantly gave up their adventuring and set about redoing his buttons.

"Really, Benny?" he asked when I was nearly done.

"We've already been here too long," I said as I did the last button.

"We have, haven't we? Much longer and people will show up to take *real* showers."

I gave a small chuckle at the cheeky joke.

He smiled back at me. "I like it when you laugh."

"I laugh."

"Not like that, you don't." Before I could ask what he meant, he followed up with his own question. "When is your next round?"

"Thursday."

"I'll be here."

King Kelani held Prince Einar's gaze for a minute that stretched into eternity. The king never conceded, never negotiated. His power had always been absolute. The suitors that had come before had been incapable of enticing him with anything grander than fleeting interest. Now the esteemed Prince Einar had played a hand he had not expected. Perhaps he'd finally found a worthy partner capable of seeing beyond his mantle.

Chapter 16

Calvin

I shoved the door open with far too much force and practically launched myself into the room. *Please still be here.* Even as I had the desperate thought, the sound of running water filled my ears. I quickly rounded the division, stripping as I went.

Benny turned as my shirt crumpled against the wall and fell unceremoniously to the floor. I greedily devoured the sight of him. Water ran down his wonderful body in rivulets that dipped and explored every defined inch of him the way my fingers itched to do.

Fucking hell, he's hot.

He was flushed as well, the pink coloring his barely tanned skin. I wasn't sure if it was because he had already started without me or from the scalding water, sending waves of steam throughout the room. Judging by how hard he was, I suspected it was the former.

"Sorry I'm late." I pulled off first one shoe and then another. "I ran into Stein and Jackson and had to double back and take a different route. And my stupid bunkmate decided tonight, of all nights, to give a shit about his grades. He spent the last three fucking hours studying and I couldn't get away without raising suspicion." Apologies poured from my mouth. "I got here as soon as I could." I stumbled as I tried to walk and remove my pants at the same time.

Finally, I was free and strode with renewed vigor towards him. He managed one step away from the wall before I reached out to cup the back of his neck and pulled his mouth the rest of the way to mine. The force of my momentum was so great we fell back against the slick wall. My body firmly pressed against all the hard lines of his while I devoured his mouth with a hunger that had grown since he had sucked me off four days ago.

I let out a groan as I remembered how hot his mouth had been and the way his hands had roved across my torso. I physically ached for him to touch me again, to touch me everywhere.

We haven't even done anything and I'm barely keeping it togeth-er.

"Did you finish?" I asked huskily, barely dragging in enough breath to form the question.

"What do you think?" He thrust his hips forward so that his very hard cock stabbed in my belly. I let out another groan and conquered his mouth again, prompting him to elicit his own delicious moan.

Fuck. He really does only want to come the one way.

"Why are there so many fucking days between Monday and Thursday?" I growled.

"It's called a week."

"It's too long."

Oh god, the feel of him is going to drive me insane.

I raked my fingers down his back and he made a sound deep in his throat, arching against me. I abandoned his mouth to nibble across his jaw and then down to where his neck met his shoulder.

My teeth grazed the increasingly sensitive skin, and he made a sound akin to a whimper. His fingers slid through my damp curls, encouraging me.

"Your hair is amazing." The breathy compliment was unexpected. I smiled against his flush skin, then placed a kiss further up his neck.

"Yours could stand to be a little longer," I whispered as I brushed the palm of my hand across his border-line crew cut.

"Why?" The breathless question hitched when I nipped at his shoulder again.

In lieu of a response, I reached back to where his hand was still tangled in my hair and tightened his grip. He let out a sensual groan as if it was actually his hair we were pulling. I released my hold and tasted his sweet skin again.

I'm going to leave a mark if I don't move to something else. Reluctantly, I pulled away from his neck.

"Don't stop." The husky request almost undid me and I struggled to get control of my spiraling desire.

He shivered as I whispered in his ear, "If I don't, you'll have a hickey."

"Who fucking cares?" He turned his face, questing for my mouth. My teeth sank into his bottom lip and I pulled. He let out a deep moan. This kissing thing was obviously working for both of us.

"You will when you have to figure out how to hide it," I said low.

His breath caught. "Do it." The insistent command sent desire coursing down my spine.

God, does he even know what he's asking?

To prevent myself from giving into the temptation, I kissed him back more aggressively. He bucked his hips forward and I ground against him.

He's so fucking hard.

I released his mouth and placed a kiss on his jaw, his Adam's apple, his peck, tasting and teasing as I went. His soft sounds of enjoyment following in my wake. I shifted to keep going and his hand cupped the back of my neck, halting my progress. He gently pulled me back up level with his lusciously swollen lips.

"That's not where I want your mouth," he said, then captured me hard enough to make me moan.

Fucking-A Benny.

My right hand slipped around to press into the small of his back. He eagerly arched into me. "I still need to make up for being late," I said between kisses.

"You came. That's all that matters."

"I always come." He gave a primal groan and tangled both of his hands in my hair.

Fucking hell.

The pure unadulterated need in Benny was going to have me coming, and I hadn't even touched either of our cocks.

Time to remedy that.

I rolled my hips forward, and our erections rubbed against each other. He made a small noise at the back of his throat.

Sounds like someone enjoys that. Good, I did too.

I dropped my head to place kisses on the sweet spot between his neck and shoulder that I was supposed to be avoiding as my hand drifted down between us. I wrapped long fingers around both of our cocks and gave a light pull. Benny's body reacted better than I could have hoped. He straightened in surprise even as his cock twitched in my hand and he moaned into my ear. I slowly worked both of us together, pulling gasps of pleasure from him with each fist.

"Fuck, that feels good," he groaned.

I slipped a finger between our cocks and dragged again. His hips bucked, and I swallowed his moan. My movements got faster, bordering on frantic.

"I've wanted to do this a while," I confessed.

"Why… why… sooner?" he gasped.

I would have laughed if I'd had the breath to spare. He wasn't the only one riding dangerously close to the edge. "I wasn't sure how you'd take it."

He gave a whimper. "Cal, please."

I knew what he was trying to ask, but I wasn't sure I'd make it at this point.

"We need to get you ready," I whispered against his neck.

"I've waited long enough." He was right, and I felt terrible. My hand drifted down his backside. "I'm good," he added.

I chuckled. "Benny," I started to scold just as my hand slid in between his cheeks and kept sliding.

"Like I said." He pressed back into my hand, the warmth of his ass easily swallowing my finger.

"Fuuuck," I exhaled.

He's more than prepped.

I subconsciously slipped another finger in, loving how he pulled me deeper.

Oh god, I'm going to come. Shit shit shit. This is the last time I wait.

"I swear to god, if you don't put your cock in my ass soon, I'm gonna…" His threat disintegrated into a strangled cry as I squeezed hard at the base and pulled my fist up our shafts.

I was a fucking masochist; I was never going to make it, but I wouldn't deny Benny what he wanted. I removed my hands and spun him around. His ass thrust back against me and my already strained control crumbled a little more. There was no pretending to try to cool down; he couldn't wait and neither could I.

I pressed the head of my cock against his hole and slowly pushed in. I bit down on my lip hard enough that I might have drawn blood. Even the sharp pain did little to distract from how fucking good he felt. His tight ring quivered around me and I could have cried. At this rate, I wasn't even going to get inside before I fucking exploded.

"For the love of god, Cal," Benny whined. "If you go any slower…"

"If I go any faster, I'm gonna come," I barely managed to respond. All of my concentration was focused on going as slow as possible and praying that Benny's impatience wouldn't get the better of both of us. I was shaking by the time I slipped past the last ring of tight muscle and found my entire length buried inside of him.

"I…can't…" Benny didn't finish. His whole body tightened as his release took over.

I cried out as he squeezed me from the inside, forcing the orgasm that I'd been fighting against. I griped his body against mine as I rode out the wave.

I'm not even a one-pump chump.

His channel quivered and then I did something I'd never done before—I immediately got hard again.

"Fuck yes," he moaned, pushing into me.

The things you do to me Benny Price.

I wrapped my arms around to rest my hands on his chest and pressed him more firmly against me, while I trailed kisses from his ear to his neck and across his shoulders. "What do you want?" I asked softly.

"What I want?" he echoed quietly as he turned his head to press his mouth against mine. The angle was awkward, but that didn't stop him from sliding his tongue inside to tangle with mine. I gave into the kiss completely. I was so wrapped up in Benny, it wasn't even fucking funny.

"Whatever you want," I whispered, brushing my lips against his. As I said it, I realized how true it was. I'd give him anything he wanted. All he had to do was ask.

He let out a sigh as he moved his hips backwards and forwards, slowly working himself on me. It was maddening. During the day, he could be a total prick, but here he was shockingly erotic. My fingers dug into his pecs. Another deliberate roll of his hips. He rested his forehead against mine and my eyelids fluttered as he stroked me with his body.

"Slow," he finally whispered, barely audible above the water. "Take me slow, Cal." He caught my eyes and I could have drowned in their light green, a stunning, undiluted Celadon that stole my breath.

Have they always been that color? I wondered as I stole a languid kiss, tasting his lips even as I thrust slowly into him. While the other quested down, I wrapped one hand around his shoulder. I wanted more of him. I wanted all of him. My fingers closed around him and he hardened at the touch. *That's my man.* The possessive thought barely even registered as I continued to drive into him at a deliberate pace while I stroked his cock.

Never in a million years would I have thought such a tedious rhythm could drive me to the edge so quickly. Despite all my efforts to keep the rhythm moderate, my thrusts grew sharper and more insistent as I chased my second, impossible orgasm.

Benny let out a moan so deep I felt it wrap around my cock and squeeze. He reached back and dug his fingers in my ass cheek. The touch almost pushed me over the precipice, as did the inexplicable desire for him to reach further.

I let out a gasp as I imagined what it would feel like to have his fingers inside of me while I drove into him. My thrusts became frantic. I wanted him to do it. Needed him to. And that absolutely fucking terrified me. His fingers dug in enough to bruise, forcing me deeper and harder against him. The feeling only heightened my fantasy. All sense of sanity slipped away as I rode him hard towards completion.

"Benny!"

His cry came a second after mine. He thrust into my hand and came every bit as hard as I did. My heart rate, like my breathing, skipped and started in ragged bursts.

I don't think I've ever come so hard in my life.

After a few seconds, he shifted beneath me so that he could turn and rest his back against the wall. "You okay?" he whispered, stroking my hair back from my face.

Fuck. I was really hoping he wouldn't notice. I was pretty sure my death grip on him was the only thing keeping me upright.

I gave a half-hearted groan. "That's the last fucking time I wait," the unfiltered honesty slipped out. *Fuck.*

"Wait for what?" he asked, placing light kisses along the side of my face while his fingers trailed down my back.

Mother of Mary, that feels good.

"I haven't gotten off since Monday." *Why did I tell him that?*

A small smile appeared on his face right before he caught me in a slow kiss that threatened to finish turning me into a puddle, and I sighed into him. "Me either," he admitted.

Something fluttered low in my belly. I ignored it and focused on the wonderful feel of his hands exploring my exhausted body. "I love the way you touch me," I said softly into his shoulder.

"How's that?" A finger trailed down my spine, and I lost my words for a minute.

"Like I'm special. Like I'm worth touching," I finally answered. He shifted slightly and I looked up.

What's wrong with me? Why am I saying all of this?

His gaze searched mine. "I don't want to be mean to you anymore." His words were so sincere, I felt a little bad for my resulting chuckle.

"We all have our roles to play."

"What do you mean?" he asked, his brow furrowed.

I looked back at him curious if he really didn't know. "You're the school bully, and I'm the flamboyant fag. That's just the way it is." I smiled in an attempt to take the sting out.

His face still clouded over.

"That's not true."

"Yes, it is," I sighed.

His fingers felt like butterflies on my face. "You're more than that. You always have been." He leaned forward and tentatively placed his lips against mine.

We stayed like that a moment until I pressed back. He immediately opened up to me and my tongue slid inside to taste him. His fingers wrapped back into my hair and he deepened the kiss, claiming my mouth in a way no one ever had before. It stole my breath and what remained of my senses. I wanted to stay lost in that kiss until graduation.

A distant sound invaded my perfect bubble of bliss.

"Shit," I hissed, breaking the kiss.

"What?" he asked, trying to recapture me.

"That's first bell."

"Shit."

"Yeah." I made to pull away, hoping my legs would hold, and realized we were stuck together.

When did he turn off the water?

"Ow," he said with a laugh as our dried skin pulled apart. He chuckled, eying the red on his chest and I looked down to see much the same on mine. I took a step and my leg threatened to buckle. Benny's hand shot out to steady me. "You okay?" he asked, concern coloring the words.

"Yeah," I nodded, pulling my hair away from my face. "Definitely not doing that again."

His smile was positively wicked. "I think it worked out," he said, quirking an eyebrow.

At that moment, I hated we were in a school full of bigots and re-pressed homophobic assholes. I didn't want to race away, sneaking down hallways to avoid being caught together. I wanted to stay. I wanted to soothe the red out of his chest and kiss that smile until he stole my breath again.

He blinked, and the spell broke.

Get a grip Calvin. This isn't you. That isn't what this is. No matter what happens in here, out there, he's still Benjamin Price.

Chapter 17

Benny

I absently doodled on my page while Professor Garza droned on in the background. There were a few token notes, but nothing relevant. Not that it mattered, Social Studies was an easy class, and I had already read ahead three chapters. I finished out the latest geometric design as my mind wandered back to the other night.

When he hadn't shown at the usual time, I'd gotten anxious; worried I had really fucked everything up by insisting on kissing him. Then he had burst into the showers, ditching clothes like he was on fire. More miraculously, he had seemed relieved to see I was still there. The kiss he conquered me with had instantly set me alight, as if his fire was catching.

I probably could have come from that alone.

Everything after that had spiraled completely out of hand; not that that was a surprise. But he had been different, wilder. I still wasn't sure which Cal I preferred: the calm, dominating Cal who knew every button to press to get me to the edge and keep me there, or the out-of-control Cal that had given me everything he had to the point he had to hold on or fall over. Truthfully, I appreciated them both, but I suspected I was leaning more towards this newer version.

My pulse quickened as I recalled the way he had kissed me afterward. Still needy, but also lingering. His arms twined around my neck, holding him up—yes—but also keeping us close. I lost myself to the memory that was quickly evolving into a full-blown fantasy.

The heat of his breath on my already flushed skin. His beautifully long fingers tracing patterns across my shoulders. Those honey-colored eyes staring into me. Calvin had never been afraid of me, but there had been something else in that look, something I couldn't quite put my finger on. *And that mouth of his. Astounding how lips that give birth to the filthiest things can also give the sweetest kisses.* My tongue flicked over my own as if I could taste him there.

"Mr. Price."

I jerked in my seat and looked up to see Professor Garza eying me speculatively.

"Are we disturbing you?" Garza asked.

Oh fuck.

I fought back the very different heat trying to creep up my neck. My gaze slid past the obviously perturbed instructor in search of a clue on the blackboard. A random string of off-kilter circles.

Eight circles. In a line. Hawaii. That's what we're covering.

"The US government presence rewrote the constitution, severely restricting King Kalakana's powers. Hawaii eventually became a territory in 1898 and the fiftieth state in 1959. Did I miss anything?" I asked, mentally crossing my fingers.

Garza's eyes narrowed before he finally turned away. I let out a silent sigh of relief.

I have got to get myself under control.

I looked down at my useless notes.

Calvin is part Hawaiian.

"As an interesting side note, there are over one hundred documented waterfalls between the islands," Garza commented, returning to the lesson.

Now there's an image.

I pictured Calvin standing beneath a tropical waterfall surrounded by flowers in every color imaginable. It was a far better sight than the mold-colored tile in the showers. He slicked back his dark hair, allowing water to cascade like a lover's caress down his gloriously naked body.

God Calvin is beautiful. He doesn't need to make art; he is art.

Those seductive eyes caught me, filled with honey and lust. They promised all sorts of wicked pleasures. I let out an involuntary groan. I desperately wanted any carnal sin that man could imagine. He gave me that rogue smile of his as if he knew what I was thinking and crooked a finger, beckoning me to join. The look alone was enough to make heat flood through me again, clouding my thoughts in a haze of desire.

"Yo, you alright?" The question was accompanied by a light touch on my arm.

"What the fuck do you want?" I hissed, just barely remembering to keep my voice down. Anger over took me as the beautiful fantasy I'd created dissolved into dust motes.

"Chill. You just seemed to be working yourself up over there." Todd gave a subtle glance to where I was tenting.

Fuck.

All the anger flowed out of me, doing its part to bring me down.

Get it the fuck together.

I met Todd's concerned look. *At least he stopped me before I made a complete spectacle of myself.*

"I'm sorry, man." I shook my head, though it did little to ease my frustration. His expression immediately went from one of indignant concern to outright shock. "What?" I asked, furrowing my brow. Then it hit me: I'd apologized.

I never apologize. For anything. What kind of asshole friend am I that an apology is noteworthy?

Fucking hell. This is all Calvin's doing.

Imaginary Calvin winked at me from his private waterfall.

Fucking hell. I need air.

I raised my hand.

"Yes, Mr. Price?" Professor Garza asked, sounding exceptionally put upon.

"I need to take a piss." His jaw ticked as snickers rippled through the classroom.

"You're excused." He didn't comment when I slung the messenger bag across my body; class was close to letting out, and I needed something to help hide my persistent hard on.

I slipped out of the room and drifted down the hallways towards the cafeteria.

If I keep checking out like that, I'm gonna be in real trouble. I have to do something.

The problem was I had zero desire to do a damn thing about it. I liked the way things were going, and frankly, could stand for a bit more. Sex with Calvin was phenomenal, but talking was nice too. Hell, just holding him was pretty fucking incredible.

To my surprise, the object of my thoughts appeared across the way, turning into the main hall from an adjoining corridor. He was already smiling, but when his gaze fell on me, he practically shone.

My stupid grin rose in response, even as something fluttered in my chest, throwing off my heart's regular rhythm.

I wanted nothing more than to cup the side of his face and capture that smile with a kiss. Then trail my hand down his arm and intertwine our fingers even as I stole another. He would give a small teasing laugh, implying he thought I was being silly, but wouldn't stop me. Together, we'd walk to the mess hall or courtyard or anywhere we could sit and be together. We'd talk about our day and our classes, all the while staying in perfect contact. I'd have to brush the hair out of his eyes, because the stuff really was too long. He'd smile and give me that look. The one I couldn't quite put my finger on. I'd get lost in his honeyed gaze and…

"Benny." My name being called from somewhere behind me brought me up short.

Now that the trance was broken, I could clearly see Anderson Gallagher walking beside Calvin—*not me*. I blinked and realized I'd already cleared half the distance between us before I had been stopped. The flutter in my chest turned painful as cruel reality asserted itself.

I couldn't just walk up to Cal and kiss him in the hall. I couldn't go anywhere near him; couldn't even touch him. Not here. Not with all of these people around. At some point, classes had let out and the massive hall was quickly filling with bodies, adding physical barriers to the invisible ones that already separated us.

"Hey man." I barely recognized the voice as belonging to Todd. Rage at the unfairness of it all burned away the remnants of pain in my chest. I twitched beneath his restraining hand. "Take it easy. It's cool. You can get him some other time."

I stole one last look at Calvin's receding form next to Andy. The same Andy who had made him smile and was about to have lunch with him like it was no big deal. *They* would sit and talk and laugh. A growl bubbled up, feeding off the anger that already had a hold of me.

"Whoa. I don't know what the fuck Bridges did to set you off, but I swear, I thought you were going to tear him apart right here in the hall," Todd laughed.

"Don't worry, we'll get him next time," Neil added.

Where the fuck did he come from?

I spun around without warning. "No one fucking touches Calvin Bridges but me. Understand?" I hissed through clenched teeth.

My two idiot friends looked at each other, clearly taken aback by the vehemence of my statement.

"Sure thing, man."

"No one but you."

"We can mess with him now if you're really that pissed. They usually head to the courtyard when the sun's out," Todd offered unhelpfully.

The thought of seeing him again had the flutters threatening to return. They were quickly tempered by my fear of what I might do to Todd or Neil for treating Cal the way we always had. Or to Andy for having the good fortune of actually being able to spend time with him.

We all have our roles. Calvin's words came back to me and I wanted to be sick.

"I'm over it. Besides, I wanna get a jump start on drills. My passes have been shit lately." They exchanged another look before I turned to make my way to the practice field. My passes had never been anything less than perfect.

Calvin

Andy glanced over at me as I stared after Benny. "Um… what the fuck was that about?"

"Huh? What?" I tore my gaze away from the trio's retreating silhouettes, wondering the same thing. "I… don't know." When I finally looked over at Andy, his mouth curled down in a wry scowl. "What?"

"That was hella convincing."

"I'm serious," I argued. "Don't have a clue. Why would I know why Price was stalking over here?" Not with death in his eyes, but with the familiar longing I'd grown to recognize when we were truly alone together.

"Maybe because you know just about everything that happens in this twisted place. What the fuck happened? Did you do something?"

My gut twisted. I had done something alright—I'd done *a lot* of somethings—and it was quite possible those somethings were catching up with me. It would seem Benny and I needed to have a chat about keeping up appearances. I tucked a curl behind my ear and tightened my grip on my bag. "Umm…"

"Calvin." Andy stopped halfway through the door to the cafeteria and looked back at me with an expression that would brook no nonsense. I scrambled for something to fill the void that would make sense *and* account for my awkward response.

"Look, we got into it the other day. Okay?" I exclaimed in a loud huff and pushed past him.

"What happened?" Andy asked as he stepped up beside me and grabbed a tray. I simultaneously wanted to groan at the worry in his voice and kick him in the shins for deciding that *now* was the time to be the perfect friend.

"He… accused me of being the one to do that prank on Nolan." *Sort of.*

Andy paled and his tray caught on a dip in the bars meant to support it. He quickly righted the plastic before food could go everywhere. "Shit. I didn't… I mean… If he's…"

I placed a light hand on Andy's arm. He looked over at me, his Emerald eyes almost Sap Green with fear. "It's okay. I took care of it." He didn't look convinced, so I knocked his shoulder. "I can handle Benny."

He relaxed a hair. "You sure about that? He seemed pretty intense in the hall."

I snorted to hide the fact that I wasn't at all sure about anything. If Benny couldn't keep his shit together and play his part, then this whole thing we had going would blow up in both of our faces. We finished acquiring our food and drifted over to the usual table. I forced myself not to keep obsessively checking the entrance for Benny and his cohort's entrance, but it didn't stop me from noticing that he never showed. Which was probably what led me to suggest we relocate to our spot by the stone wall outside the second we were done eating. There was only one place Benny would be if it wasn't here.

For all the years Prince Einar had kept distance between himself and King Kelani, who could fathom that a day would come he'd long to approach the king. Not for border disputes or threats to sabotage supply lines, but to bask in the king's radiance. Would that there was no need to keep their newly forged alliance secret. But rival nations would not sit idly by upon learning that their greatest obstacle had further fortified his rule.

Chapter 18

Benny

I was completely obsessed with Calvin's mouth. From the moment he'd placed his lips on my back, I hadn't been able to think about anything else; I wanted those damn things everywhere. I couldn't even come anymore without imagining them on my body. Even more than on my flesh, I craved to feel those lips on mine. I'd been nervous about asking for it. Terrified it would ruin everything. What if he freaked out? What if he said no? But he hadn't. And while he was far from confident when he'd agreed, it was absolutely worth the risk.

I smiled to myself, recalling how he had wrapped around me to deepen that first kiss, similar to what he was doing now. Calvin's nails scrapped along my scalp, grounding me in the here and now. I groaned and pressed into him harder.

God, I love how he pulls on my bottom lip like that. I gave a moan and rolled my hips forward, seeking even more contact.

When our cocks rubbed against each other, he gasped, and I grabbed the chance to tangle my tongue with his. He arched into me and I left his delicious mouth to taste other parts of him. He groaned again and dug his fingers into my back as I found the tender spot on his neck.

"Fuck me," he hissed, then promptly caught the bottom of my ear between his teeth.

I made a strangled sound somewhere between a cry and a moan, and immediately ground against him again. He gave another groan before catching my mouth in a kiss savage enough to steal both our breaths.

He pulled away gasping for air even as he arched back. I took the invitation and followed the curve of his neck with my lips. His leg bent as he hooked his knee on my hip pulling me closer still.

I love how he always wants more of me.

I let out a groan as I dug my fingers into his thigh. There was a low whine deep in his throat as he tangled his hand in my hair. The stupid stuff was finally growing, but it still wasn't long enough for him to do much besides run his fingers through it. Still, I imagined it was more and moaned in response.

"God, Benny," he panted.

My hand slid higher up his leg as I tried to grip it tighter. He groaned again and a fresh wave of desire swept through me. I was already so close to losing my senses and we hadn't even played with our cocks yet. My hand quested down. Calvin let out a strangled moan as my fingers wrapped around his length.

"I want you," he gasped, breathless.

Fuck yes.

I released him, and he immediately caught my mouth in a kiss hard enough to bruise. I eagerly returned the tangle, reflexively pulling his leg higher.

"Something different tonight," he said when he finally released me.

I would have been more intrigued if he hadn't sounded so uncertain.

"Oh?" I queried, taking his hand in my free one and bringing it to my mouth. His eyes hazed with lust as I took his middle finger into my mouth and wrapped my tongue around it.

"Not that either," he responded shakily.

"Rimming?" I echoed his guess from eons ago.

His eyes sparkled, and his confidence seemed to return. He moved his stolen hand to wrap around my neck and claimed my mouth, biting my lip again for good measure. He was completely out of breath by the time he released me.

"What do you want, Cal?" I asked, returning to that sweet spot on his collar. I drank the water flowing over him as if I could somehow drink him up, too.

"Inside," he moaned, practically crawling up my body.

I hesitated, not sure if he meant what I thought he meant.

When I didn't respond right away, he added, "I want you inside of me."

"No," I said quietly, regretting the word even before I said it.

I let his leg slip through my hand back to the floor as he shifted his hand to my chest.

He pushed me back slightly, forcing me to look at him.

Much as I didn't want to, I met his gaze. All the playfulness from before was gone, as was the lust; seared away by the anger that now burned in its place.

"What do you mean 'No'?"

Oh yeah, he's pissed.

"Exactly that. No," I repeated.

What is wrong with me?

His eyes sparked, and his jaw tightened. Mounting rage wrinkled his brow and pulled at his mouth. "I have given you everything you have ever asked for. Repeatedly. I ask for one thing, and you have the balls to stand there and calmly tell me no, as if what *I* want doesn't matter?"

My heart sank to plop uncomfortably in my stomach.

How do I make him understand? It's not that simple.

"One fucking thing." He shifted and water fell between the distance he'd created. The cold of the spray was in stark contrast to the fire burning in his eyes. "Why?" he asked. The sinister tone seemed more than the one word could possibly convey.

"Because this is still just sex to you." Of the dozens of explanations to choose from, I had no idea why I went with that one. I had thought he was angry before; I was wrong.

He shoved me and I stumbled back a couple of steps.

"What the fuck is that supposed to mean!" he shouted, moving out from under the chill water. "That's what it's always been, Price."

I flinched at the sharp way he said my name.

Calvin stormed over to where his clothes were stacked. He didn't even bother trying to dry off as he started to get dressed. He got frustrated when they stuck and started shouting again. "One fucking thing, Benny! One. Fucking. Thing. And that's your fucking answer? Un-fucking believable!" He violently pulled his shirt down, nearly ripping it. "This whole fucking thing was a mistake. I don't know what the fuck I was thinking." He stepped towards the exit, then spun back around and got in my face. "Congratulations. You're not gay, you're just an asshole!"

My face burned at the rebuke, and I still had nothing to say for myself.

His gaze searched mine another moment, then he turned on his heel and marched out of the showers, slamming the door behind him.

When the hallway disappeared behind the closed door, air finally rushed into my lungs. I gasped as I fell against the wall and slid to the floor. The freezing water continued to fall all around me, highlighting my isolation. I hung my head in my hands, still searching for the words I should have said to him.

What have I done?

Chapter 19

Benny

"Fuck off already," I snapped at Todd and Neil, who had done nothing more heinous than breathe.

"What crawled up your ass and died?" Neil asked.

On any normal day, I would have verbally torn him apart for having the balls to talk to me like that. Today wasn't a normal day. Yesterday hadn't been either. As it was, it took everything I had not to claw at my scalp and growl out my frustration. What the fuck had I been thinking? Why would I tell Calvin no?

On the surface, I could admit that it petrified me what switching things up would do to our tenuous dynamic, but deep down, I knew it was more than that. I just didn't know what.

What is wrong with me?

I thought about how fast he'd hidden the hurt of rejection behind a mask of anger until the anger overtook everything else. I couldn't even blame him for shouting and storming out while I stood there like a total and complete ass.

I should have chased after him.

But what would I have said?

I glanced up to find Todd and Neil hovering a modest distance away and eying me like I was a ticking bomb ready to explode at any minute. They weren't wrong. I'd managed to go four days, avoiding so much as a glimpse of Calvin. Four. Whole. Days. Which was exactly four days longer than I'd ever gone without seeing him since we'd started at Ulwich ten years ago, bar holidays and summers. Going so long without seeing him before wouldn't have been easy. Doing so now that things were… complicated was significantly harder. Every night I wanted to go to him. He was there. I knew because I checked. Every night. I wanted to explain my reasons for denying him, except I didn't understand them myself.

With a shout, I drove my fist into the nearby support. Thankfully, it was wooden and didn't crack my entire hand wide open, but it still hurt like a motherfucker. Todd and Neil flinched while I embraced the throbbing agony radiating up my arm. Anything to distract from thoughts of Calvin. The pulsing pain encompassed everything like a second heartbeat.

Calvin's heartbeat. Beating in almost perfect time with my own. I could feel it in his lips when they pressed against mine. Feel it when he buried his length inside me. Feel it where he placed his hand over my heart and pulled me tight against him.

I clenched my aching hand into a fist and grunted more at the pain of the memory than at the pain that lanced across my knuckles.

"Um, you okay?" Todd's hesitant question was the final straw. No, I wasn't okay. I wasn't in any way, shape, or fashion, *okay*.

"I've gotta go. I'll catch up with you two later."

Neil stepped forward, but stopped shy at actually blocking my path out of the lockers. The place had been my sole refuge and one of the few places actually safe from Calvin. I could think of a couple others that might do the trick, but couldn't take the risk that he might know about them as well. "You sure you don't wanna go see the nurse?" His gaze flicked down to my massacred hand.

"It's fine," I growled and took another step, but not before Todd latched onto the inspired idea.

"Don't know, boss. Heard that new nurse has a hell of a pair of knockers."

Neil glanced over at his buddy. Sometimes I could swear the two shared a brain. "She may be a little older, but who cares when you've got a full pair pushed in your face?" They snickered as one and fist-bumped. A poor choice of celebration as witnessing the move only made my hand throb harder.

"I don't want some old lady's tits in my face." *But a pair of young ones might do...*

"Aw, she's not that old," Neil argued. "Forties at worst."

I frowned at their pathetic attempts at enticement and pulled out my phone.

"Who you callin'?" Todd asked, peering around to glimpse the screen. Instead of answering, I dialed and waited for the call to pick up. Two rings later, I got my wish.

"Sup?" I tried not to think of the pressure releasing around my chest as relief, but that's what it was.

"Can you meet me at the heart?"

"When you thinking?"

"Now?" I held my breath as I waited for an answer.

"Be there in thirty."

I let out the breath and didn't even care about the curious looks Todd and Neil were giving each other about my unusual behavior. "See you then, Savannah."

Todd threw up his hands. "I see how it is. You blow us off for your own tits on demand."

I had no intention of explaining to either of them that wasn't how this was at all. Instead, I offered a leer and let them believe what they wanted as I sauntered past and made a beeline straight East toward the girl's school.

Thirty minutes later, the telltale crunch of leaves announced another person approaching. I abandoned my perch against the tree carved with a heart and arrow that had most likely been made years ago by some star-crossed lovers between the schools. Savannah and I weren't that by any means, but the spot was easy enough to find when you knew where to look and was dead center between Ulwich and the girl's school.

When Savannah emerged from the trees, it wasn't the risque outfit she'd been sporting in town she wore, but the much more proper presentation of a distinguished young lady of society. Her buttons were done all the way, not a one of them straining. Her shirt was tucked into her plaid skirt, that wasn't even rolled to make it shorter. She even wore her school tie and had on a neat, trim blazer. She looked great and although the image was in stark contrast to the rebellious one she often donned, she still looked every inch herself.

An unfamiliar pain stabbed at my heart, and I launched myself at her. She let out a grunt as I wrapped my arms around her waist and squeezed tight enough to make her wheeze. Rather than pull away or tell me to ease up, she rubbed my back and gave me a light squeeze in return.

"Hey, what's wrong? Did something happen?" Her soft voice washed over me and I fought to rein in the sudden tide of emotion. So many things had happened, I didn't even know where to start.

I gave her a last squeeze and pulled away, only to rake my hands through my over-grown hair for want of something to do with them. "Yes. No. I don't know. I fucked up… maybe. No. Pretty sure I fucked up. And I…I don't know what to do. I don't know how to fix this." I met her blue gaze when I ran out of words. The concern I found there at once hurt and soothed something inside me. Savannah would figure this out. She could fix it.

She has to.

"Come here." She grabbed my wrist and led me over to a stump worn smooth with time. "Sit. And start at the beginning." I did as she asked, but only her hold on my arm kept me from popping right back up again.

"There's this guy at school—"

"Benny, did you hit him?" She pointedly looked at my scraped knuckles. "I know they're all a bunch of putzes, but your father will kill you if you get into a fight at his stupid alma mater."

"Trust me, murder is definitely in my future if he ever finds out about this, but I didn't hit anyone."

"O-kay… so, what's going on?"

I looked at her out of the corner of my eye, her ponytail pulled over her shoulder like a river of gold. "Do you remember Calvin Bridges?"

She snorted and leaned back to rest on her arms. "You mean the guy you've been obsessed with since you started at that fucked up school?" I shot her a look, and she rolled her eyes. "What? We both know it's true."

I huffed and rested my forearms on my knees, my gaze focusing on the forest floor. It didn't do any good to argue with her, especially since she was right. "Yeah, him." I twisted my hands together and wondered why I was stalling. Of all the people in the world I could talk to, I trusted Savannah the most. We'd grown up together, and she knew literally everything about me.

So why am I anxious?

"Well, what about him?" she prompted when I remained quiet.

"I… I mean we…" She raised an eyebrow at my uncharacteristic stammering. "We've been fooling around," I finished in a rush. "A couple of months now," I added, my face heating as I kept my gaze firmly fixed on the ground.

"Aww, Benny, are you blushing? That's so fucking adorable," she cooed.

I shook her off. "Shut up. No, I'm not. Don't be such a fucking twat."

She brushed her hair back over her shoulder and smirked at me, clearly not buying my shit. "The young prince finally decided to pursue the elusive king."

I sat up and met her knowing gaze. "Seriously, Sassy? You're gonna go there? Now?"

She shrugged as if it was of little significance. "I mean, writing those stories was *my* idea to help you deal with your obsession. At least that two-bit quack was useful for something." I envied her ability to be so flippant about therapy. That was certainly a luxury I would never have. Even if I could convince my father to let me see someone, I'd never be able to trust that the sessions would truly be private. "So…"

"So what?"

"Oh my god, Benny. For fuck's sake, tell me all about it." She leaned forward, her eyes alight with eagerness, and I couldn't help but chuckle.

"Well, the sex is fucking incredible. Like damn." She beamed and gestured for me to keep going. "And I… uh, I kissed him."

Her eyes said it all. She knew exactly how long I'd wanted to kiss Calvin Bridges. "And how was it?"

A smile twitched at my lips as I dropped my gaze back to the leaf-riddled ground. "Really good." When she didn't immediately have something to say, I looked back up at her. This time, her eyes were filled with a touch of wonder. "What?"

"Nothing. It's just… you really like this guy."

I opened my mouth to argue, but couldn't make the words come. "Shame I fucked it all up."

Her face fell and all the previous joy disappeared. "What happened?"

"He asked something of me I don't know if I can give him."

"Care to be more vague? You didn't call me out of Debate so you could pussyfoot around the issue."

"Shit, Sassy. You didn't have to ditch Debate." If I'd known, I never would have insisted she meet me so soon. Savannah had fought hard to be on the team and even harder for her position as captain, it was one of the few extracurriculars she'd been able to choose for herself.

She placed a hand on my knee and squeezed. "It's no trouble, I promise. You wouldn't have called if it wasn't urgent. Now, out with it. What did he ask?"

"He asked to switch." Her brows drew together in a deep V that matched the frown tugging at her mouth. "It sounds stupid to say out loud and I'm not even sure why I said no. If it was literally anyone else, I wouldn't think twice about it, but not him."

She considered me for a long minute. "Anything else?"

I knew what she wanted, the underlying reason I wouldn't top Calvin, but some secrets weren't mine to tell. I shook my head. "I don't know how to fix this. He was so angry and I… I don't know…"

"Oh, Benny. I think I have an idea." I looked up at her with unexpected hope and found a knowing look in her baby blues. "Casual has never been enough for you. That's one of the main reasons we didn't work. You always want more and you hate sharing."

"Savannah—"

"No, hear me out. You know I'm right. You need more than casual sex." She tilted her head and seemed to weigh her next words. "I think you two should date."

"Are you out of your damn mind!"

"Face it, Benny, you've been half in love with the guy for years. It only makes sense you want more of a commitment."

"Being obsessed and being in love aren't the same thing."

"No, they're not. But facts are facts. Your world has practically revolved around that guy since day one and when you finally gave in, it only got more pronounced. I don't think I've ever heard you tell a story about that place that didn't somehow come back to Calvin. You can deny it 'til your last breath, but if you had seen the goofy smile on your face just from *thinking* about kissing him, you wouldn't have a leg to stand on."

I thought back to that day in the hall when I'd been beside myself with anger solely because Andy could spend all the time he wanted with Cal and I couldn't. "I really hate you sometimes."

"No, you don't, you love me, and you love that I call you out on your shit. Date him, Benny, it's what you want." I continued to scowl at her, even though I knew she was right. Leave it to Savannah to find the heart of a problem with almost nothing to go on.

I gave up my futile battle and dropped my head in my hands. "It would never work. We'd get caught. I don't even know how we haven't gotten caught already."

"I seriously doubt that no one has ever managed to date at that repressed school." I blinked as I realized that once again, she was right. People had gotten away with dating right beneath everyone's nose. Even better, I knew them. Except I couldn't very well ask Andy how he'd pulled it off, especially after he'd threatened me not once, but twice. That left Connor.

I could do that.

A tiny spark of hope blossomed in my chest, then promptly went out. "He'll never go for it."

"You don't know until you ask." Unexpectedly, she threw her arms around me and squeezed. "It's so nice to see you happy." I snorted. At the moment, I was a far cry from happy. She pulled away and punched me in the shoulder. "Don't give me that. We were great in our own way, but you never smiled like that when we were together. Now, when do I finally get to meet the infamous King Kelani?"

I threw my head back and laughed. My first answer was when hell freezes over, but then it occurred to me I wanted her to meet him, to get to know how wonderful he was. "One step at a time. He actually has to agree to date first."

"I'm sure you can convince him." She winked and bumped her shoulder into mine. "Then you can introduce us."

I reached for her hand and gently squeezed her fingers. "Thank you, Sassy. You're an amazing friend."

"I know." She gave me a self-satisfied smirk. "Now, what's the deal with the hair? Since when did you stop buzzing it?"

My eyes went wide before I could check my reaction to the laissez-faire question and heat surged up my neck to burn on my cheeks.

Her mouth fell open. "Oh. My. God. *He* asked you to grow it out."

"What? No. That's stupid."

She giggled in vicious delight. "He totally asked, and you did it. Imagine that, Benny Price willing to change his appearance for someone else."

"He didn't ask," I continued to argue while fending her off. She paused, her hand inches from my head, my fingers around her wrist the only things keeping her from her destination, and raised another eyebrow. "He didn't *ask*," I grumbled.

Her attack relaxed as she smiled back at me. "You really are gone for this guy."

"Sassy."

"I'm not teasing. I just… maybe I'm a little jealous."

"Why?" I frowned as I released her, suddenly concerned that maybe our breakup hadn't been as mutual as I thought.

"Because you're willing to fight for what you want. You always have been, and I hope… I hope someday someone can look at me the way you look when you think about him."

"You will," I said as I pulled her in for another hug. She squeezed back. But we both knew the truth. Whoever Savannah ended up with would be purely for social gain. For that matter, so would I.

Chapter 20

Calvin

He has to show. He just has to.

I laced my fingers behind my head as I paced the room again. Three different fucking nights I'd shown, and he hadn't; I'd waited for hours, one night even to the first bell, and still nothing.

He's definitely avoiding me. Why do I have to overreact about everything? Maybe if I'd taken a breath and actually explained why I asked what I did, then maybe he wouldn't have been so quick to say no.

My jaw tightened, and I fought off a fresh wave of anger as I recalled what else he had said.

How could he think that? It hasn't been just about sex. Not for a while.

I liked Benny, like, really liked Benny. And it didn't matter that it was stupid or didn't make sense or that Andy was right. None of it changed how I felt. What had started as a game had evolved into something else. Even mad at him, I had still dreamed of being able to sit and laugh together, to not have to say goodbye at the end of the night. Sometimes in my dreams we talked for what could have been hours, learning about each other in a new way, and others we wouldn't say a word, just lie wrapped in each other's arms. The usual longing sprang up at the thoughts.

I'm a fucking mess. I have to make this right. He'll understand if I tell him. He has to.

But why should he?

The renegade thought slashed through my stubborn optimism. I certainly hadn't given him any reason to believe me or even want to hear me out. That he'd failed to show for over a week stood testament to that. I let out a cry of frustration that echoed back at me from the washed-out green tiles.

But that's why I'm here now. If he won't show at the usual time, then I just have to try an unusual one.

I yanked at my school tie, tearing it loose. I fucking hated the damn thing and everything it stood for, not to mention the constricting button down. Angrily I pulled the shirt loose, taking out my frustration on the only thing handy: my clothes.

I should have at least swung by my room to change and drop my bag. I glanced at the discarded pack, once again toying with the idea of at least pretending to do schoolwork. I shook my head and resumed my pacing.

I couldn't risk going back to the room and getting held up. What if I missed him?

It was a dim hope that he would even bother to check the showers at all. Still, I clung to it.

Please show.

"Yeah, but Neil will always be second string, unless you're planning on getting injured soon."

"As if. All I'm saying is that he can't expect to leave the bench without putting in more effort. You know?"

I spun around at the voices. There in the doorway stood Connor Hendricks and, holding the door open, was Benny.

All of my calm evaporated as I realized what I was looking at: Benny was with Connor. Connor and Benny were in the fucking showers. Together. Suddenly, him not showing at the usual time made a whole lot more sense. He'd moved on.

Benny quietly met my accusatory glare.

"Are you fucking kidding me!" I yelled. My body was shaking, I was so pissed.

Connor gave Benny a questioning look, which he missed, as he was still staring at me. Finally, Benny ducked his head and said to Connor over his shoulder, "I'll handle this."

I puffed up with rage. *Over my dead, flamboyant fucking body is Benjamin Fucking Price going to handle* me.

Connor shot me an anxious look. "You sure?"

"Yeah. Finish the round for me? I'll get him back in his room," Benny finished, his gaze returning to me.

Since when does he do the round with someone else? Is that the excuse they're using?

My thoughts were in serious danger of spilling out in an exceptionally elevated tone. Between the tile and the open door, people clear across the school would be able to hear me.

Connor placed a hand on Benny's shoulder and if I could have breathed fire, I would have. "Yeah. I got it. Just don't do anything stupid," he said, sparing me one last look before vanishing back into the corridor.

I managed to keep it together long enough for the door to close before unleashing. "Connor? Are you fucking serious!"

"It's not what you think," Benny said at nearly the same time. I ignored him.

"Is *that* why you've been avoiding me? Or have you just not known I was here? Did you even bother to check!"

"I knew you were here." The flat statement was like adding kerosene to my already blazing bonfire.

"So, what? You just moved from one fucking fag to the next! Did you choose him because you knew he'd be up for it? Or does it even matter?"

"It's not like that."

"Like hell it's not! You're willing to fuck him, just not me, is that it? What the literal fuck, Benny!"

"If you would stop shouting, I could tell you," Benny said calmer than a stone as he walked deeper into the room.

I trailed after him, unwilling to let him out of my sight now that I had him. I rounded the divider hot on his heels, a fresh rebuke ready. "I can shout all the fuck I like. You don't get to tell me what to do."

"I know that."

"Then what makes you think you can do it now!"

"I'm not. I'm asking you to let me explain. Why do you always have to be so dramatic?" he asked, leaning against the tiled wall, the picture of chill. It was infuriating. *He* was infuriating.

"I am not dramatic!" I shouted, immediately recognizing the irony of such a response. My mouth snapped shut to prevent more outrage from spewing out of me. I counted to three, then managed to say without yelling, "Fine. You want to explain, then explain. What the fuck are you doing here with fucking Connor Hendricks?" The tail end of the question rose in both volume and pitch. At this rate, I was going to leave general shouting and enter the realm of screeching. I fisted my hands in a vain attempt to get myself under control.

"Honestly? I was trying to figure out how he and Andy kept it quiet for so long, but I chickened out and started talking about the team instead."

"Why the hell would you want to know something like that? And why would you ask Connor? He's a fucking idiot! I'm the one who came up with the damn code. You could have asked me!"

"Why am I not surprised?" Benny mumbled to himself.

"What?"

He took a deep breath and caught my eye. "Because I wasn't sure how you would take it."

"Take it? Take what? Why wouldn't I be able to take whatever it is?" I asked, waving my hands around.

Benny gave me a knowing look. "You mean, besides the fact that you tend to overreact?" He neglected to say like how I kind of was right now and added, "You're a little hard to pin down, Cal."

It was the first time he'd said my name in weeks and I hated to hell how it felt like a balm on my burning skin. I didn't want to be side-tracked into feeling better; I wasn't done being mad at him.

"I do not overreact," I said flatly. He stared at me and I wavered. "Okay, maybe I overreact a little," I conceded.

That's the most he's gonna fucking get.

He didn't blink.

I huffed. "Are you going to answer the fucking question or not? Why would you want to talk to Connor about him and Andy?"

"Because I want to date you, Cal. I want more of you than just hot shower sex and making out. I want to get to know you, spend time with you. Out of here." He gestured at the surrounding room.

"Date me? But you've been avoiding me."

"I wanted to give you a chance to cool off."

"What about Connor? You were *here* with Connor." I glanced towards the door where Connor had vanished; where he'd dared to place a hand on Benny—*My* Benny. "You're not fucking Connor?" I asked, still feeling uncertain.

"I'm not fucking Connor," Benny replied with the ghost of a smile.

I stared down at the tile floor and scrambled to get my thoughts back in order. None of this was going the way I'd planned. "But… you said no," I finished finally, lifting my gaze to meet his.

I hate feeling like this, so unsure and anxious. This is what Benny does to me. How can I possibly want more of it?

Benny's small smile melted into his suddenly sad expression.

"Cal, I'm sorry. I—"

"I need to tell you something," I cut him off. Without waiting for any sign of acceptance, I stepped towards him. "You have to let me explain why I asked," I elaborated. My heart beat so hard against my ribs it was a miracle it wasn't echoing back.

Benny searched my face for a moment. "Okay."

I'd never heard such a magical fucking word. I closed the remaining distance between us in two long strides and mashed my mouth against his. My hands went up to his head, where I slipped my fingers in his hair. It was still pretty short, but it was long enough now that I could tighten my fingers and hold his face even closer as I tangled my tongue with his. Benny gave a soft moan, and I ate it up, hungry for more. My chest was heaving and air was just a memory by the time I pulled away. "I'm sorry. Two weeks is a long time to go without kissing you," I said, still trying to get my breathing regular.

His hand slid up my neck to cup my face, and I could have melted. "I know," he said, snaring me.

I lost myself to it as his arms wrapped around me. I barely even noticed when he spun us so I was pressed into the wall. My body reacted all on its own, arching into him, craving as much contact as it could get. I reluctantly broke the kiss and dragged in a lungful of air. His own hot panting warmed my face. Benny could kiss like no one else, but I had to do this; he had to know. "I need you to understand," I said, still a little breathless. "It's... it's not just about sex." I looked at him, getting nervous again. My speech had sounded pretty great when he wasn't actually standing in front of me. Now that he was, I wasn't sure I could go through with it.

Man up, Bridges.

I took a steadying breath. "I mean, I know that's technically what I asked for, but you need to know why that's a big deal. At least, why it's a big deal for me." I waited for him to interject or call me stupid, but he just waited to hear me out. I swallowed and went on. "My first time... doing *that*—my first time doing anything—wasn't exactly great. It was with—"

"Warren Singleton," Benny finished.

I stared at him in horror. "Wha- How do you... How do you know that?" I asked, leaning away as far as the wall would allow. An emotion I couldn't place passed across his face. Sadness? Regret? Shame?

"He might have said something." Benny didn't look pleased to be sharing.

"Said something?" I echoed. If I hadn't been so overwhelmingly stricken, I would have started shouting again.

"It was in the locker room not long before he left."

"How many people know?" I asked, my voice rising.

"Shh," Benny soothed, concern clouding his face as he brushed my hair back. "Not many. There were just a couple of us there. No one really believed him. He was an ass known for telling tall tales. Everyone just chalked it up to that."

I felt like I was going to be sick.

He bragged about it.

No matter what Benny said, I didn't believe it was just a couple. *All these years…*

"It's okay, Cal. You don't have to explain anything. I know," Benny whispered, then pulled me into a hug. I clung to him as his words sank in.

There are people out there who know. People who know Warren raped me and they did nothing about it.

I squeezed Benny tighter and buried my face in his shoulder.

"I'm sorry." His soft words brushed against my ear and reminded me why I was here.

I released my death grip on his neck and leaned back. I stole a smaller kiss to steady my nerves before continuing. "Then you know why it was a big deal for me to ask." It wasn't a question, but he answered it anyway.

"Yeah," he said softly. "I didn't want you to think that was something I needed from you, because it's not."

"I know. Just like I know you would never ask it of me. But…" I swallowed. "But it *is* something I want from you." I caught his faded green eyes and fought back my uncertainty. "I can't exactly undo my first-first time, but I would really like my first time bottoming—by choice—to be with you."

There, I said it. The words are out.

We stayed perfectly still, staring at each other for a long minute. "Okay."

That really was starting to feel like a magical word. I smashed my mouth against his, obliterating the last of my anxiety about having this whole wretched conversation. His hands wrapped around me and I moaned into the touch.

God, how I've missed this.

My arms wrapped back around his neck as I struggled to get as much contact with him as humanly possible. Suddenly, he pulled away.

"What?" I asked, my doubts immediately resurfacing.

"But not here."

"Not here? If not here, then where?" I asked, confused.

"We'll meet in my room," he said, returning to tempt me with another kiss.

"Are you insane? Do you have any idea how risky that is? What if we get caught?" I asked, completely incredulous.

Benny, of all people, should know better.

"You're being dramatic again."

I bit off the rest of my argument.

"Besides, if we meet on one of the nights I do the rounds, then who will catch us?"

That's a fair point.

"Fine. Be stubborn and crazy. You're on a round tonight. Let's go," I said.

He chuckled and brushed his lips across mine. "Not tonight. Tonight, you just go back to your room."

My mouth opened, fully prepared to argue, only to be silenced by a kiss that would not be denied. "I missed you," I sighed when I was finally at liberty to talk again.

"I missed you too."

"So date, huh?" I asked with a crooked grin.

"Yeah, or something like that," he responded, leaving me to grab my satchel.

"I might have a few ideas," I said, shouldering the bag.

"I bet you do."

Kel's smile may have started dubious, but the king quickly regained his usual air of confidence. Einar mirrored the expression and gently took the king's hand to formally seal their courtship. The ambitious prince placed a bold kiss on the king's knuckles and vowed to ensure this courtship to be one for the ages.

Chapter 21

Calvin

I stared off into the distance, still not sure what to make of the whole thing. Date Benny? Did I want that? The answer that continued to shock me was yes. Not just yes, fuck yes. There was just one problem—I'd never dated anyone before.

Can't possibly be that hard. Can it?

I glanced over at Andy. He'd been able to do it for over a year and no matter what he said to the contrary, he might as well be dating Mitch now. Sure, I'd come up with the basis of the code they used, but the actual dating part had been all of them.

"What are you doing this weekend?" Andy asked, looking up at me, no doubt having sensed my irrational stare.

Here it was, my opportunity to come clean and maybe ask for some advice. So in true Calvin style, I looked right at the opportunity...and completely ignored it. "Nothing." I shrugged as if it would make my lackluster answer more believable. Andy blinked those intense Phthalo green eyes at me, but didn't call me on my obvious shit. "You?"

Oh, my fucking God. Did my voice just crack? Jesus fucking Christ. I'm going into town with Benny, not marrying the asshole.

Thankfully, the most Andy did was quirk an eyebrow. "Not much. Finish a book. Study with Mitch."

I wonder if Andy has told Mitch what "studying" really means…

"Sounds...like fun." Andy's expression immediately morphed into a glower. "Don't say it. I remember the deal. I can't give you grief about anything when I'm not sharing either." Except thanks to Benny, I knew exactly what he wasn't sharing and wanted to give him so much fucking grief. But I wouldn't, because then I would have to answer questions about the shit I'd been up to.

… like agreeing to date Benny.

Calm down. It's not a big deal. It's lunch, that's all.

I glanced over at Andy again and almost caved. If anyone could put me at ease about this whole mess, it was probably him. Then again, if this little escapade blew up in my face, the fewer who knew about it, the better.

I cleared my throat and stood up, even more awkward at how abrupt it was. Andy looked up at me, his book perched on a knee. "It's getting late. I should go." His face clouded over and I could have smacked myself. It was only ten o'clock, and I'd literally just said I wasn't doing a damn thing with my weekend. For someone who prided themselves on keeping a low profile when it came to illicit activities, I was doing a shit job of it now. "Right. Uh, see you later."

"See you later," Andy echoed as I spun on my heel and all but fled the library so I could obsess about what to wear for half an hour, then race to town. Where I would meet Benny. For lunch. On a date.

Fuck me.

Benny

My gaze traveled over Calvin's body with reckless abandon. While it wasn't like I'd never seen him out of his school uniform, everything about his ensemble screamed sex... and nerves. He reached up to pull at the collar of his deep purple shirt for the third time since I'd spotted him. The tee bled into dark wash skinny jeans that made my own pants tighten. Fuck, he looked incredible, even with the heather gray peat coat, oddly light against the darker, winter colors. He stopped outside the cafe and looked around, his honeyed gaze not settling for more than an instant as he perused the area.

I chuckled to myself and pushed the door of the cafe open. "You planning to just stand there, or did you want to eat something?" He whirled around and I swear to God he actually jumped.

His gaze raked over the facade of the quiet little building, then took in the street once more. He walked swiftly inside and yanked the door shut before it could close naturally. "I'm here. Now what?"

"Now, we get something to eat." I placed a hand on the small of his back and gently steered him over to the counter with its healthy display of decadent sweets. He glanced from the glass to me. "Whatever you want, my treat. Actual food is on the board." I pointed to the chalkboard declaring the day's specials, along with the regular selection.

He licked his lips and stared at it, but didn't say anything. The grumpy attendant from before took one look at me and scowled. His gaze also traveled to the door, no doubt to see if my inappropriate companion had returned. Little did he know that the anxious man before him could give Savannah a run for her money in terms of impropriety.

"What can I get you?" the attendant asked when it was clear no one else would be joining us.

I glanced over at Calvin. His dark curls were in fine form and just as rebellious as ever. I resisted the urge to curl one of them around my finger and instead asked, "What'll it be?"

His dark brown eyes held a hint of panic as his gaze flicked to me. He opened his mouth, but nothing came out. Not a quip, not a snarky comment, not so much as a syllable.

More than a little shocked, I turned my attention to the board. "How about... a turkey club and a... chicken avocado wrap." Hopefully, one of the two would suit Calvin and I'd simply eat the other. My gaze fell to the sweets, that much like the man beside me, I couldn't seem to resist. Also, much like Calvin, it all looked too good to choose. "And two eclairs."

"Bear claws," Calvin piped up out of nowhere.

I smiled and corrected myself. "Sorry, make that two bear claws."

"Will you two be dining inside or on the patio?" the attendant asked as he accepted my card, thankfully without dropping it this time.

"The patio, if that's alright."

The attendant smiled pleasantly and nodded, though I couldn't help but think how much less pleasant he would be if he knew the two young men before him were on a date or if Calvin was acting more like himself.

"Thank you," I said as I took the receipt and led the way out the back door to the four-season private patio. I took a seat at one of the many empty tables and Calvin did so as well, his gaze shifting around almost frantically as he settled into his chair.

"Are you sure this is a good idea? What if someone sees us?" he asked under his breath while he leaned back to see through the narrow gap between the rail and wall to glimpse the main street beyond.

I couldn't help but chuckle at how hard he was trying to see. "You of all people should know hardly anyone from the school comes to this part of town. After all, the church is only a block or two from here. And even if someone did happen by, the odds of them seeing us are slim to none."

He huffed and straightened up. His fingers plucked aimlessly at his coat, which he'd neglected to take off, while his gaze kept searching the otherwise empty patio. "What do we do now?"

I frowned slightly, a little worried about the fact that he couldn't seem to settle down. "This is it. We sit, eat… relax," I added with emphasis. He shot me a look and immediately returned to scanning the area. "What's the matter?"

His nails dug into his sleeve, and he clenched his jaw. "I haven't done this before."

"Haven't done what?" I scoffed. "Eat at a cafe? Granted, this one is a bit of a hole in the wall, but—"

"Date." His eyes snapped to me, their brown depths holding a familiar challenge. For a second, I let myself get lost in them. I loved that look. He had so much spirit, so much fight. He'd never taken shit from anyone, least of all me. That look alone had kept me in his orbit like a moth drawn to a flame, willing to get burned for a glimpse of the sun. Then what he said sunk in.

"What? You've never…" His eyes narrowed before darting away and I immediately stopped talking. Was it really possible that he'd *never* been on a date before? Now that I finally understood the source of his weird behavior, it was kind of adorable. Calvin Bridges was nervous.

He cleared his throat and tugged at his sleeve some more. Before I could say anything, a server arrived with the food. They set it down and thankfully walked off without lingering to make idle chatter. Calvin glanced over at the two plates and without looking up asked softly, "Which one is yours?"

"The one you don't want."

He reached out and hesitated, then pulled over the chicken and avocado wrap. "Thank you," he mumbled, his head still bent. He took a bite, and I half expected him to make a quip like Savannah had about having to work it off. Instead, he glanced up briefly from the wrap and said, "This is good. How is it I've never come here before?"

"They're a little off the beaten path and don't look like much from the street."

He nodded, and we each took a bite. After another minute, he took a drink of water and asked, "So what exactly does this *dating* thing entail?" The way he said dating made it sound like a curse, and I had to fight back a smile.

"Nothing too complicated. It's generally a lot easier than people make it out to be. Like I said before, we sit, eat, chat."

"Chat about what?" The question held a hair more of his usual fire.

"About whatever. Though the idea is to get to know each other better. Likes, dislikes, ambitions, fears, that sort of thing."

"What, like friends?" he snapped.

I did my best to hide my wince. We may have known each other for years, but friends were something we'd never been. I took a deep breath and bought time by taking a few bites of my club. "How about we start simple and see where that takes us? I'll ask you questions about yourself and you answer… or you don't." He finally looked at me, lips parted in surprise, doubt flooding his beautiful brown eyes. I reached across the table to still the hand in danger of fraying his sleeve, and he froze as my fingers settled over his. "You don't have to share anything you don't want to." I waited a beat, then settled back in my chair. "Tell me what your favorite thing to paint is."

"Why do you assume I paint?"

I shrugged. "For starters, everyone knows you're one of the best artists at the school. Your work is often displayed in the annual alumni event. And I don't just know you paint. I know you prefer oils… because you told me."

"Oh." He tucked a stray curl behind his ear. Unsurprisingly, it popped free. "I like landscapes, though lately I've been focusing on portraits."

"Why portraits?"

He choked on his latest bite and his response came out raspy. "Jankowski says I need a more rounded portfolio if I want to attend AIC."

I blinked in surprise. "Chicago, huh? Why there?"

He snorted and shrugged out of his coat. It flopped over the back of his chair, and he pushed his sleeves up before retrieving his wrap. "Because they're the best. Second choice is Yale, but that's a last resort." To hear anyone talk about Yale as a last resort was beyond laughable, but coming from Calvin, it not only fit, I didn't doubt for a second that he'd get in no question.

"What do you want to do once you have your art degree?" I pushed.

His mouth twisted to the side. "Ideally, be super famous and have my artwork coveted around the world. But realistically? Anything to do with art. Like seriously anything. I'm not picky."

"How are the portraits coming along?"

His eyes widened. "They're, uh, coming." He cleared his throat and waved a hand in the air, clearly dismissing the topic. "What about you? You gonna be a career-Middie?" he asked as he reached across the table to steal a piece of fallen bacon from my plate. He popped the stolen goods in his mouth and looked back at me, where shock was most likely stamped across my face. "Don't get me wrong, I'm not knocking it. You definitely have what it takes to go pro or at least collegiate. Your transitions are on point and you certainly have the endurance." He winked, and I didn't even have it in me to respond appropriately to the obvious sexual innuendo.

"You know what position I play?"

He frowned. "Of course, I do. What, I can't be gay *and* like sports?"

"No, no, of course not. That's not what I… I'm just surprised."

He waved a piece of lettuce at me. "No, surprising is how you didn't get fucking beamed by the ball when Roger body checked you last week." For a hot minute, I was worried that my jaw had actually fallen off and landed on my plate.

How long has he been watching me play? That happened during a friendly game. It hadn't even been a legit practice.

He smirked and settled back in his chair. "I actually rather like lacrosse, beyond the obvious reasons." His gaze slithered over me and I nearly swallowed my tongue.

"How come you never went out for the team?" I asked before I could rethink the logic of such a question.

Sadness chased away the heat in his lingering gaze. "How do you think that would've gone?"

Absolutely terrible. Forget my own reasons for not wanting him anywhere near the lockers, because I wouldn't be able to control myself if A, he looked at me or B, he looked at someone else, there was the fact that most of the team comprised narrow-minded homophobes. He could have been the best player on the team and they still would've torn him apart.

"Exactly," he said when I didn't respond.

"What position would you have played if you could have?" I didn't ply him with false platitudes about how he should have tried anyway. We both knew what a horrible decision it would have been.

"What's the matter, Benny? Afraid of a little competition?" His eyes sparked with challenge. Of course, he would have been a midfielder. "Now you know I like sports. What about you, any creative bones in that ridiculously sexy body of yours?"

I was too distracted by the compliment to consider my answer before it flew out of my mouth. "I write a little."

His dark brow arched. "That so? And what does the illustrious Benjamin Price write about?"

The reality of my ill-conceived confession hit me and I struggled to make it disappear. "Nothing. They're stupid stories. Trifles." I pushed one of the bear claws over to him and took a sizable bite of my own to stop the words.

"I'd be interested to see some of these... trifles," he said, the words like a seductive purr as he plucked his treat from the table.

No. Hell no. Hell fucking no.

"Tell me more about these portraits you're working on. The subjects anyone I know?"

His cheek twitched. "Well, I've been ordered to do a self-portrait and you know me."

"Why, when you say self-portrait, does it sound like the worst thing ever? Would think that'd be fairly easy."

He let out an exasperated breath and dusted his hands of crumbs. "Because it *is* the worst thing ever. Self-portraits are self-aggrandizing, vapid, indulgences of an over-inflated ego."

"Tell me how you really feel," I chuckled.

He gave me a pointed look with a touch of mirth at the edges. "I am, if you would listen. Now, as I was saying. Pompous artists create self-portraits. They think they're better than other subject matter. Who cares what the artist looks like? It's how they see the world that people want to experience, not their own perception of their self-importance."

"Is that what you aim to reveal in your art? A different perspective?"

A wistful smile played over his lips. "I aim to show people what they can't see for themselves." His passionate response immediately begged the question of what he was so afraid to discover about himself. However, now that I finally had him relaxed, there was no way I was about to throw a wrench into everything by actually asking.

"In that case," I leaned forward on my elbows and laced my fingers together, "I look forward to seeing this year's gallery."

That wicked smile that might as well have been a baited lure designed especially for me appeared once more. "Don't hold your breath."

Once Calvin actually relaxed, the date became everything I'd hoped it'd be. Not to mention, learning about him was substantially easier when he was the one supplying the information. And while he'd surprised me with some of the things he already knew about me, I'd managed a few surprises of my own. Clearly, he didn't believe I'd been paying attention all of these years.

"I'm sorry, I can't see it," he said with a wide smile, his empty plate long forgotten before him. "Hard rock or maybe even classic I could understand, but jazz and blues? Nope. Not possible. You sure you're not secretly a heavy metal buff? That at least would make more sense."

"And your devotion to Streisand is logical?"

He gasped and held a hand to his chest. "You take that back. The illustrious Barbara is beyond reproach."

I bit my bottom lip to hold back an idiotic grin. "Stereotype."

"Hypocrite," he fired back.

I let out a huff and rolled my eyes. "We just can't help ourselves, can we?"

He threw his head back, exposing the column of his throat, and laughed. The rich sound sent low-key want pulsing through me. This is what I wanted, all I had ever wanted, to just *be* with him. The laughter trailed off and he looked back at me, a carefree smile light on his lips. I could get addicted to smiles like that paired with his warm, brown eyes sparkling with happiness.

Who am I kidding? Is there a part of him I'm not already addicted to?

"I don't suppose we can." While the words were in direct response to my observation, they also seemed to hold more, not quite innuendo, but something deeper. "Ten years is a long time to know someone without really knowing them." The tip of his finger drew designs in the ring of condensation created by his glass of water.

"Old habits die hard?"

His gaze lit back up to me, seeing me the way he always had. The want grew to a buzz beneath my skin like I'd had a couple glasses of wine at a social mixer. "No one said they had to die altogether. It's part of who we are now. I don't see any reason to change who I am. Do you?" he asked softly.

"Yes," I said without preamble or fluff.

He tilted his head to the side and his dark curls swayed while he continued to pull at the water on the table. "I don't think you do. Not who you are, anyway. Maybe how you approach the world. But I've never found anything wrong with *who* you are." His steady gaze, without reproach or judgment, filled me with unexpected warmth.

Maybe if more people had looked at me like that in my life, then I wouldn't have come out so damn rotten.

Suddenly, the joy on his face clouded over. He leaned across the table, coming out of his chair slightly in order to reach my face. His hand cupped my jaw while his thumb stroked my cheek. "What's the matter?"

"Nothing," I managed, though the word came out thin.

"That's right, nothing, because there is nothing wrong with you, Benjamin Price. That's not to say a little self-improvement isn't warranted." His gentle smile turned cheeky, and he patted my face before resuming his seat. I struggled to wrap my head around what had just happened and how close I was to selling my soul to get it to happen again. My tongue darted out to wet my lips, and Calvin's gaze immediately dropped to my mouth. Lust radiated off of him, adding to the palpable shift in mood.

"Let's get out of here." I stood up a hair too fast and had to steady the table.

There was literally nothing decent about the lascivious look Calvin gave me as he peeled himself out of his chair and took his sweet time putting his coat back on. By the time the damn thing settled on his shoulders, all I wanted to do was grab his lapels and yank him close so I could mash our mouths together. If I wasn't convinced the attendant would find a way to get me barred from this place if he saw something like that, I would have.

"And where do you plan on taking me, Mr. Price?" Calvin crooned, his voice unabashedly laced with sex and promise as he smoothed his coat along his sides. Normally I hated it when people called me Mr. Price, a fact Calvin was well aware of, but the way he said it had blood rushing south and left me lightheaded.

"A walk," I croaked out by the grace of God alone. "We're going for a walk."

He immediately dropped all pretense of advance. "A walk. Why?"

"To cool down."

His lips twitched, and his eyes glinted with wicked glee. He took a step forward and placed both hands flat on my chest. The heat from his palms might as well have been a brand for how they burned into me. He leaned closer to whisper in my ear. "What's the matter, Mr. Price? Something got you all hot and bothered?" I nearly choked on the groan I was desperately trying to hold back. We absolutely needed to leave before I not only got banned from this tiny haven, but thrown into jail for indecent exposure.

I grabbed his hand and proceeded to drag him out the side gate toward the main street, where hopefully the threat of witnesses could keep my rampant libido in check. His laughter bordered on a giggle as he let me man handle him, but ceased altogether when we reached the thoroughfare. Just like that, his anxiety resurfaced. "It'll be fine," I reassured him. "No one from the school comes over here."

He took a deep breath and nodded, then took a step to come abreast of me. We meandered a few blocks in relative silence that miraculously wasn't awkward. I could count on one hand the number of people I'd ever had companionable silence with in my life.

Suppose I shouldn't be surprised Calvin is one of them.

As if knowing I was thinking of him, he cast me a furtive glance and I realized he was chewing on his lip. "Something on your mind?"

"Maybe."

"After ten years of being bold and in people's faces, *now* you wanna play coy?" I teased.

"Shut up." He pushed my shoulder, and I laughed. "I..." He glanced over at me again, uncertainty in his eyes.

"What is it? Did you hate it? You did and you don't want to do this again." The different options poured out of me until he held up a hand to stem the tide. I snapped my mouth shut and waited for what he wanted to say. If he didn't want to date, I'd understand—I'd be disappointed as fuck, but I'd understand and respect his decision.

His mouth drew into a grim line, and my internal list of self-recrimination queued up. Why did I always have to push? Why couldn't I be satisfied with what we had? Why wasn't it ever enough? Why did I let Savannah talk me into this? At his words, though, all the thoughts scattered.

"We still have to keep up appearances. I know you don't like it, but things at school have to stay the same. You know that, don't you, Benny?"

I did know that. I hated it with every fiber of my being, but I knew that. Unwilling to voice it, I simply nodded.

Calvin let out what sounded suspiciously like a relieved breath. Then, without warning, he grabbed my arm. "Come with me," he said like I had a choice, given his vice-like grip. He tugged me into a narrow alley between two buildings and kept walking at a good clip, his long legs eating up the distance with confidence, as he turned first one corner, then another and another. Right when I couldn't stand it anymore, he turned a final corner into a sun-filled alley behind some commercial stores I'd never heard of and threw me against the wall.

No sooner did my back collide with the aged brick than his mouth was on mine. My gasp of surprise turned into a moan as he curled the fingers of both hands in my hair and completely dominated me. I slipped my hands beneath his coat to caress his sides. He took that as his cue to press more firmly against me. His tongue tangled and teased while he ground against my already straining erection. My resulting groan bounced loudly in the narrow space, but I didn't give a shit. The whole goddamn town could show up, and I still wouldn't care, as long as Calvin was kissing me like this. In fact, if he didn't stop, I was liable to come in my pants.

"Jesus fucking Christ," he gasped, his voice ragged from lack of air. "Sitting across a table from you for three hours was like fucking torture." He didn't wait for a response before reclaiming my mouth with a determination that made my knees weak. I clung to him, digging my fingers into his shirt, desperate to reach what I knew lay beneath. His mouth traveled across my jaw to catch my earlobe between his teeth.

"Oh God, Cal," I moaned, aching for more even though I knew I couldn't have it.

"Benny." The harsh whisper of my name cradled my ear and sank deep inside, turning my need acute. All I could manage was a half-strangled grunt as I clawed my way back from the precipice. Abruptly, Calvin's hands were gone from my face and undoing my buckle. Reason made a valiant effort to return, then promptly shattered into a million pieces when his skilled hand wrapped around my aching dick, the pleasure of it bordering on pain.

Oh God. Fuck. No no no no no…

I squeezed my eyes shut at the same time his fingers tightened around my shaft. Multicolored stars danced across my lids and I forced them back open just in time to see Calvin drop. His lips wrapped around me and I bucked off the wall. The intense, wet heat of his mouth swallowed me down, taking me deep. This time, the stars danced right across the far brick wall. Logically, I knew I should stop him. This wasn't the place. But I couldn't. I couldn't tell him no again. Whatever Calvin wanted, he could have.

I reached a hand out and tentatively brushed the curls from his face, already so close I didn't know how I was even hanging on. Seeing his lips stretched around me threatened the tenuous hold. His mop of dark curls bounced as he bobbed his head, each pass adding to the sweet, unbearable ecstasy. Then he looked up. His dark gaze latched onto mine and it was like someone gut punched me with a sledgehammer. My breath caught in a groan and my fingers reflexively tightened in his hair as I shot my load down his throat. He didn't move, didn't pull away, didn't even fucking blink, just knelt there holding my gaze captive while he took everything.

At last, I sagged completely depleted against the wall. While I was aware of him touching me, it felt more like an out-of-body experience, like it was happening to someone else far away from my fog of satiated bliss. He leveraged my belt loops to pull himself back up and caught me with a more sedate kiss that still managed to stir the embers of my desire. When he pulled out of the kiss, his lips were wet and the remnants of tears from his eyes watering were drying on his face. Without thinking, I reached up and wiped them away.

"I had a great time today," he whispered, and stole another sweet kiss.

Doubt wrapped around my heart. *Was that why...* I shook my head. "You didn't need to—"

He placed his lips against mine again to silence me. "I know. But I really, really wanted to." Another kiss and he stepped away, magically still as put together as ever, while I felt like I'd been fucking wrecked. He tugged his coat straight, though it didn't need it, and looked back at me with that perfect honey brown gaze, a soft smile curving his mouth. My chest ached for that smile.

Savannah was wrong. I'm not half in love with him.

"See you around." He winked and turned to leave. I stepped away from the wall and he spun back to catch my arm, his touch light but firm. "Oh, and Benny, I would absolutely love to do this again." The smile in his eyes told me he wasn't exclusively talking about the sex.

"Me too."

His smile broadened and seemed to fill him until he rivaled the sunlight falling around us. He gave my arm a gentle squeeze and once more turned away, this time walking down a side alley with the confidence of someone who knew exactly where they were going. I stumbled back into the wall and clutched my chest over my pounding heart. I may not know where I was going in this life, but I knew I would never tire of Calvin Bridges.

Chapter 22

Calvin

The door to the haunted classroom swung open, and I'd never been so relieved to see Andy in the four years we'd been friends. "Thank fuck you're already here," I said as I forced the door back closed.

Andy looked up from his book, a quizzical expression on his face. "I still don't understand why we couldn't meet in the library like usual." He slipped a bookmark between the pages and set the paperback aside.

"Because what I want to talk about, we can't talk about in the library, or outside, or anywhere else someone might overhear us." I wrung my hands and glanced over at the blocked-out window of the door. "If someone did…" I didn't want to think about how epically bad it would be if anyone heard this conversation.

"What did you do? Are you in trouble?"

"No. Yes." I dropped my bag on the dusty desk and let out a frustrated huff. "It's complicated. But it's also not. Honestly, I'm not really sure what to think anymore. This whole thing was supposed to be a laugh, a fun way to pass the time. Except now… And what the fuck does that mean—it's just about sex—anyway?

Besides which, I met him in the middle. Dating isn't exactly my forte and honestly, if the sex wasn't so good, I wouldn't have even considered it. Who would have guessed dating Benny would be nice, of all things? But why won't he top me, Andy?" I looked over at Andy every bit as lost as I'd been the last couple of weeks. His mouth hung open and his bright emerald eyes were wide. "Are you listening? Don't just sit there. I need help."

"Back up. Did you say you've been fucking Benny?"

"Yeah, didn't I mention that? Keep up. That's not the point."

"Benny," Andy repeated. "Benjamin Price."

"Yes, moving on."

"How long have you been sleeping with Benny?"

I rolled my eyes. "First, no sleeping is happening. I can promise you that. As for how long, a couple months, but the dating thing is new," I clarified.

"You… you're *dating*… Benjamin Fucking Price!" Andy shouted.

"Would you keep your voice down?" I snapped. "If I'd wanted the whole damn school to know, I wouldn't have asked you up here."

"Fuck the school. How could you not tell me you were fucking Benny?" Andy demanded to know, his face turning blotchy red with indignant outrage.

"Oh, you mean like how you told me you were fucking Mitch?" I countered. All the red drained from his face while his mouth opened and closed without uttering a sound. "And for the record, pretty sure Benny knows too."

Andy swayed in place, and I rushed over to steady him. He blinked at me as I held him, his gaze distant. "How… how did you know?"

I let out a sigh and made sure he wouldn't fall over before stepping back. "Benny actually helped me put it together. He mentioned that you'd been in that fight with Mitch and the others from the team. Which you also didn't tell me." I scowled at him, still pretty pissed about that as well.

His eyes narrowed to glare right back. "That doesn't mean—"

"He also said that after you two disappeared, he saw Mitch coming into practice later that afternoon."

"So what?"

"From the East Woods." The little color Andy had gained paled once more. I gave him a knowing look and leaned against the nearby bookshelf. "Still want to deny something is going on between you two?"

He shook his head and stumbled back on shaky legs until he bumped into an old desk. He sat down heavily and looked up at me. "So… you and Benny… again. What started that?"

I shrugged. "Don't know. Went up for my usual shower one night and he just sort of showed up. He seemed surprised to see me at first, but he stuck around, then he showed up again. I kept waiting for it to stop, but he kept coming back." I crossed my arms and bit the inside of my cheek while I studied the ground.

"Okay, so you two have been fooling around for a while. What's this dating business about? And did I hear you correctly about actually *wanting* him to top you?"

I raised my gaze to Andy once more. He still appeared shaken for sure with his hands clasped before him tight enough to white knuckle, but he clearly was attempting to keep it together. "The dating thing is…interesting."

"Why are you dating at all? Wasn't aware that was your thing."

"It's not, but it's not all bad. Believe it or not, Benny isn't actually a total prick, or at least he isn't outside these walls." I gestured to the room and the school in general. "As for the why…" I trailed off, my face unexpectedly heating. "I guess I look at it as a compromise of sorts. Quid pro quo. He wants to date. I want him to top me."

"You lost me again. Why would you need to trade anything?"

Embarrassment blossomed inside of my chest and made me queasy. "Because when I asked, he said no."

"He knows," Andy deduced, without missing a beat.

"He knows," I echoed. "But the reason he gave at the time was that it was because this was still just sex to me. What the fuck does that even mean? What's wrong with sex?" I asked, my voice gaining strength and a noticeable edge.

"Is it?"

"Is it what?" I lashed out, my embarrassment morphing into frustrated anger.

"Is it just sex?"

All the wind left my sails, a tempest dissipating to leave my metaphorical boat adrift in the vast ocean. "I…" *don't know.* The words were right there on the tip of my tongue, but I couldn't bring myself to say them aloud.

He sat back in his seat and gave me a look that seemed to peel back my layers of bullshit with all the mercy of a palette knife. "Sounds like a hell of a lot more than sex to me."

My hand fisted. "What are you trying to say?"

"Something you clearly don't want to hear. There's only one reason I can think of that you'd be twisted up about anyone. Face it, you're falling for him."

I barked out a humorless laugh. "I am *not* in love with Benjamin Price."

Andy raised an eyebrow at the vehemence of my denial. "I didn't say you were *in* love with him. I said you were well on your way."

I blanched and cut my gaze away to glare out the windows at the outside world.

"The Calvin I know wouldn't date, wouldn't even barter to get what he wants. He'd move on to someone more willing. That tells me something is special about Benny for you. You're not treating him like your other conquests."

"Speaking from experience?"

"That was uncalled for," Andy snapped, giving me a glimpse of that infamous Irish anger he did such a good job of keeping in check. "You know damn well shit is complicated between Mitch and me. Always has been."

"Planning on elaborating?"

"Are you?"

I opened my mouth, fully prepared to give him a piece of my mind concerning his own hypocrisy, then deflated. Wasn't that why I'd asked him up here after all? Because I was feeling out of my depth? "What do you want to know?"

Try as he might, Andy couldn't school his surprise fast enough. "Really?"

"Yeah." I slid down the shelves and slumped to the floor. "And don't worry. If you're not ready to talk about what's going on with you and Mitch, then you don't have to. But I..." I stared at my hands, then curled and uncurled my fingers. "I don't know what I'm doing, and that..."

"Freaks the hell out of you," Andy said as he took a seat beside me.

I stared at him in shock unsure of when he'd gotten up or why he was willing to help at all given how long I'd kept this from him or how I'd thrown my knowledge of what he'd been up to with Mitch in his face.

He smiled and bumped my shoulder. "Let's forget the fact that this is *Benny* we're talking about and start at the beginning. Minus details, please. There are some mental images you can't unsee." He winked and I smiled in return. Thank fuck for Andy.

Benny

"Fancy meeting you here."

I started at the unexpected greeting and spun away from my desk to find none other than Calvin Bridges leaning against the doorjamb of my room, dark curls framing his handsome face and a sinister grin quirking his lips up in a half smile. My grin stretched my lips as the light Calvin seemed to carry with him filled me like a second sun. A split second later, logic asserted itself and I launched out of my chair.

In three long strides, I was by his side, his devious smirk filling my vision. I grabbed his arm and yanked him inside, my gaze searching the miraculously empty hallway beyond before I slammed the door shut. "Are you out of your damn mind? What were you thinking coming here?"

He shrugged as he wandered across the small room, taking in the space. "Funny how I've never actually come over here in all these years." He had a point there, though I suspected his reasons weren't all that different from the ones that had led me to avoiding his as well.

"It's the middle of the fucking day."

"Your point?" he asked as he trailed a finger along a poster of the Chicago skyline.

"Exactly that. Are you insane?"

"Maybe I wanted to practice the route." His brown eyes gave up their perusal of my walls and snapped to me. Instantly, a ball of nerves twisted in my gut. It would seem my efforts at distracting him and hoping he'd simply forget all about wanting me to top hadn't done shit.

Should have known better.

"At any rate, no one saw me coming here and no one will see me leave." He meandered toward the desk and the slew of books open on it. "Such a diligent student," he teased as he reached forward to thumb one of the pages.

My gaze slipped past him to the open journal entry I'd been working on. In a few steps, I inserted myself between him and the desk. "This is a little brazen, even for you," I said as I closed the notebook behind my back and slipped it under a textbook.

"You think so?" he asked, stepping close enough that I could feel his body heat. I bit back a groan of anticipation in an effort not to encourage him. It was all useless though. All Calvin had to do was look at me to know how badly I wanted him.

"What exactly was your plan?"

"What do you think?" Another half-step and my back pressed into the edge of the desk.

My breath faltered and my eyelids fluttered at his nearness and the promise practically radiating off of him. "Cal." What was intended to be a rebuke or note of caution came out a whisper that bordered on a whimper saturated with longing.

"Yes, Benny?" he whispered back. His breath mingled with mine as he closed the distance and captured my mouth before I could come up with anything.

My fingers dug painfully into the wooden desk at my back while he curled his own long fingers around the back of my neck and held me where he wanted me. His tongue delved past my lips to steal the moan I was trying so hard to keep in check. Unadulterated want pulsed through my veins and kept me at his complete mercy. My arms ached with the effort of keeping them behind me and became the only thing holding me up as he conquered my mouth with reckless abandon.

He pulled at my bottom lip before ghosting kisses across my jaw. "What are you thinking about, Benny?" The low whisper directly in my ear sent a shiver down my spine that landed in my already aching dick. I swallowed hard and tried to think about anything but what I wanted right now. He wrapped his tongue around the shell of my ear and my knees threatened to buckle. "Are you imagining me spinning you around and fucking you right here?" His hand slithered between us and squeezed my straining erection through my trousers. I grunted, but couldn't seem to form words. "Are you fantasizing about me sinking into your tight ass? Stretching that tight little hole of yours with my hard cock?"

The filthy whispers caressed my ear, the heat of his breath only adding to the sensory overload. But as much as I wanted all of that and then some, it was broad daylight. "Cal… Cal…" I struggled to find my voice as he continued to palm my dick and my eyes tried to roll back. Much more and I'd come right here with no more than a few words and a light brush, the only mercy of which was I had clothes on hand. He lowered his head to suck lightly on my neck and the groan I'd been fighting so hard against rolled out. Finally, I forced words out. "My door doesn't lock any better than yours. Anyone could walk in here at any given moment."

He gave up the hickey I knew he would never give me, no matter how much I wanted him to and looked at me with lust-filled brown eyes. "You should do something about that, then."

I didn't even think twice. I extricated myself, grabbed my chair and dragged it over to the door where I promptly used it to brace the handle. Fuck if it was weird and would attract all sorts of attention if someone tried to get in and couldn't.

This is a bad idea. A really, really bad idea. It's the middle of the day. What if Neil or Todd decide to drop by? There will be no mistaking the sounds coming out of here.

At least no one will be able to see that it's Calvin. But how will I get him out without anyone knowing he was here to begin with?

I was so lost in my thoughts, I didn't realize until it was too late that Calvin had snagged the poorly concealed journal until I looked up and found him holding it open. Horror rushed through me, evicting any lingering desire. "Wait."

He glanced up, a knowing smile twitching at his lips. "Would this perchance be the writing our dear Benny is too modest to claim?"

"Don't. Give it back." I stepped forward, intending to snatch it before he could read too much, but he spun out of reach.

"King Kelani looked out over the balcony at his vast kingdom below," he read aloud. "His subjects scurried about their daily lives mindless of the compassion of their benevolent ruler. Would that Kel had someone to share his lonely kingdom with, but to rule absolutely was to rule alone." Calvin glanced up, his smile wider. "I don't know what you're so worried about. This is actually pretty good."

"Cal, please." I held out my hand in the vain hope he'd pass it over. No such luck. He flipped a few pages back to another passage.

"White silk hung in elaborate folds from King Kelani's sleeves as he met with the latest supplicant. The trade agreements settled without quarter or malice, but with a firm stoicism that bespoke of a wisdom beyond the young ruler's age. Many had made the mistake in the past of believing the ostentatious prince would become a weak and malleable king. However, Kelani had assumed his role with a dignity and form unbeknownst to his predecessors. After all, what need had he for an army when he held sole control of all the supplies essential to his hostile neighbors?" The laughter dancing at the edge of his words as he read aloud vanished as he blinked at the page in confusion. Without a word, he began flipping back through, pausing only long enough to read a few lines before finding another page.

"Cal."

"What is this? It… it…"

"Cal," I tried again.

He looked up, and I saw he'd already made all the connections. "Cal," he echoed. "Kel… I'm Kel."

"It's not…" I gave up as soon as I started. It would do no good to deny it. That journal was exactly what he thought it was. We stared at each other for a long minute, then his gaze dropped back to the page.

"Looks like just about everyone is in here. The Councilor is obviously Andy. Hostile neighboring nations are definitely the homophobic assholes like Brian and John." He set the journal aside and leaned against the desk in a much more casual perch than the one I'd had a scarce few minutes ago. "A king, huh?" he asked with a crooked smile.

"Shut up."

He snickered and pushed off the desk. Once more, he closed the distance between us and I stood there, too mesmerized to move. "What about you, Benny? You gonna tell me who you are?"

"No. Absolutely fucking not."

He laughed, and the sound slipped past my mortification to settle warmly in my chest, then just like before, he leaned forward to steal a kiss. This time, I didn't pretend like I had restraint and wrapped my arms around his waist as I gave into it completely. Sadly, the kiss was much shorter lived, though once again he leaned in to whisper in my ear. "Whatever you say, Prince Einar."

I jolted with surprise and he used the opportunity to slip free. He paused at the door, where he'd already removed the chair while I regained my senses. His hand wrapped around the knob and a desperate need to keep him here if only for a few seconds longer rose in me. "You free this Saturday?"

The smile he gave me wasn't the one I wanted, the one I craved. It was small and a little sad. "Actually, already have plans that night." He glanced back toward the door. "Really should get going. Just wanted to make a point." He offered a wink, then slipped out without so much as a whisper of fabric to betray his passing.

I sat heavily on the desk. My fingers closed around the damnable journal and chunked it across the room hard enough to dent the drywall on the far side. "Fuck."

Chapter 23

Calvin

The church filled with the usual hum of voices as we waited for Saturday Mass to begin. My fingers rubbed together absently as if I held a phantom rosary. Father Miles had greeted me along with several other parishioners when we'd arrived an hour before. I'd hoped coming so soon would have given me a chance to speak with Father Miles in private before the sermon, but no such luck.

Not that it would have done much good.

What could he possibly tell me I didn't already know, or that Andy hadn't said himself? I let out a sigh and stared down at my empty hands, still seeking something that wasn't there.

This is why I avoid feelings. They're a complicated mess that drag everyone down.

Things had been so much simpler when it was only sex. Fun, light, no expectations. It would go on as long as it went, and then it would be over. A fun story to look back on. It pained me to admit it, but I was woefully incompetent when it came to navigating my own feelings. Others' weren't so bad, but mine? Easier not to have them.

After Andy's accusation that I could be falling for Benny of all people, I'd gone out of my way to prove that wasn't the case, take back control, reassert the unusual balance between Benny and myself.

That had gone spectacularly horrible.

I'd had this grand plan of freaking him out—which I had—but I never could have anticipated the way he'd look at me. That soft smile he almost never shared, glowing in his eyes as he turned to find me in his doorway bold as brass. His pure joy at seeing me had hit me in the gut full force and it had taken everything I'd had to keep the smirk on my face and casually walk into his room rather than race over to him. Not even getting him riled up had changed things. All I'd really established was that I knew of all the right buttons to push and that Benny made me reckless. For God's sake, I'd nearly given Benny a fucking hickey.

What is wrong with me?

I stared up at the stained glass in the ceiling. The early evening meant the sky beyond was too dark to truly appreciate their beauty, but the colors still managed to be striking with the illumination from within the church.

And that damn journal. What was that about?

Page after page of a fantastical story about a young king ruling with confidence and a wisdom beyond his years.

Alone.

I squeezed my hand and longed for the press of worn olive beads against my fingers and the inherent comfort they brought. The truth of his assessment as me being cold and calculating hurt more than anything. Except I wasn't those things with Benny, not anymore. Even though I'd gone to his room with the explicit purpose of proving I was, it wasn't the same as it was, hadn't been for a while. Coming to terms with that, however, and understanding this evolution was fucking with my head.

Maybe I should have skipped Mass and gone out with him.

The look on his face when I'd said I had other plans had physically hurt my chest. I didn't want him to be sad or disappointed. I wanted him to smile at me like he had when I'd shown up, so fucking happy to see me he couldn't hide it.

That's it, I'm bailing. I'll atone with Father Miles later.

I stood up and turned to exit the pew and ran smack into someone. "Sorry," I mumbled with my head down in shame at getting busted trying to sneak out mere minutes before the sermon was due to start. With a heavy heart, I slumped back down.

"It's okay. Is this seat taken?"

My head snapped up at the familiar voice and my jaw fell. "What are you doing here?" I asked a little too loudly, earning myself several reproachful hushes. Abashed, I ducked my head once more and scooted over to give him more room to sit. He did so without hesitation, taking his time unraveling his thick scarf from around his neck to reveal the faint blemish still marring his warm ivory skin.

"Is this okay?" he asked softly once he was fully settled. I glanced over at Benny, still in shock to see him here. He gave me that smile that glowed in his eyes and made my stomach flip-flop.

"Yes." The word leapt out of my mouth with abandon. His smile widened, and more shushing ensued as Father Miles stepped up to the pulpit. I glanced behind me at the middle-aged woman basically giving me a death glare. When I spun back, Benny was still looking at me. I dropped my voice and asked again, "Why are you here?"

"Because I wanted to see you."

"But you're not religious," I countered.

"You are." That smile again.

"Eh-hem," the woman behind us cleared her throat rather aggressively. I scowled at her, and she glared right back. With a huff, I turned forward once more as Father Miles' steady voice reached out to the congregation and Benny did his best to smother a chuckle. I rolled my eyes and sagged against the bench.

When something warm brushed along my finger, I jolted in my seat and nearly came out of my skin. It wasn't until I looked down that I realized that my hand had found its way beneath the substantial bulk of Benny's scarf. The soft touch came again, and my brain finally connected what was going on.

I licked my lips and looked over at Benny. His light green gaze met mine, filled with calm and patience. I glanced back down at our concealed hands and swallowed thickly. Then, before I could psyche myself out, I hooked my finger with his. A sense of rightness settled in my chest. I let out a shaky breath I prayed he didn't notice. He tugged lightly against my finger, then gently rubbed his thumb along it and my heart fucking soared.

Fuck you, Andy. Fuck you for always being right.

I did my damnedest to focus on the sermon, but my thoughts kept straying to the man beside me and the intimate glide of his thumb along my knuckle. Each pass chipped away at my concentration until my awareness of Benny beside me consumed everything. I blinked in confusion when the tiny spot of warmth that had become my world disappeared. It wasn't until I glanced over at Benny that I realized the congregation was already dispersing.

Fuck me. I missed the whole damn thing. Hopefully, Father Miles doesn't ask about it when I come in for confession next week.

Shaking my head at my distraction, I followed Benny out of the pew, my gaze riveted on the thick hunter green scarf as he wrapped it back around his neck to ward off the chill awaiting outside. The woman who'd been giving us a hard time slipped in between us, which allowed several other people into the aisle, creating even more distance. I choked on my mounting frustration as I lost all sight of Benny amid the press of bodies and bubble of voices.

Determined to ditch the lingering crowd as fast as humanly possible, I ducked off to the side and tugged my peat coat tightly closed before stepping through one of the smaller doors into the frigid winter beyond. My gaze traveled over the lazy river of people vacating the church, but no hint of Benny emerged.

Fuck. Maybe I imagined the whole thing.

I rolled my eyes. *Great. What the fuck does that mean if I'm fantasizing about Benny coming to church with me? Fuck you, Andy. Fuck you so much for putting these thoughts in my head.*

Despite the concern that I might have dreamed up the whole impossible experience, I continued to search the crowd. I rubbed my freezing hands together and brought them to my face to blow on them. My breath misted in a white cloud and did little to add warmth.

Fuck this. I'm crazy for standing here like an idiot.

I was about to tuck my hands into my pits when a voice warmer and more seductive than mulled wine stopped me. "Here, let me help with that." Benny tugged off his gloves, and I vaguely wondered why I hadn't thought to put my own on as he stepped forward and wrapped my hands in the very real warmth of his.

"Hey," I said at last, which wasn't at all the smooth quip I'd intended.

"Hey," he said back with that smile that melted my insides despite the fucking sub-zero weather. He glanced around at the dispersing people and looked back at me. "What do you say we get out of here."

I nodded, unable to muster up actual words.

"You gonna be okay?" he asked, giving my hands a gentle squeeze.

"I have gloves."

He quirked an eyebrow. "And where would these gloves be?"

"In my pocket," I replied like the dunce I apparently was now.

Jesus Fucking Christ, pull yourself together. Just because Andy says a thing doesn't make it true.

Without preamble, Benny liberated my gloves along with my forgotten scarf and all I could do was stare at him in wonder as he first tugged on each fitted finger, then wrapped my scarf around me. With each loop of the insanely long scarf I'd thought was fashionable, I turned to more mush, unable to tear my gaze away from Benny's pure Celadon eyes.

Except he is. Oh fuck, Andy's right. I'm falling for Benny.

Some darker part of my mind cruelly pointed out that I was a lot farther along that path than I wanted to entertain, but I could barely admit this little bit. I couldn't handle what the rest implied.

"There," he said, tugging the scarf, "much better." His gaze finally came to my eyes, and I saw what I so often saw when he looked at me these days, desire, want, things I was too terrified to label, but didn't stop them from fluttering with abandon in my chest. I was already leaning forward, eyes half-lidded for a kiss, when my brain finally caught up and a reminder of where we were stabbed through me.

"We should go."

"I have just the place." He grabbed my hand with his equally gloved one, though fuck if I knew when he'd put them back on, and led me down the nearest side street. Once he was sure I was following, he released me and glanced over. "I still can't believe I didn't know you were Catholic, not to mention a practicing one."

"What? Because I'm gay, I can't also believe in God?" I snapped, still shaken by my own unwanted revelation.

Benny's brow furrowed with genuine concern, and I immediately wanted to take back the harsh rebuke. "That's not what I meant at all. I think it's great you have faith. I was merely stating my surprise that *I* didn't know."

This time, it was my face that screwed up in confusion.

What was that supposed to mean?

Before I could ask, he halted by a door and pulled out a set of keys. I glanced around and didn't recognize the area, impressive and a tad disconcerting given how much I'd wandered the back alleys and small streets of the town over the years. "Where are we?"

He glanced up at the nondescript facade. "No place fancy." Still confused, I followed him into the subtle warmth and immediately felt my nose defrost. Before I could ask again where the fuck we were, he launched up a narrow flight of stairs and only paused to open another door at the top. "Here we are." The lights flicked on to fill what appeared to be a modest studio apartment with soft, yellow light.

I began removing my scarf by rote as my gaze traveled over the room, taking in the perfectly made queen bed, the microscopic kitchenette, intimate table set for two. I did a double take. The plates were very clearly set out for dinner and even had a candle ready to be lit sitting between them. In the background, a bag marked with the logo of the popular Chinese joint in town sat on the counter. I turned my gaze back to Benny. "What is this?"

He shrugged and offered a sheepish smile. "I thought you might be hungry after Mass and didn't want you to worry about being seen in town."

My heart squeezed at the thoughtfulness as I continued to shrug out of my coat. "What if I hadn't wanted to come?"

He shrugged again, his own winter gear already divested and hanging on the coat rack. "Then it would have gotten cold. I could always come back for it later." He added my things to the rack. "We don't have to stay if you don't want to. Like I said earlier, I just wanted to see you."

Fuck it. Fuck all of it. I couldn't take it anymore. If I didn't do something soon, my chest was going to explode. "Benny."

He turned back to me, clearly braced for a negative response. "Yeah?"

"I hope that microwave works."

"What?"

I closed the distance and smashed my mouth against his with zero finesse. He let out a muffled sound of surprise that turned to a moan as I slipped my tongue past his lips to tangle with his. My fingers curled through his hair, so much longer than it had been three months ago, and urged him deeper. His fingers gripped into my side and I groaned with barely contained need. "Supplies," I gasped out at last.

"Side table," he managed between hungry kisses.

I abandoned his mouth only long enough to get a good heading, then snatched at his pliable lips once again as I dragged him back toward the bed and everything else we needed. My fingers traveled up his soft shirt and set to work, fumbling open the buttons until I found the desired flesh beneath. Benny's breath caught as I pushed the fabric from his shoulders and he immediately reached to tug my shirt free. Our arms tangled a moment as I sought to liberate him from his undershirt and he struggled to yank off my sweater. I laughed and gave up my pursuit to help.

"Fuck," he hissed when it fell clear. "Still no undershirt. Are you crazy? It's like twenty degrees outside."

"I told you. I don't like them." I ran a hand up his now bare chest, my fingers gliding with ease through the light, silky strands of his chest hair, then dropped it to his buckle. "I like undressing you," I said as I flicked the tongue of his belt out and stole another eager kiss.

"Why's that?" he asked, more than a little breathless.

So many reasons.

I teased his lips with another kiss while I mentally ran through the list. It was intimate, not transactional like my previous encounters had been. It let me explore his body the way my fingers longed to. It made all the rest of the world fall away so that it was only us. I tugged on his pants, simultaneously popping the button loose, and leaned in close as I slid my hand inside to cup his plump cock. "What do you think?"

Instead of answering, he groaned and captured my mouth hard enough that we fell back on the bed in a tangle of limbs. His kiss didn't stop there. The fiery brand of his lips pressed into my throat and ventured down my chest. He paused to nip and suck lightly at a nipple and I arched into the lavish attention with a moan he echoed.

While I was distracted, he set about undoing my pants. He abandoned his determined pursuit to torture the rest of my torso, sucking kisses down my abdomen that made my stomach quiver with expectation. His fingers hooked over my briefs and removed them, along with my pants, with practiced ease. He ran his hands up my legs as he settled back on the bed that was substantially more inviting than the meager cot I'd procured for the haunted room.

I looked down at him and groaned at the hunger I found there, not as he looked at the cock I knew he loved, but at me. My head fell back into the pillows, which I promptly tossed aside as he wrapped a hand around me and gave a decisive stroke. He leaned down to place a tender kiss on my inner thigh, then lapped at my balls. Blood pulsed through my aching cock and a drop of pre-cum squeezed out.

I registered the firm muscle of his tongue licking up my shaft to steal the drop right before the intense heat of his mouth swallowed me whole. A strangled moan caught in my throat as I bucked off the mattress, lost to the intensity. He groaned around me, more than capable of taking whatever I could dish out. The vibrations rippled through my sensitive cock to my core and I tangled fingers in his hair, both to cling onto something and eager to encourage him.

He moaned again as my hold tightened and swallowed around me before returning to his rhythm. The ecstasy of release danced within reach, tingling in my spine and tightening my balls. I fought against it as I flailed for the drawer and the promised lube within. Out of the corner of my eye, I noted the drawer was stocked with a hell of a lot more than lube, including a healthy supply of condoms. I ignored the rest and snagged the bottle right as Benny took me deep. The intense pleasure of it threatened the tenuous hold of my pending orgasm.

"Stop," I gasped out, not sure if I could last a second longer.

He immediately pulled off and looked up at me with eyes blown wide with lust and colored with a hint of concern. Before he could voice any doubt, I leaned forward to conquer his spit-slicked lips then used my hold on his hair to roll us. Confusion shone in his light green eyes for a second. I popped the lid free of the lube and leaned down to press my lips against his once more. His doubt melted away as his mouth and body molded against mine. Hoping the lubricant wasn't too cold, I rubbed my thumb gently along his entrance. He moaned into the kiss and I pressed my middle finger in, only encountering the mildest resistance before sliding as deep as I could.

"Oh, god, Cal," he gasped as I added another finger and curled them delicately against his prostate.

"You like that?" He gave a whimpered moan in response and I slowly thrust the fingers in and out, being sure to stroke the bundle of nerves. "You like me stretching you open, don't you? Like me inside of you. Making you mine." His eyes rolled back, and he arched into my hand, squeezing my fingers with his gloriously tight ass while his hands fisted in the sheets. "Fuck, you feel so good. So tight and greedy for me." I dropped my head as he tightened around me again. My gaze caught on the fading bruise staining his neck that I never should have given him and my mouth moved toward it as if pulled by some magnetic force. I licked at the marred flesh and sucked lightly on the mark as I scissored my fingers in and out of Benny's willing body.

"Wait."

The breathless command instantly froze all of my movements. I pulled back from his neck, thoroughly chastened. I knew better. What the fuck was I thinking, deliberately marking him like this?

He angled his head up and pulled a featherlight kiss from my lips. "I didn't mean stop altogether," he whispered, then added with a cheeky grin, "Just warning that I was going to come if you kept that up."

I slowly removed my fingers and saw the loss of them on his face. "We can't have that now, can we?" I snatched at his lips, then rocked back on my heels. My hand closed around one of the discarded pillows and I pulled it close. "Get that tight ass in the air." Benny dutifully lifted his hips, and I placed the pillow beneath them. That done, I wrapped a hand around my length and stroked enough to add a liberal coat of lube to it before guiding it toward his already clenching hole.

I smothered a moan as I pressed slowly in, keeping an eye on Benny's face. I'd never had the pleasure of watching my partner as I sank into them, had never wanted it before, but I very much wanted to see Benny's reactions. I watched as his face tightened from the burn of the initial breach, saw his flushed chest flex, then relax as he remembered to breathe. I sank a little deeper with each shallow thrust and saw each gain register until the cringe on his face dissolved into sheer fucking ecstasy when I bottomed out. My pleasure at being so incredibly deep barely even registered, I was so enraptured in his reactions.

Fuck, Benny. What have you done to me?

I didn't need an answer to the question; I already knew it. I gave a slow, deliberate roll of my hips, gliding out and back in, then did it again and again, taking my time building Benny's pleasure, because as much as he liked it fast and dirty, he also loved it slow and purposeful. He squeezed around me and I gave up my hold of his thighs to fall on my arms over him. My gaze fell once more to the almost-hickey on his neck. This time I didn't hesitate. My mouth closed over the mark and I sucked hard as I thrust into him. Benny gasped out a groan and snaked his arms under my shoulders and dug his fingers into my back.

I moaned and my thrusts got sharper and sharper until the slow pace I'd been maintaining became a frantic pound. My arms ached from holding me, but I couldn't bring myself to move because it would mean Benny would let go. I shifted my angle and swallowed Benny's cry of pleasure with a sloppy, savage kiss he eagerly returned. The need for release saturated every fiber. Electricity surged up my spine. Heat coiled low in my belly. And an unbearable ache I'd do just about anything to hang onto built to blinding heights.

"Cal!" Benny shouted, clamping down tight around me as his orgasm ripped through him to pulse in hot streams onto his chest. I didn't even manage another thrust before I shattered apart with my own cry and collapsed on top of him.

Benny

I let out a contented breath and combed my fingers through Calvin's silken locks, one hundred percent positive I couldn't be more in love with him if I tried. He shifted on my chest and let out a groan that sounded like he'd run an entire game with two overtimes. And, fuck, if that wasn't exactly what he'd done. I still wasn't sure if my legs would hold if I tried to stand or finish disintegrating into jelly.

I glanced over at the setup on the table. All my grand plans to make topping Cal special like he deserved had gone up in smoke faster than sage brush in a draught the second he'd rolled us. Not that I was complaining. Jesus Christ, man could fuck like no one else. I placed a tender kiss on the top of his head and he let out a stuttering sigh. My hand slid from around his waist where it had been keeping him close and I shifted to roll him off of me.

"Where 're you going?" he mumbled into my chest.

I chuckled and tilted his relaxed face up to steal a kiss. "You stay here. I'll be right back." He groaned as he rolled to the side, but didn't protest. I slipped into the bathroom to relieve myself and cleaned up a bit before returning with a warm towel for him. To my surprise, he was no longer laid out on the rumpled bed, but standing. He offered me a smile that suffused my chest with an entirely different heat than the one from earlier and my lips stretched into an echoing grin.

"How you doin', stud?" he asked as he stepped forward to steal a kiss and the towel I'd brought.

"Stud, huh?"

He hiked his shoulder in a half-shrug and finished cleaning up. When he was done, he grabbed his briefs from the pool of his pants and tugged them on. I shamelessly followed the motion, and he snickered before stealing a quick kiss. "About that microwave…"

"It works." I wrapped the loose sheet around my waist and wandered over to heat-up the food. We didn't bother with the candle or even the plates and table, but settled on the floor amid the heap of pillows and plucked at the food straight from the cartons. It came as no surprise to me that Calvin was proficient with chopsticks, though I despaired at his need to put soy sauce on everything.

"Don't judge me," he said, snapping his chopsticks at me before stealing another piece of chicken from my carton.

"Is it judgment if you're wrong?"

He snorted and dunked the already sauced chicken into his veritable bowl of soy. "Maybe I like salty things." His eyes glinted wickedly, and I bit my lip to keep from laughing. He finished chewing and sealed up the cartons nearest him, then leaned back on his arms to take in the room. I mirrored him in closing up the remaining containers. When I was done, he asked, "So you gonna tell me what this place is or not?"

"It's exactly what it looks like. A studio flat above a shop," I said as I stood and took the leftovers back to the kitchenette.

"You know what I mean. Whose is it? How do you know about it? Why are we here?" he asked in one continuous stream as he followed me back to the bed. I replaced my stolen sheet and slipped beneath it. He settled beside me and poked me in the ribs.

"Ow," I laughed and turned on my side to face him. "What was that for?"

"You going to answer the question?"

I rolled my eyes and propped up on my elbow. "What do I get if I do?"

His mouth twisted in a frown. "First off, you should tell me anyway, but fine, I'll see your terms. You answer my question and I'll answer one of yours."

Ooh, I loved this game. "The place belongs to my friend Savannah. She rents it out to students to make extra cash on the side, since her parents are always cutting her off."

"Savannah, huh? Couldn't help but notice the… extra in the side drawer," he added with a smirk.

"If you're not so slyly asking if Savannah and I were involved, the answer is yes, but that was a long time ago. We're much better as friends. Do you need a list of my other partners?" I asked with a raised eye brow at the same time, hoping that didn't count as my question.

"No. Do you need mine?"

I slid a little closer and glided a hand over his firm stomach. "No. I know you would tell me if you thought it was relevant."

"I would," he said softly as his fingers trailed along my side, tracing the patterns only he seemed to know.

"My turn." He smiled, but didn't cease his drawing. "What are you doing?"

"Hm?" he hummed while his fingers continued to play.

"Whenever you touch me, it's almost like your drawing. I'm curious what."

"Oh, that? Nothing in particular, mostly just memorizing."

"Memorizing what?" I asked, leaning into him, completely enthralled.

"You. One of these days I'm going to sculpt you in clay and I want to make sure to get it right."

I frowned down at him. "What, like some Patrick Swayze-Ghost bullshit?"

Calvin's hand stilled as laughter rolled out of him. His eyes danced with humor as he finally sobered up. "For the record, I would make a fantastic Demi Moore, but no, not like that. Think more Pygmalion." As he said it, his hand resumed its sensuous roving.

I searched my knowledge of history for the name and almost laughed when I found it. "That's the Greek guy who had his ivory sculpture brought to life by the gods, right?"

Both of his eyebrows rose in obvious surprise. "It is."

I frowned at him in mock insult. "Are you calling me the perfect woman?"

He laughed again and used his hold on my waist to tug me closer for a kiss. "Obviously."

I got lost in the sweep of tongues and let my hand trail lower until it hit the band of his underwear. I was on the verge of asking if he still wanted me to top when he asked a question of his own.

"When did you know you were bi?"

I didn't think he was asking because having doubts about his own sexuality so much as he was simply curious. "Truthfully?"

"No, lie to me," he quipped with a relaxed smile and no sting.

"I used to think everyone was. It wasn't until right before I came here that I realized that wasn't the case."

"What happened?" His hand glided up my chest, distracting me from my response.

"My father," I said without thinking. Too late to take it back, I elaborated. "He found out my mother was "encouraging" my eccentricities."

Calvin's frown deepened. "I'm not following."

I let out a sigh and rubbed my thumb along his lower abs. "Benjamin Wallace Price the Third is a man with very decided opinions and didn't want any son of his to be, as he put it, a fucking fairy. He offered my mom a choice. She could raise me as she saw fit and fend for herself, or she could take a sizable settlement and disappear." My fingers curled on his stomach as my own rolled with rancid anger. "She took the money."

"Benny." The soft compassion in his voice tightened my chest.

I shook my head, eager to return to the lightness we'd been enjoying. "It was a long time ago." A smile tugged at my lips as I looked into his honey brown eyes, the same eyes that had first captivated me across a crowded room full of strangers, eyes that had seen the real me. "Of course, any doubts I may have had vanished when I got my first crush on a boy."

His eyes sparkled as a smile spread across his lips. "Oh? And who was that?"

I looked down at him, a little surprised, then leaned close to taste his smile. "Do you really not know?"

His eyes widened as my meaning sank in. He delicately wrapped a hand around the back of my neck and pulled me down for a more thorough kiss. I moaned softly into him, my hand drifting lower to palm his thickening cock. He ground up into the touch and slipped his fingers into my hair. "When do we have to leave?" he asked.

I moved to free him from his briefs. "We don't. We can stay as long as you want."

His tongue swept past my lips in a deep kiss that ignited all the parts of me that had belonged to him for as long as I could remember. He drifted his hand back down my chest to my hip and tugged it toward him. I broke from the kiss long enough to reacquire the lube from the stand, then tugged his briefs the rest of the way off. Calvin pulled his legs free, then guided me to straddle him. I leaned back down to get lost in his mouth again as he slipped an already lubed finger in my ass. The teasing touch had me moaning into him and eager for more in a matter of seconds.

"Calvin," I panted, his in so many ways I wasn't brave enough to voice for fear of losing him.

He tugged at my lips one last time, then pulled his fingers free. Without prompting, I straightened up and reached back to guide his thick cock to my entrance. My breath hitched as I slowly lowered myself down, but I couldn't bring myself to look away from Calvin's captivating eyes. Their honey brown both seared my soul and grounded me. I didn't bother to fight the moan or subsequent flush that rose when I finished settling. He thrust up slightly to meet me and I loved how full I felt, loved even more that it was him that made me feel this way.

His hands glided over my thighs as he stared back at me with a reverence that made my heart flutter and heat rise in my cheeks. They continued their journey, caressing my hips and coasting up my chest to hover over my struggling heart, then settled back on my waist. We stared into each other, years of history and understanding passing in the silence.

I fought the overwhelming need to tell him how I felt, how he'd stolen my heart ten years ago with a half-smile and a shy wave. The words pushed at my chest, demanding freedom, but I held them back, determined to hang onto this perfect moment for as long as I fucking could. His fingers tightened on my hips as he searched my face like all the things I couldn't tell him were written there for him to read.

He released my side and lifted a hand to curl around my neck once more. I leaned down to meet him halfway, eyes already half-lidded in anticipation. "You're a masterpiece," he whispered just before our lips connected. I moaned into him as his fingers tightened almost possessively in my hair, then gentled. He laid back down and all I could do was get lost in his eyes as I finally started to move. For at least one night, there wasn't anyone else, no overbearing fathers, no oppressive expectations, nowhere we had to be, just us lost in each other.

Chapter 24

Benny

I glanced down the hall for probably the hundredth time and checked my sigh of disappointment. Empty. Still.

How long does it take to have a year-end meeting with your art teacher for fuck's sake?

I shoved my hands deeper into my pockets and leaned back against the wall, hiding me from view to resume my impatient waiting. Though at this rate, all the people I'd spent the last hour evading would stumble across me before Calvin deigned to emerge. True, I could have given him this surprise anytime, but after going to mass with him and our night at the flat, I wanted him to have this now, though a part of me wondered if he already knew about it.

Finally, the click of a door latch filled the expansive hallway, and I hazarded another peek. Calvin stood outside the art room; large sketchbook tucked under his arm as he bid goodbye to Professor Jankowski.

I wonder if he'll ever show me the art he doesn't share with the rest of the world.

Not that I hadn't seen his work before. His landscapes were so surreal they looked like they belonged in a fantasy world, but it didn't take a genius to know Calvin had plenty of art that never reached the eyes of others. The door latched closed, and he turned to make his way down the hall toward where I'd been waiting. I ducked back out of view and listened to his footfalls as he approached. When he was close enough, I reached out and yanked him down the smaller hallway.

He let out a squawk of indignation and barely caught the sketchpad before it could crash to the ground. I cupped the side of his face and pressed our lips together to prevent the tide of expletives undoubtedly coming my way. There was little doubt in my mind that a goofy grin stretched across my face as I released him to take in his perturbed expression. Fuck if this man didn't tick every box I had.

"Are you fucking insane?" he hissed, hiking his sketchpad higher under his arm while his gaze darted around for witnesses I already knew weren't there. Truthfully, yeah, I was probably a little insane, being crazy about Calvin made me reckless and the more time I spent with him, the less I cared.

"I wanted to show you something."

"And it couldn't wait 'til light's out? What the fuck is so important you need to risk exposing us?" Despite his angry tone, at the mention of 'us' my heart did little flip-flops I'd given up trying to ignore. At the end of the day Calvin wasn't upset about getting caught. He was upset that *if* we got caught, then we'd have to stop… and he clearly wasn't ready to do that. "Why are you smiling like a goddamn idiot?" he snapped.

"I have a surprise for you."

He straightened up as light chased away the darkness that had been clouding his features. "A surprise?" His eyes narrowed again. "I swear to fucking god, Benjamin Price, if you scared the shit out of me so you can show me your dick, I'm going on strike."

I smothered a laugh, because sound carried and *that* would definitely lead someone to where we were standing far too close for people who supposedly hated each other. Damn, Calvin was cute when he was angry. I brushed the curls away from his face, enjoying their silky caress as I tucked the rogue strands behind his ear. "I promise I didn't ambush you to show you my dick."

The spark in his eyes dimmed a little, and I almost laughed anyway at his sullen disappointment. "Then what is it?" he asked, a tad more irritably. Part of me still worried that despite what he said this really was still about sex for him while I'd already jumped in with both feet, but the dates he kept going on and our night in town gave me hope that I'd win him over, eventually.

"Follow me." I did a quick double-check to make sure no one else had walked up while I'd been distracted, then ventured down the side hall, making my way back toward the main atrium and offices there. Behind me Calvin muttered to himself about unnecessary secrecy and a certain someone being obtuse and why should he follow me, anyway. That he continued to bitch to himself as we traversed little used hallways in this part of the school further solidified my belief that he didn't know where I was taking him.

Finally, we pulled up in front of a heavy door with a patch of bleached wall beside it where a plaque had once been mounted. He squinted at the bare spot and the intricate detailing on the otherwise nondescript oak door and frowned. "Where the fuck are we?"

My suspicions confirmed, I produced an old iron key and unlocked the door. "Why don't you come inside and find out?"

He narrowed his eyes at me, then boldly strode past into the long-forgotten room beyond. I'd done my best to clean the place up, but there was only so much I could do without arousing suspicion and it was a far cry from its former glory.

"Benny."

At his gasp, I looked up from gently closing the heavy door. Wonder dominated his face and his lips parted in wordless awe as he took in the small space. His gaze danced from the dusty pews and large cross dominating the table at the far end to the elaborate stained glass set in the far wall. The afternoon sun peered through the painstakingly cleaned surface to create a riot of color that stretched from the floor to halfway up the wall.

"What do you think?" I asked, pushing my hands in my pockets once more, suddenly anxious that he wouldn't like it.

He spun around to face me, his brown eyes wide while his mouth opened and closed without emitting a single syllable. In all the time I'd known Calvin, I'd never thought it possible to actually make him speechless. He ripped his gaze away from me to stare at the room again. "I don't understand. How did I not know this was here? How did *you* know it was?"

I shrugged and leaned against the wall next to the door. "When the school decided to avoid any religious entanglements in the seventies, they removed the placard and shut the chapel up tight. I had to memorize blueprints of the school for those ridiculous tours. That's how I found it."

Calvin gently set his satchel and sketchpad on one of the still very dusty pews and looked back at me. "And the key?"

I smirked. "I'm a Price not a saint. No one will miss it." I held it out and his hand shook as he reached for it.

"Why are you giving it to me?" Confusion swirled in the honey-eyed depths of his eyes as his fingers wrapped around the iron and he took a step closer.

"I thought you might like a place where you could worship in private without anyone finding you or having to go all the way into town."

He licked his lips and swallowed hard. Fear trickled through my happiness. Had I overstepped? He'd pointed out before that I wasn't religious. Was this a weird thing to do? Suddenly he stepped forward, key still in hand, and mashed his mouth against mine. My hands reflexively went to his sides to keep us both steady and pull him closer.

Calvin

Every ounce of feeling currently overwhelming me poured through me into Benny. His hands wrapped around my waist and I pressed my entire body into him, desperately seeking an outlet for all the emotion bubbling inside. Fuck if anyone outside of my family had ever done anything so sweet or thoughtful for me before. And damn this sensitive asshole for making me feel like this.

My fingers tightened around the relic of a key, grounding me as I panted for breath. It still wasn't enough. Even kissing Benny senseless didn't come close to scratching the surface. I wanted—no, *needed*—to make love to him until neither one of us could move for hours. My fingers tightened even more to the point I feared I might actually snap the ancient iron as the word I'd been avoiding with blind determination finally forced its way to the surface.

Fuck me, I'm in love with Benny.

Damn you Andy and damn you too Benny.

I pushed away from him enough to pocket the key before I could break it or, heaven forbid, lose it. A quick glance at Benny showed him looking at me with those soft green eyes the color of algae on a crystal spring, undiluted and pure. *Fuck.* I licked my lips and debated returning to kissing him within an inch of his life. Come to think of it, that sounded like a splendid plan and an even better way to keep avoiding what I didn't want to admit. Feelings always ruined everything. Life was better, less complicated, when they weren't involved.

"I take it you like it," Benny said with a smirk.

I leaned forward to taste his lips again and steal a kiss he didn't deny me. "You could say that." His hands dipped beneath my shirt to caress the bare skin beneath as I kissed him deeper. I moaned into him and pulled away. "I'm not having sex with you in here. I may be depraved, but even I have limits and sex in a place of worship—even a neglected one—is a hard limit."

Benny's brows scrunched together. "I didn't bring you here so you would have sex with me and I have never once thought of you as depraved."

My heart fluttered alarmingly, and I took a half step back. "Why did you?"

His face relaxed, and he offered me a sad smile. "Like I said, I thought you would appreciate it and could find peace here."

Goddamn it, Benny.

My eyes stung, and I took another step back, officially taking me beyond his reach. He remained leaning against the wall, silently watching me freak the fuck out. What was he thinking? Was he judging me? Did he think I was nuts? Why couldn't I keep my shit together? I took a shaky breath that did absolutely nothing to quiet my pounding heart or steady my nerves. I seriously sucked at emotions. "Fuck."

"What's the matter? I'm sorry if this wasn't okay. I didn't mean to upset you."

I shook my head as the stinging behind my eyes intensified. "Stop."

"Cal." My heart lurched painfully at the concern in his voice.

"Don't call me that." I couldn't take this. My breath came in quick bursts as I fought to get myself back under control.

"I don't understand. If you don't like me calling you that, why didn't you say something sooner? I would have stopped."

I shook my head again, though if it would have been possible to squeeze my heart, that might have helped more, because that wasn't it at all. I loved it when Benny called me Cal, absolutely fucking loved it. It was intimate and made me feel special, treasured. "Stop," I gasped out. "Just stop it."

"Stop what?" Benny asked, sounding more confused by the second. And, oh God, I hated that, I hated making him feel unsure, because fuck it all, I was in love with the fucker.

"Being nice to me. I can't… I can't…" I struggled to keep air in my lungs long enough to finish the thought, but how could I? I couldn't be in love with Benny. I just couldn't. Being in love brought heartache and pain. Happily ever after wasn't real and even if it was, guys like me didn't get them. Not because I was gay, but because I was *me*. And here he was making me believe it was possible, making me want it, stupid hearts and all.

He straightened up against the wall, and a wave of hurt crashed over his face. "Well, fuck." Those two words might as well have been a dagger being plunged straight into my heart for how much pain they caused.

"No. It's not… I…" I scrambled to find some way to explain that didn't involve the truth, but as Benny pushed off the wall and turned toward the door, I ran out of options. "Wait!" He looked back at me and frowned. "Wait," I repeated calmer, then pinched the bridge of my nose. "Shit. Fuck. I can't believe I'm going to do this."

"Do what?" he asked as he resumed his position against the wall.

I dropped my hand and looked toward the ceiling in search of divine inspiration. All I found, though, were cobwebs and the knowledge that I couldn't avoid this forever and keep Benny too. "Okay. I need to tell you something."

"So tell me already. What's with the big fucking production?"

I winced at the anger in his words. "You don't understand. It's not that easy."

"Spit it out already."

"Okay. Okay," I repeated, more for myself than him, aiming for more calming breaths that did absolutely fucking nothing.

"Fuck this. Find me when you feel like sharing." He shifted to leave again, and I surged forward to stop him.

"Okay, I'm sharing. But first you have to promise not to get mad." He snorted and rolled his eyes. "I mean it, Benny. Promise you won't get mad, because I need to tell you something, but I'm pretty sure you're gonna get mad. Like next level pissed."

"Tell me what it is already."

"Promise first."

"Fine, I promise. What's the big deal?"

"I love you," I blurted and instantly a weight lifted from my chest, only to have anxiety rush in to fill up the space when he didn't say anything. "Did you hear me? I said I'm in love with you, asshole." I pushed hard against his shoulder, but he remained as immovable as ever.

"I heard you."

"And? Why aren't you mad? You're supposed to be mad."

He raised an eyebrow. "Do you want me to be mad?"

That took the wind out of my sails. "Well… no. But… but why aren't you? I feel like you should be."

His eyes softened, and a small smile tugged at his mouth. "Because I love you too, asshole." Five words. Five words is all it took for Benjamin Price to turn all the bones in my body to jelly. Five, because I wasn't counting the part where he called me an asshole. Thank God I was already standing so close to him or I'd have landed on the floor when I keeled over instead of latched onto his mouth while his arms wrapped around me.

My fingers scraped across the back of his neck as I urged him deeper, delving my tongue past his lips to steal his breath as much as he was stealing mine. He tightened one arm around my waist while he threaded fingers gently through my hair. When we finally pulled apart, my lips were swollen from the fierce kiss and we were both breathing hard. "Why didn't you say anything before?" I finally asked.

His lips quirked up in a half smile as he continued to comb through my hair. "Why do you always have to be so dramatic? If I hadn't thought you'd run for the hills, I'd have told you weeks ago." I opened my mouth to protest the assumption and closed it again when he raised an eyebrow in challenge.

"Fine," I huffed. "I'm a little dramatic, but I… I don't do emotions. Love is complicated and messy. Casual sex is so much easier."

"Maybe, but it's not half as rewarding." His mouth closed back over mine in a sensuous kiss that went all the way to my toes. I melted into him, finally recognizing the way Benny touched me for what it was—love, Cupid's arrow, little bubble hearts, big ass fucking card, love.

"I'm still not having sex with you in here."

He chuckled softly and the warmth of it spread through my chest to continue thawing my once carefully frozen heart. "I didn't tell you I love you, so you'd have sex with me."

"Why did you?" I asked, tipping his nose with mine and lightly brushing his lips.

"Because I do."

I arched into him at the admission and tangled our tongues once more. We kept both our hands in semi-respectable positions despite the evidence that both our bodies craved more than the heavy make out session. Even that toed the line of too risque for a chapel, but I figured as long as all clothes stayed on, God wouldn't find it too grievous an offense.

Chapter 25

Calvin

I opened Benny's door, not surprised to find him pacing the dimly lit room. The curtains hung open, allowing just enough moonlight in to illuminate the obvious anxiety on his face. I sighed inwardly and slipped into the room, gently closing the door behind me. As the latch clicked back into place, Benny spun around and attempted to hide his concern with a forced smile.

"Hey," he said and seemed to rock in place, as if unsure if he should step forward or stay there.

I smirked and decided for him. "Hey yourself." I pressed my body against his, enjoying the way his muscled physique pushed back, and brushed a light kiss against his lips. When that failed to ease the tension bunching his shoulders, I dropped my head to place a kiss on the side of his neck. He shuddered as I sucked on the sensitive skin. Finding all of Benny's erogenous zones had become somewhat of a mission for me, but I refused to let his subtle moan distract me from my true purpose this evening.

"Any trouble getting here?" he asked as I tugged him toward the bed, still kissing the side of his neck.

"What do you think?"

"Right. Yeah. Stupid question."

I chuckled into his throat at how nervous he was acting. Not even the first time we'd been together had he been such an uncertain ball of anxiety, at least not as far as I could tell. Maybe he had been and I simply hadn't known him well enough yet to recognize when he was low key freaking out.

"What's so funny?" He whispered into the shadowy darkness.

I lifted my head to meet his gaze. "You. Relax. It's not like we've never had sex before."

He took a deep breath and let it out in a huff. "But this isn't like that. We haven't…"

"Switched. The word you're looking for is switched. It's still not a big deal. Think of it as simply trying out a new position. If we like it, then we add it the other things we like to do. If we don't—"

"If we don't," he interrupted, worry coloring the words.

"If we don't," I continued, catching his eye, "then we don't add to the list of wonderful sexy things we do to each other." A small laugh escaped him and some of the tension eased away. "Now kiss me already before I change my mind and leave you with your hand."

His laugh was a little stronger this time, and he did as I asked, covering my mouth with his in a slow, deep kiss that had me aching in no time. I slid my hands down his back and into his pajamas to squeeze his ass unable to help myself. Man really did have an ass made for squeezing, and pounding, and gripping. I moaned as the kiss took on new life and my desire to be buried deep inside the man I loved briefly won out. Much as I wanted to do this, there was no denying I was a natural top. It was simply the way I was built, and I doubted one night of switching would suddenly make me verse. Still, stranger things had happened, like actually wanting Benjamin Price of all people to top me in the first place.

"On the bed," I said, following my command. Benny drifted after me, his mouth greedily chasing kisses. I tugged on his bottom lip with my teeth and settled back on my elbows. He made to lean down and keep kissing me and I shook my head. "Uh uh, I want that hot, wet mouth of yours wrapped around my cock." I could feel his hungry gaze on me as it traveled down to my tented pants.

Benny rebelliously stole one more kiss, then hooked his fingers on the waistband of my lounge pants and pulled them down. My cock bobbed free and throbbed when he moaned like a starving man. He settled between my thighs, then leaned down and licked me from base to tip. My head fell back with a groan as he wrapped his lips around my length and took his sweet ass time swallowing me down. His hand joined the mix, stroking while his tongue swirled around the swollen head and darted across the slit.

I hissed and fisted my hands in the sheets. Much as I wanted to watch and give Benny exactly what he desired, if I did that, then this evening would be over far too soon and doubted I'd be able to convince Benny to try again, love or no love. I reached blindly for the lube I'd noticed on the nightstand when I'd come in while Benny took me deep again. My hips curved off the bed, seeking more of that glorious heat, and I used the opportunity to draw my knees up.

"Here," I gasped, all but flailing the bottle at him. My cock came free with a pop and he stared at the bottle as if he didn't know what he was supposed to do with it, even though he'd been the one to leave it out. "You need to prep me." I waved the bottle at him again and he accepted it with jerky movements, glaring at it. The high from his giving me head was quickly wearing off in the face of his scowl. "What are you worried about?" I panted. "We've talked about this."

"I don't want to hurt you."

"You won't. Have I ever hurt you?"

"It's not the same," he grumbled,, and I couldn't help but laugh.

"Please, Benny," I said with a smirk, "it's not like I've never played with my ass. How do you think I got so good at it?" More muttered grumbling, but at least it was accompanied by the cap flicking open this time. "How about this? Think about what you like and just do that?" I was about to give up hope when he finally squeezed some of the liquid out and rubbed it between his fingers. Then he lowered his head back to my flagging erection and expertly brought me back to life. I curled my fingers in his hair that was finally long enough to grip properly and encouraged him to keep going.

His slick fingers gently massaged my balls, and the familiar tingle wrapped around the base of my spine. My grip on his hair tightened in warning and then relaxed as he abandoned them to pursue a different prize. The tip of his finger circled my entrance and slipped inside at the same time he swallowed my cock down as deep as he could. I groaned at the dual sensation and shoved a fist in my mouth to stifle the sound. Benny grunted as I squeezed around his finger then worked the digit in and out of me with agonizing slowness. Between my efforts to stay as relaxed as possible so Benny wouldn't panic and not coming from being blown within an inch of my life, I didn't think I could last much longer. If this is what I did to Benny, point me, all the fucking points me.

I smothered a sharp cry as Benny added another finger and stroked my prostate. "Fuck, yes," I moaned as I arched into his hand. "Oh God. Fuck. Again. Do it again." He obliged, sucking on my head as his fingers massaged deep inside me. "That's it. Just like that. Fuck." My fingers tightened in the sheets and I panted through the ecstasy as my orgasm danced dangerously close. It wasn't getting any better than this. "Fuck me. Shit. Fuck. God." I couldn't even curse straight as Benny continued to fuck me with his fingers and his mouth.

By the miracle of God, he pulled off before I completely combusted. His fingers slipped free, leaving my stretched ass clenching air. I moaned in desperation of my denied release while Benny tore off his pajamas that I'd entirely forgotten about and repositioned himself. My fingers ached to bury in his hair and guide his mouth to mine, but instead I lay there gasping for breath and trying to cool down so I didn't come from an unlikely breeze of air. Maybe I should have anyway, because the second Benny's cock touched my rim, I closed up tighter than a steel drum and no amount of telling myself to breathe could get me to relax.

"Cal?" Benny's warm hands caressed my thighs. I reached out lightning fast to grab his wrists and keep him from moving while all the fear I'd worked so hard to get past warped and twisted inside of me, fear I thought I'd conquered years ago. "Cal," he tried again, even softer.

"Just… just wait," I squeezed out through strangled lungs. Talking proved to be a major mistake as a sob quickly followed.

"Calvin. Talk to me."

I shook my head violently from side to side.

"What can I do to help?"

My chest stuttered as I fought through another sob. "A minute. I need… a minute."

"We don't have to do this. Not now, not ever." Benny's quiet concern did nothing but spread guilt through my rampant anxiety.

"I know," I sobbed. "But…"

"But what, Cal? We don't have to do anything you don't want to. You know I don't need this."

Tears poured freely down my face as blubbered, "But *I* want this. It's *my* body, Benny. I should be in control of it, not the other way around."

"What do you need me to do?"

I took one shuddering breath and then another as I struggled to come up with a way to feel less powerless.

"You're in control here. We only do as much or as little as you're comfortable with," Benny reassured me.

Control, that's what I needed, to be in complete control of what was happening. Suddenly, I had an idea. "Lay on the bed." He quickly got up, and I swiveled around to take his place on my knees at the end of the bed. When he lay down, I straddled his thighs and took another steadying breath, already feeling the tension in my chest ease with the reversal. Benny reached out for me, though, and I recoiled. "Don't. Don't touch me. Hands on the bed frame above your head." Even in the dark I could tell Benny was confused, but he did as I asked without comment and the anxiety eased again.

"This better?"

"Yes. Is that okay?"

"Whatever you need, Calvin, I'm here for you." Damn if that didn't make me love him more. I'd kiss him if I wasn't positive I'd turn into a sobbing disaster too afraid to ever try this again, because clearly my trauma was still as ripe as it had ever been.

I patted the sheets until I found the lube again. My slicked fingers sought out Benny's very dead erection. I gently tugged, but it wasn't until I leaned down to place a kiss where his groin met his hip that his cock twitched with any signs of life. It took a few minutes of dedicated attention until he started plumping back up in my hands. My heart hammered as I considered what I was about to do.

"Fuck," I hissed and leaned across his statue-like form. "I need to see you." The lamp switched on, revealing Benny with both hands curled around the bed frame, the flush of arousal darkening his chest. He watched me as I took him back in hand, his lids fluttering as I tightened my slick grip and stroked hard. "Tell me how much you like it."

The groan that rolled out of him was exactly the encouragement I needed. His knuckles went white and the muscles in his arms flexed as he worked to keep his hands to himself. His head tilted back, exposing the column of his throat, as I continued to work him like I knew he liked. While his gaze was elsewhere, I reached around to see if I needed to be prepped again after my episode. Fortunately, it only took a little more stretching to get me to the point that I could accommodate Benny.

I released his cock and repositioned myself over it. I could feel Benny's eyes on me, but I didn't dare look at him for fear of losing my nerve. Instead, I devoted all of my attention to slowly lowering myself down, every centimeter of distance giving myself the same reassuring guidance as I'd given so many others over the years. Take your time. Don't forget to breathe. Relax. Go as slow as you need to. Deep breath in, now let it out. With that last one, Benny's cock breached my entrance. I repeated the list of instructions over and over until, at last, Benny was all the way inside. My last deep breath came out in a whoosh and I could have laughed for joy. I'd done it. I'd actually done it. And now that the hard part was over, I could work for the more fun bits.

My teeth sank into my bottom lip as I slowly pulled up and slid back down. It took a few unsteady tries before I found the right balance and was able to shift enough that each slide stroked my prostate. I let out a low moan and ventured a squeeze. Pleasure arced like lightning up my spine and my head fell back as I continued to fuck myself on Benny's pulsing cock. Suddenly, I realized he was shaking. I forced my attention back to him and kept rolling my hips.

His features were tight beneath the lamplight, his whole body vibrating with the effort of holding perfectly still. I tightened around him and ground down hard. The muscles in his neck bulged and his hips jerked with the urge to drive up and meet me. I leaned back and gripped his thighs for support as I rode him hard, my cock bouncing with each drive of my hips.

"Oh God," I moaned, hovering closer to a precipice I hadn't expected. "Touch me. For the love of God, Benny, please. I need you to touch me." I gasped as he wrapped one hand around my aching cock and gripped my thigh with the other. It only took a few thrusts into his tight grip for me to crash down on his cock and shatter into a million pieces. I squeezed around him as ribbons of cum spurted out of me to splatter on his chest. Benny let out a grunt, and I collapsed spent beside him.

Benny

I ran fingers lightly up and down Calvin's back as he panted for breath beside me. I'd never had a dry orgasm before and was not in a rush to repeat the experience. Calvin's slow torture of my cock to bring it back to life and then my inability to actively participate as he rode me past the point of reason had the poor thing still throbbing hard.

"Are you okay?" Calvin asked where he lay curled on his side into me.

"I should be asking you that."

He reached out and traced a finger in the cum on my chest. "I honestly didn't think I'd climax."

I gently snagged the hand on my chest and brought his finger to my lips where I sucked off the release, then kissed his palm. He moaned and curled a hand around the side of my face in order to turn me toward him for a different kiss. I rested my forehead against his and rubbed my thumb along the back of his still captive hand. "*Are* you okay?"

He let out a shaky breath and nodded. "I am now. Thank you and… I'm sorry."

"Please don't be sorry. We knew this wouldn't be easy."

He groaned and buried his face in my shoulder. "Maybe you did. You sure you're alright? Did you even come?"

"Yeah, I think so. Sort of anyway."

Calvin snorted and shifted to reach for my very obvious erection. "You think?"

"If you love me at all, please don't touch my dick. I'm so over-stimulated, I think it's more likely to fall off than do anything else."

"I'm sorry."

I pulled him closer. "I already told you not to be. I'm fine. I'll be fine. You're the one I'm worried about. Don't ever freak me out like that again. Jesus fucking Christ, I thought I'd hurt you." He winced and I curled into him in blatant disregard of my abused dick. I grunted at the unsurprising pain that radiated through me. "Hey, look at me." I tilted his chin up to see those honey eyes that had captivated me over ten years ago. "I love you."

His gaze searched mine for a moment before he snuggled closer. "I love you too." He leaned forward and brushed my lips with a tender kiss. Without a second thought, I cupped the side of his face and kissed him back, slow and gentle at first, then with gradually increasing intensity he returned with fervor.

"How long can you stay?" I asked when the kisses slowed to mere presses. I'd only spent one complete night completely wrapped up in him and could already tell I was completely addicted to it.

He smiled knowingly and leaned back to glance at the digital clock on the nightstand. "A little while longer, but not much." Instead of saying exactly how much longer he burrowed back in my embrace, and let out a sigh.

"So, is this something we're going to be adding to the list of things we do?"

He chuckled into my shoulder. "The snuggling for sure. As for the other... no. Not now at least."

I let out the breath I'd been holding, because I really wasn't sure if I could go through that again.

"No need to sound so fucking relieved," he teased, smacking me on the chest and getting his own drying cum all over his hand.

I snickered. "Serves you right for trying to beat me up in my own bed."

"Don't know what you're laughing about. You're gonna clean it up." He held his hand up in front of my face and arched a challenging eyebrow.

Per the unspoken challenge, I gently wrapped my fingers around his wrist and proceeded to lick him clean. His stifled moans were reward enough for the daring move, and my rebellious dick threatened to come back to life after finally deflating. I willed the damn thing to stand down and released his now differently wet hand. Calvin leaned forward and stole a kiss that made me hate he had to leave.

A short while later, we were both properly cleaned up and dressed once more in pjs. He stopped a short way from the door and turned to offer a small wave that I returned. I watched him ghost soundlessly down the hall until he disappeared, then closed my door with a sigh, already looking forward to when I'd get to see him again.

Prince Einar watched as King Kelani stood at the balcony and surveyed his vast kingdom beyond. It was unprecedented for the King to remain in the Summer Palace during the Solstice. Yet here he was. With Einar.

With the rest of the court away, Einar didn't hesitate to step up beside the young king. Their alliance was still tenuous, but he had hope that it would persevere. He placed a hand upon the king's lower back in a familiar gesture that had gotten countless before him exiled, or worse. But the King had no sharp words for him, only a smile that rivalled the rising sun.

Acknowledgments

Special thanks to my alpha readers for pushing me to explore Benny and Calvin's story. These characters evolved beyond my wildest dreams. And a final thanks to my beta readers Mx Alex, Stephanie, and Ashley for helping me make this story everything it could be.

Andy

I tightened my coat against the cold and pushed into the warmth of the main hall. Behind me, countless students milled around in the courtyard as their drivers unloaded their luggage. The shouts of greeting and laughter disappeared when the great doors shut behind me. My nose tingled as heat suffused the frozen tip. I wiped at the phantom drip that thawing always brought and looked around at the handful of students clustered inside.

No one spared me more than a pacing glance before returning to their conversations with friends they hadn't seen in almost three weeks. I didn't pay them any mind; there was only one pair of eyes I was interested in and they weren't here.

Stop it. Even if Mitch was here, he wouldn't be waiting for you. Get a grip.

Sadly, all my attempts to "get a grip" over winter break hadn't been very successful. I still dreamed about him every night, still looked forward to seeing him any chance I could, to hearing his laugh. I'd even dug out some old pictures of the two of us while at home. Heat crawled up my neck as I thought about how much…

attention I'd devoted to those old photos. My grip tightened on the handle of my rolling suitcase and I launched forward.

Safely in my room, I let out a relieved sigh as I unwound my obscenely long scarf—thank you, Calvin—and shrugged out of my coat. I dusted off the remnants of snow from the gray wool and then from my hair before it could melt. The luggage landed with a muffled thud on the bed and I flashed to Mitch hovering over me, holding me close while he—

"There you are, you sneaky little scamp."

The memory blasted apart. I looked up to find Calvin perched in the doorway. "Hey," I said, grateful my voice didn't crack. "Didn't see you at drop off."

He sauntered into the room. "That's because I didn't get dropped off."

I paused mid-unpacking to stare at him in disbelief. "You didn't go home for the holidays?"

"Nope." He shoved my suitcase aside and plopped on the bed.

"But… but you always go home for the holidays. You fucking love Christmas, not to mention any excuse to leave this hellscape."

He shrugged and feigned a sudden interest in his cuticles.

I gave an exasperated cry, then stomped over to the door and slammed it shut. Unpacking could wait and with any luck, my dorm mate, Lucien, wouldn't return until later. "Alright, spill. What on earth could have possessed you to stay?" I sucked in a breath as a horrible possibility occurred to me. "Did something happen to your mom?"

Calvin clucked his tongue and rolled his eyes. "Always so dire, Gallagher. I *chose* to stay."

"You did not."

"Oh, I definitely did, and it was *so* worth it." He let out a happy sigh and flopped back, missing the open suitcase by a fraction.

"You still haven't told me why."

He rolled his head to face me, the goofiest smile plastered across his face. "Benny."

"Are you fucking serious? You gave up the holidays with your family to fool around with... Benny," I asked incredulously, remembering to lower my voice at the last second. Shut doors could only muffle so much and those fuckers didn't lock.

Calvin propped up on his elbows. "Not just to fool around, though we did a fair bit of that," he added, his happy smile turning wicked. "Turns out, he never goes home for winter break if he can help it. Family drama and all that." He waved a dismissive hand, though I suspected there was a lot more to it than that.

I crossed my arms over my chest. "Still waiting for a why."

"Ugh, would you let me tell the story? So, impatient." He sat back up and spared me a playful glare. "Like I was saying, Benny didn't go home for the holidays and I didn't want him to have to spend them alone."

"Uh-huh."

In an uncharacteristic moment of visible nerves, Calvin averted his gaze and chewed on his bottom lip.

I straightened and let my arms fall. "What? What is it?"

That goofy smile he'd been sporting earlier twitched at the corners of his mouth as he looked up at me. "I told him I love him."

I held my breath, not sure how I should react. While I personally didn't agree with Calvin's fascination with Benjamin Price, that didn't give me license to be an asshole.

"And he said it back." Calvin barked out a laugh and covered his mouth with his hands as he disintegrated into happy giggles.

All the air I'd been holding surged out of my lungs like someone had punched me in the gut. Here I was, trying desperately to figure out some way to stay Mitch's friend and not lose myself, and Calvin was living my dream. The guy he was in love with loved him back. Something I would never have, because the guy I loved was straight, and I... wasn't.

"Oh my God, you have to see this." Calvin popped back up and started rummaging through his pockets. I took advantage of his distraction to wipe the devastation from my face. Finally, he pulled out something that looked like a necklace. "We got each other Christmas gifts."

"He got you jewelry?" I asked as I squinted at the smooth wooden beads.

"It's not jewelry, it's a rosary. To replace the one I left at home."

I wasn't sure what was more shocking, that Benny had gotten Calvin a rosary or that Calvin had one to begin with. "And you got him a gift as well," I said slowly, struggling to keep up with what had been going on with my friend while I'd been distracted by my own woes.

"Well, made not got." He shrugged and carefully tucked the rosary away. "But he seemed pretty pleased with it, so I'm not stressing." He leaned back on his arms again, his smile seemingly now a permanent part of him. "What about you? How were holidays with the folks?"

"Um, holidays were... fine." I flashed to endless dreams of Mitch's hands on my body and quickly shook them off. "Shannon was a total pain in the ass per usual, but as she keeps reminding me, that's a sister's job. Mom and Dad were their usual festive selves. All in all, nothing of note," I bold faced lied. But I wasn't ready to come clean to Calvin yet about how he'd been right—I couldn't just be friends with Mitch.

Calvin's smile settled into a suspicious frown. "Uh-huh. Did you come out?"

I gritted my teeth. He asked me that after every break and my answer remained the same as it had for the last four years. "No."

"No need to get defensive." He held up his hands in mock surrender. "You're acting cagey is all. What about James? Where was your hot stuff, big brother during these mind-numbingly boring celebrations?"

I rolled my eyes. While I was most definitely not Calvin's type, my brother was. Course, it didn't hurt that he topped me by a good seven inches. "Meat head shipped out for a tour in Sudan at the end of November."

"No fucking way. He actually enlisted? I know you said he'd talked about it, but I honestly never thought he'd go through with it. When the fuck did he manage that?"

"Apparently, sometime last year, and never bothered to tell anyone." I scowled at the frayed corner of the comforter. Once again, I was the last to know anything in my family. Suppose it came from being the youngest, but that didn't make it suck any less.

Mitch

I barreled down the corridor just shy of a full sprint. Thanks to the team congregating at the drop off circle like leopards waiting to pounce, I had to go the long way around and hadn't been able to meet Andy like I'd wanted. I'd harbored a small hope that he'd be waiting for me, would be as eager to see me as I was to see him, but he was smarter than that. Knowing him, he was already unpacking in his room. And since everyone else was still camped on the school's front lawn to catch up with friends as they arrived, this was the perfect time for us to connect without prying eyes.

I chewed my lip as I ate up the seemingly miles of hallway separating us. Reconciling with Andy dominated every thought, and after the incredible night we'd shared last semester, I finally felt like I had a real shot. The soft way he'd moaned my name had inspired hope and, truth be told, endless nights of hard-ons.

A smile cracked my cheeks as I finally spied his door. The sandstone colored plaster actually looked bright for once, instead of its usual oppressive dark. And while I seriously doubted it, even the wooden wainscoting seemed to shine as if freshly polished. I willed my pounding heart to calm the fuck down and did what little I could to school my grin. My fingers wrapped around the cool bronze of the handle and I took a fortifying breath.

This was it. After four and a half years, I was finally going to tell Andy the truth.

I twisted the knob and pushed the door open before I could lose my nerve. And stopped dead. Every happy thought that had propelled me here, every ounce of optimism that I could actually mend what I'd broken, died a horrible death in point-two seconds flat.

Andy stood beside his bed, snowflakes still clinging to the ends of his auburn hair. He turned to face me in slow motion, confusion and anxiety stamped plain as day across his freckled face. I shifted my focus from his stricken expression to Calvin Bridges, who lay propped on his elbows. On Andy's bed. Where he was smiling. Well, not anymore. His cheerful expression had dimmed to one of curiosity when I burst into the room. And he hadn't moved from where he was comfortably sprawled out. On Andy's bed. The bed where we'd… Where Andy had…

This was a mistake.

"Mitch." Andy's voice snapped me out of the trance I'd fallen in and I blinked for what felt like the first time in days. "What are you doing here?"

Fuck my life. All the progress I thought we'd made last semester gone in an instant.

"I… uh…" I floundered, tearing my gaze away from Calvin's knowing smirk. I longed to look at Andy, to have him deny my worst fear, but couldn't bring myself to meet his furrowed gaze. Had he lied to me about him and Calvin? What was it he'd said? Calvin's a friend. But I was Andy's friend too, and some of the things we'd done had been more than friendly.

I swallowed down the urge to spew the breakfast I'd been too excited to finish. Acid rolled around in my stomach as Calvin joined the faceless shadows of Andy's sexual experiences that haunted my nightmares.

"Mitch, are you okay?" Andy asked, taking a step towards me.

I reflexively took a step back to maintain the distance between us and involuntarily looked over at Calvin again. "Sorry, I should have knocked. I didn't realize you'd have company." I risked a glance at Andy and found his green eyes clouded with confusion. He darted a look at Calvin and I fought the urge to do the same. "I'll… I'll just go. Leave you two to… it."

For the love of god, stop talking and fucking leave already!

Knowing I should leave as fast as humanly possible and actually doing it, however, apparently wasn't going to happen. I continued to stand there, my feet glued to the ground, and my mind blanking out in a desperate attempt to avoid thinking about Andy and Calvin together and failing fucking miserably.

"You know what? I actually have some errands to run." Calvin popped off of Andy's bed like he was fucking popcorn. "You boys catch up. I'm sure you have a lot to talk about," he said with a sickeningly sweet smile as he patted Andy's cheek.

The death glare Andy gave him could have burned a hole in the wall, but Calvin sauntered toward the door and coincidentally me, whole and hale. But it made sense Andy would be mad. I'd ruined their afternoon by showing up completely unannounced and uninvited.

Calvin paused in front of me, and I dutifully cleared the entryway. "Don't have too much fun without me," he crooned, and blew Andy a kiss over his shoulder. Andy rolled his eyes and his normally plush lips twisted into a scowl. Calvin offered me a wink and waltzed out of the room, leaving me all alone with an obviously irritated Andy.

"Look, I'm sorry. I shouldn't have come in here like that. Definitely should have at least knocked. I'd hoped to catch you out front, but it's a fucking disaster out there and snowing and—"

"Did you need to talk to me about something?" Andy snapped, effectively cutting off my babbling.

I thought briefly about why I'd come here, about what I'd thought about almost non-stop since Andy had moaned my name. Then I thought about his absolutely stricken expression when I'd showed up out of the blue... unwanted.

"Mitch?" The concern in his voice tugged at the part of me that only he seemed able to reach. "Are you alright?" He took a half-step towards me and I danced a full one back.

"Y-yeah. I'm good," I lied, rubbing the back of my neck. A quick look at his narrowed eyes said he wasn't buying it.

"So, what's up? How were your holidays?" Small talk. Andy was doing small talk and I could have fucking died.

"Good. Yours?"

He shrugged and moved to unzip his luggage. "Same old same."

"Suppose that's good," I said, like I had any idea what that entailed these days. "My mom is good," I offered, unsolicited.

"Mine too," he responded by rote and I sent up a silent prayer for a meteor or something so this awkward ass conversation could end. He pulled out a small stack of clothes and I spied the dark jeans he'd worn the day we'd gone to the bookstore in town together.

Fuck, his ass had looked good in those. I shook my head to clear the traitorous thought.

"Was there something you wanted to talk about?"

I dared to meet his gaze and got snared in his emerald eyes like I always did. My tongue might as well have been wool for all the good it did me. His copper brows arced gracefully on his forehead while I struggled to get enough moisture in my mouth to speak.

"I… uh… I was hoping we could maybe keep studying togeth-er?" I stammered out at last.

He tilted his head to the side and seemed to consider me. "Study?"

"I mean, I know the tough subjects are over and I'll have to deal with like a shit ton of practice and you're probably also really busy, but it's been nice having grades I can be proud of for a change, that I actually earned and—" *Shut. The. Fuck. Up.* My mouth snapped closed, and I pressed my lips together to keep it that way.

"Sure…" Andy dragged out, his gaze distant. Abruptly, he refocused on me, and I felt like an ant beneath a magnifying glass at noon. "We can continue studying."

"Really?" I asked, not entirely positive he meant it or if I had some kind of masochistic tendencies I wasn't aware of.

He hiked a slim shoulder. "Yeah, why not? I'm assuming you'd still like to avoid having to take an athletic scholarship, right?"

A tightness in my chest eased. Andy actually wanted to help. That was awesome, though how I was going to deal with this new wrinkle of Calvin and Andy being friends with benefits without turning into an absolute caveman was beyond me.

I'll figure it out. I still have to fix this.

Slightly encouraged, I nodded. "Yeah. Yeah, that would be great. I'll… uh… see you around." I spun on my heel to beat a hasty retreat that fingers crossed wouldn't look like fleeing the scene before my tongue could start wagging again.

"Hey, Mitch," Andy called after me.

I fought to keep my flinch from showing and turned to look at him. "Yeah?"

"Don't mind Calvin. He's just really excited about this guy he's seeing. Apparently, they had a very… eventful… holiday."

"Oh—okay," I stammered, to cover my surprise.

So Andy and Calvin aren't seeing each other like that.

Andy shrugged like it was no big deal. "Anyway, I'll see you around."

"Yeah," I said, my lips twitching in an almost smile as an ember of hope reignited.

About the Author

Sam Bolanos (she/they) is a genderqueer author and founder of Chaotic Neutral Press LLC. They believe in love, equality, and the Oxford comma. When not playing with her three dogs, who you can follow on Instagram @austendogs, or spending time with her incredible husband, she's probably agonizing over edits or escaping into her latest fantasy.

Welcome to the adventure!

Newsletter: subscribe
Website: Booksbysbolanos.com
Facebook: @Booksbysbolanos
Twitter: @Booksbysbolanos
Instagram: @sbolanosbooks

Series

<u>Paranormal Stories</u>

War on Darkness
Darkness Defined (MM)
Order of Light (MM)
Knights of Nyx (MM)

Moons of Mystery
Sara's Moon (MF)
Charline's Solstice (MF)
Diana's Eclipse (MF)

Contemporary Romances

Ulwich Preparatory Academy
Our Last Fall (MM)
Our Secret Winter (MM)
Our Epic Spring (MM)

Oak Haven Romance
One Brave Thing (Enby/M)
All the Hype (MM)